KAY HOOPER

"A master storyteller."
—TAMI HOAG

"A chilling read."
—CATHERINE COULTER

"A scary page-turner."
—IRIS JOHANSEN

BANTAM BOOKS

The darkest evil is the
hardest to see....

SHADOWS

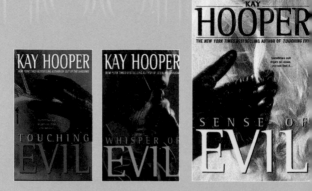

"Peopled with interesting characters and intricately plotted, the novel is both a compelling mystery and a satisfying romance."—*Milwaukee Journal Sentinel*

"Kay Hooper has crafted another solid story to keep readers enthralled until the last page is turned."—*Booklist*

"Joanna Flynn is appealing, plucky, and true to her mission as she probes the mystery that was Caroline."—*Variety*

AMANDA

"*Amanda* seethes and sizzles. A fast-paced, atmospheric tale that vibrates with tension, passion, and mystery. Readers will devour it."—Jayne Ann Krentz

"Kay Hooper's dialogue rings true; her characters are more three-dimensional than those usually found in this genre. You may think you've guessed the outcome, unraveled all the lies. Then again, you could be as mistaken as I was."
—*The Atlanta Journal-Constitution*

"Will delight fans of Phyllis Whitney and Victoria Holt."—*Alfred Hitchcock Mystery Magazine*

"Kay Hooper knows how to serve up a latter-day gothic that will hold readers in its brooding grip."
—*Publishers Weekly*

"I lapped it right up. There aren't enough good books in this genre, so this stands out!"
—*Booknews* from The Poisoned Pen

"Kay Hooper has given you a darn good ride, and there are far too few of those these days."
—*Dayton Daily News*

HIDING
IN THE
SHADOWS

Kay Hooper

BANTAM BOOKS
New York Toronto London Sydney Auckland

HIDING IN THE SHADOWS

A Bantam Book / October 2000

ISBN 0-553-57692-5

Published simultaneously in the United States and Canada

Bantam Books are published by Bantam Books, a division of Random House, Inc. Its trademark, consisting of the words "Bantam Books" and the portrayal of a rooster, is Registered in U.S. Patent and Trademark Office and in other countries. Marca Registrada. Random House, Inc., New York, New York.

PRINTED IN THE UNITED STATES OF AMERICA

OPM   10   9   8   7

FOR MY FAMILY

DINAH

Kane MacGregor looked up from the morning news-paper as she came into the kitchen, and reflected not for the first time that Dinah Leighton was the only woman he'd ever known who managed to create the illusion of incredible bustle while never moving faster than a lazy stroll. It was a peculiarly endearing trait.

"I am so late," she said by way of greeting, drop-ping her briefcase into a chair across from him at the table and going around the work island to pour her-self a cup of coffee. He always made the coffee in the morning, favoring a gourmet blend rich with taste, a selection Dinah accepted cheerfully even though she considered the beverage merely a simple and efficient means of getting caffeine into her system as quickly as possible. "You turned off the alarm again." She didn't sound annoyed, just matter-of-fact.

"After all your long hours recently, I thought you could use a little extra sleep. Besides, it isn't all that late. Just after nine. Do you have a meeting this morning? You didn't mention anything last night."

"No, not a meeting." She spooned enough sugar into the coffee to make him wince, and poured enough cream to make him wonder why she even bothered with coffee. "I just . . . They allow visitors only twice a day, and I'm always too late in the evening."

It was Thursday. He'd forgotten.

"I'm sorry, Dinah. If you'd reminded me—"

The smile she sent him was quick and fleeting. "Don't worry about it. I still have time, I think." She put two slices of bread in the toaster and leaned against the counter.

Kane looked at her, wondering as he had wondered often in recent weeks if it was his imagination that Dinah was a bit preoccupied. He'd thought it was because of the accident, but now he wasn't so sure. She tended to get wrapped up in her work, sometimes to the exclusion of other things. Was that it? Just another story that had drawn her interest and engaged that lively mind?

He wanted to go to her, but didn't; he was experienced enough to recognize the warning in both her actions and her body language. She had not touched him, had not even come near him, in fact. She was across the room with the island *and* the table between them and showing him most of her back.

She might just as well have worn a no-trespassing sign. In neon. It irritated him.

"Will you stop on the way to work?" he asked, keeping the conversation going while he decided whether or not it was time to do something about this.

Dinah checked the wide, leather-banded watch she wore and nodded absently. "For a few minutes."

"You don't have to go twice every week."

"Yes," she said. "I do."

"Dinah, it wasn't your fault."

"I know that." But her voice lacked certainty. She seemed to realize it, because she cleared her throat and quickly changed the subject while she buttered her toast. "Anyway, we'll be going in opposite directions this morning. Just as well, I expect. Steve has me chasing after that building inspector for an interview and the wretched man is never in his office, so I'll need my Jeep."

Steve Hardy was Dinah's editor at the small but well-known magazine where she worked, and he tended to push her almost as hard as she pushed herself.

"Another exposé?" Kane said lightly. "Bribery and kickbacks in the city?"

She laughed. "I wish. No, this is just for a series on our local officials. You know—a day in the life of, and how, exactly, your tax dollars are being spent."

"Easy stuff for you."

Dinah shrugged. "Easy enough."

Kane watched her load the toast with grape jelly and take a healthy bite. She was, he decided, very watchable no matter what she was doing. She wasn't beautiful, but damned close. Regular, not-quite-delicate features that fit together well, the best of which being a pair of steady blue eyes that sometimes saw more than one would guess. Her pale gold hair was cut casually short in tousled layers—"wash and wear," she called it—and her tall, voluptuous body was clothed in a simple tunic sweater and jeans. Dinah didn't care much about clothes, and it showed. On the other hand, what she wore hardly mattered because the enticing figure underneath was what caught the eye. The male eye, at any rate.

His eye, certainly, more than six months ago.

It hadn't taken them long to get intimate, but getting to know each other had become a much more complex, drawn-out process. And a cautious one. Both were fiercely independent, with busy careers and cluttered lives and rocky past relationships that had left scars, and neither had been in a hurry to delve beneath surface passion.

It had been enough, for a while.

But even wary relationships either evolved or fell apart, and theirs was evolving. Almost against their wills, they had been drawn together to share more than a bed, tentatively exchanging views and opinions and comparing tastes and basic values. They liked what they had discovered about each other.

At least, Kane thought so.

They were not quite living together, but after nearly four months of my-place-or-yours, Kane had been wondering if he should be the one to suggest they stop the shuttling back and forth almost every night.

And then, a little more than a month ago, the accident happened and Dinah began to distance herself from him. He had assumed the cause was Dinah's worry for her friend and the ridiculous guilt she felt.

For the first time, though, he asked himself if that was the case.

"I'll probably be late tonight," Dinah said, eating the second piece of toast.

"More research?" It had been her excuse so often of late. Was it time for him to pick a fight and clear the air between them?

"Just something I need to check out. I'll probably be closer to my place than here by the time I get finished, though, so—"

"Why don't I meet you there?" he interrupted, unwilling to hear her suggest another night apart. There had been several recently. Too many. "Eight? Nine?"

Her hesitation was brief. "Eight. I should be through by then."

"I'll bring Chinese," he said. "Or would you rather have something else?"

"No, Chinese is fine. Sesame chicken."

"And no egg rolls. I remember."

Dinah sent him another brief smile, but her mind was clearly elsewhere.

Kane sipped his coffee and watched her. He could accept that her job was important to her; his was to him, after all. So it would hardly be fair of him to protest her abstraction, to demand all her time and attention for himself. But was that really it?

An easy story about the city officials of Atlanta was the sort of thing she could do with her eyes closed. But she had more than once juggled two stories at a time, one of them unknown even to her editor; it was her way of combining the routine work of a magazine writer with the more gritty and urgent instincts of an investigative journalist.

"Dinah?"

Finishing her toast, she sent him a glance, brows lifting inquiringly.

"Why don't we go away this weekend. Maybe drive out to the coast?" He had a beach house, a peaceful retreat that both of them found a welcome change from the hectic pace of the city.

Her hesitation was almost imperceptible. "I wish I could. But I have an appointment on Saturday."

"Can't reschedule?"

"No, I'm afraid not." She smiled regretfully. "There's an assistant D.A. I'm supposed to talk to, and she's got a big case coming up, so her schedule is full. It has to be Saturday."

Kane thought she was lying to him. "Well, it was just a thought. Maybe next weekend." He let the exasperation in his voice lie there in the silence between them.

Her eyes flashed, but her voice remained calm when she said, "Relationships are hell, aren't they?"

"Sometimes."

"I gather you're feeling neglected?"

"Dinah, don't try to make me feel and sound like the typical selfish male."

"There's nothing typical about you," she murmured.

He decided not to ask if that was a compliment. "Look, I know work gets the best of both of us from time to time, and that's as it should be."

"But?"

"But there's more to life than work."

Her lips twisted in an odd, fleeting smile. "I know."

"Then *talk* to me, dammit."

"I don't talk about my stories, Kane, you know that."

"I'm not asking you to betray a confidence. I just want to know what could be so important that you barely have time to eat or sleep these days. And don't give me that bullshit about the story on city officials. That isn't what's making you toss and turn at night."

Disconcerted, she said, "Am I doing that?"

"Yes. Since the accident."

"Well, it's that," she said, grasping the handy reason with relief. "The accident. I've been worried about her, and—"

"It isn't the accident. Or it isn't only the accident. So it has to be a story. Or it has to be us."

"I don't know why you would think—"

"Dinah. I know when something is off-kilter in your life. And what affects you affects me. Tell me what's wrong. I can't fix it until I know what it is."

She looked across the room at him, and something changed in her face. She went behind his chair and bent to put her arms around him. Her warm, smooth cheek pressed against his.

"I really don't appreciate you, do I?" Her voice sounded shaken.

He lifted a hand to her head, letting his fingers slide into her silky hair because he loved it and she never minded. "No," he said a bit dryly. "I'm a prince."

She chuckled. "You certainly are. And I have been neglecting you, I realize that. I'm sorry."

He looked down at her hands on his chest, the fine-boned strength of them, the red-polished nails that showed her one vanity. "So what's going on? Is it just work, or have you met a better prince?"

She hesitated, then moved around him to lean a hip against the table and smiled down at him. "Let's just say I've stumbled onto a story with a lot of potential. A story that could make my reputation."

He frowned. "Your reputation is already made."

"Locally, sure. Even regionally. But this . . . this could put my name on the national map."

Kane felt a prickle of unease. "What kind of story is it?"

"You know better than that."

"I'm not asking for details, Dinah. Just a general idea. Is it criminal? Political? Business?"

"Criminal and business. Maybe wanders into the political arena as well, although I'm not sure about that yet," she replied, still smiling.

"Jesus. Dinah—"

"Don't worry, I know what I'm doing." She reached over and brushed the backs of her fingers down his cheek in a familiar caress.

He didn't allow it to distract him. "Just don't tell me you're on your own in this. If Steve doesn't know—"

Her smile vanished. "He's my editor, Kane, not my nanny."

"That isn't what I meant and you know it. If there's a criminal element in this story, things could get very nasty in a hurry."

"I know that." Her voice was patient. "I have been doing this for a number of years, in case you've forgotten." She went to pick up her briefcase, the tension in her shoulders obvious; that alone told him he'd crossed the line.

She was already moving toward the door; it was too late to apologize, to explain that he was worried only because he cared, not because he doubted her instincts or abilities.

"Just be careful," he called after her.

"Always," she tossed back lightly. And then she was gone.

The silence of the apartment settled over him. With a new anxiety in his mind, the morning seemed darker and much less peaceful than it had only minutes before.

Unlike Dinah, Kane seldom had to cope with downtown traffic, which, in Atlanta, could be truly horrendous. His company was on the outskirts of the city, a five-story stone and glass structure of considerable beauty set on five acres of sprawling grounds just as lovely. It was an engineering and architectural firm founded by his father and his mother's brother, named MacGregor and Payne; Kane hadn't felt the need to change the name, despite the fact that his uncle, Jonah Payne, had died a bachelor, leaving his share of the business to his nephew.

Kane had been in charge since his father, John MacGregor, had taken an early retirement more than ten years before, happily setting off with his second wife to see the world, then choosing to settle in California when his traveling was done.

Kane enjoyed the work, although lately he seemed to concentrate more on administrative details than on the engineering and architecture he loved.

Which was probably why, after Dinah left that morning, he decided on the spur of the moment to visit the construction site where MacGregor and Payne was building new offices for the mayor's support staff and other city officials.

"Kane? What are you doing out here?" Max Sanders, the owner of the Mayfair Construction Company, approached Kane's car briskly. He was wearing a hard hat and carrying a rolled-up set of blueprints, neither one detracting from his superbly cut dark suit—though the liberal coating of dust didn't help. Behind him rose the steel skeleton of what would be an impressive building, which today was crawling with construction workers. Huge earth-moving machines working inside the foundation were kicking up waves of dust.

"I could ask you the same thing," Kane said as he got out of his car. "Since when does the boss get his nice suit dirty if he doesn't have to?"

"He has to," Max replied with a grimace. "Somebody misread your plans and fucked up at least three of the support beams. Something the foreman said to me yesterday bothered me, so I came out this morning. Good thing I did, too."

"It can be corrected?"

Max nodded. "Shouldn't lose more than a day or two. And I've warned Jed he'd better be more careful from now on." Jed Norris was the construction foreman.

"How did he come to misread the plans? He's been in the business long enough to be an expert."

"Well, that might be part of the problem. He thinks he knows how things *should* be, so he doesn't always consider somebody else's opinion."

"Blueprints are opinions?"

Max grimaced again. "What can I tell you? I had a talk with him, Kane. He's too close to retirement to want to fuck up his twilight years, so maybe that'll be enough. I'll keep an eye on things, though, don't worry."

Kane was concerned; the job was highly visible, and if anything went wrong, reputations could end up with mud all over them. But he wasn't about to tell another man how to do his job, and once construction began, his own responsibilities were purely advisory and explanatory.

"I'll leave it up to you, then," he said. "If you find something wrong on the blueprints, give me a call. Otherwise, it seems you have everything under control. So I'll get out of your way."

"You just don't want to get *your* nice suit dirty," Max retorted, his slightly wary expression vanishing, then saluted Kane with the roll of blueprints and headed back toward the site.

Kane had just opened his car door when Max returned. "By the way, did Dinah find you yesterday?"

Kane frowned. "Yesterday?"

"Yeah. About, I don't know, two in the afternoon, maybe? I dropped by here for a look-see, and she came around about fifteen minutes later. Said she thought you might have been out here instead of at the office. I showed her around since she seemed curious. She didn't stay long, though. Did you two meet up later?"

Kane nodded. "Yeah, thanks, we did."

"Okay, great. See you, Kane."

" 'Bye."

Kane didn't know why Dinah had come out there, though it wasn't the first time she had shown up at a construction site looking for him—and finding him, once or twice. But she hadn't mentioned it last night.

Then again, he hadn't mentioned dropping by her office the previous week hoping to find her there.

The detour cost Kane only half an hour. It was just after ten-thirty when got to his office. As usual, his secretary, Sharon Ross, presented him with a dozen messages, which meant he'd spend the remainder of the morning on the phone.

"Shit," he said elegantly.

Sharon grinned. "I can pretend you didn't come in today."

Kane was tempted, but since he only enjoyed ditching work when there was a fun alternative—and today, there wasn't—it didn't seem worth the bother. "No, I'm officially in today, Sharon."

She nodded. "I didn't add it to the rest, but Dinah called about two minutes ago."

Kane said *shit* again, but silently. He would have liked the opportunity to finish his discussion with Dinah; being at odds with her screwed up his whole day. "Did she leave a message?"

"Yeah, she said to tell you she just found out her cell phone battery was dead, so not to worry if you don't talk to her until tonight. She's going to be on the run and out of her office most of the day."

"Okay. Thanks, Sharon."

In his office, Kane pushed Dinah out of his mind and concentrated on work. Two hours later, he was frowning down at an engineering schematic of a gravity-defying design when the door opened and Sydney Wilkes strolled in. She looked serene and cool as always, which was not unusual on a nippy October afternoon but earned her astonished stares in the heat of an Atlanta summer. Her business suit was immaculate, the beautifully tailored style and mustard color flattering her tan and pale blond hair, and she walked with the easy confidence of a woman who is beautiful and knows it.

Kane swiveled his chair away from the drafting table and looked at her with lifted brows. "Bored, Syd?"

"Is that the only reason I ever visit my favorite brother? Because I'm bored?" Her voice was rich and lazy.

"I'm your only brother—and yes, usually." But he smiled to remove any sting from the words.

She smiled in return, the pale gray eyes they shared amused and tolerant. "All right, so nothing much is going on today in the residential arm of MacGregor and Payne, and I thought you might like somebody to buy you lunch. I ran into Dinah yesterday, and she said she'd be tied up all day, so . . ."

An architect herself, Sydney had chosen to special-ize in residential work, whereas Kane's preference was commercial; it was an easy and profitable partnership. There were only three years between them—at thirty-two, Sydney was the younger. Her marriage had kept her working only part-time until her husband's accidental death more than two years previously; she was now fully involved in the family firm. As for her personal life, though there was certainly interest from just about every male she encountered, she had been unwilling, so far, to begin dating again.

"Well," Kane said, "if you're buying . . ."

Lunch was pleasant, and the remainder of the afternoon hectic. In fact, he wasn't able to leave the office until after seven-thirty. Determined not to be late, he rushed to pick up the Chinese food and get to Dinah's apartment, but even so it was well after eight when he got to her building.

Dinah's Jeep wasn't in its parking space.

Both relieved and irritated, Kane parked his car and went inside. The security guard knew him well enough just to wave a greeting.

He let himself into Dinah's third-floor apartment with his key, fumbled for the foyer light, and took the food to the kitchen. As usual, the place was very tidy; not only was Dinah naturally neat, but she had a cleaning service come in once a week—and by the fresh scent of lemon in the air, Kane knew the apartment had been cleaned today.

Maybe that was why it felt so . . . empty. He went around the living room lighting lamps and turned on the television. He changed out of his suit into jeans and a sweatshirt, and waited.

By nine o'clock, he was hungry and angry.

By ten o'clock, he was worried.

He couldn't remember Dinah being so late before without calling. And even if her cell phone did have a dead battery, there were pay phones, weren't there? All over the city, there were pay phones.

Kane called her office and got her voice mail; he left a brief message asking her to call him if she came in or checked in before coming home. She never carried a pager, so his options were limited.

All he could do was wait.

By eleven he was going often to the front window to look searchingly out at the busy streets. By midnight he was pacing the floor.

He only just stopped himself from calling her boss. He reminded himself that Dinah was a grown woman, no fool, and able to take care of herself. She would certainly be unhappy with him if he pushed the panic button when she was just tied up with something and had forgotten to phone.

He told himself that several times.

The streets outside got quieter and grew shiny in the streetlights because it had started to rain.

It got later.

And later.

And Dinah never came.

FAITH

She opened her eyes abruptly, as though waking from a nightmare, conscious of her heart pounding and the sound of her quick, shallow breathing in the otherwise silent room. She couldn't remember the dream, but her shaking body and runaway pulse told her it had been a bad one. She closed her eyes and for several minutes concentrated only on calming down.

Gradually, her heart slowed and her breathing steadied. Okay. Okay. That was better. Much better.

She didn't like being scared.

She opened her eyes and looked at the ceiling. Gradually a niggling awareness of something being different made her turn her head slowly on the pillow so that she could look around the room.

It wasn't her room.

Her other senses began waking up then. She heard the muffled, distant sounds of activity just beyond the closed door. She smelled sickness and medicine, the distinct odors of people and machines and starch. She noted the Spartan quality of the room she was in, the hospital bed she was lying on—and the IV dripping into her arm. All of that told her she was in a hospital.

Why?

It took a surprising effort to raise her head and look down at herself; her neck felt stiff, and a rush of nausea made her swallow hard. But she forced herself to look, to make sure all of her was there.

Both arms. Both legs. Nothing in a cast. Her feet moved when she willed them to. Not paralyzed, then. Good.

With an effort, she raised the arm not hooked to the IV until she could see her hand. It was unnervingly small, not childlike but . . . fragile. The short nails were ragged and looked bitten, and the skin was milky pale. She turned it slowly and stared at the palms, the pads of her fingers. No calluses, but there was a slight roughness to her skin that told her she was accustomed to work.

Afraid of what she might find, she touched her face with light, probing fingers. The bones seemed prominent, and the skin felt soft and smooth. There was no evidence of an injury until she reached her right temple. There, a square adhesive bandage and a faint soreness underneath it told her she'd suffered some kind of cut.

But not a bad one, she thought, and certainly not a big one. The bandage was small, two or three square inches.

Beyond the bandage, she found her hair limp and oily, which told her it hadn't been washed recently. She pulled at a strand and was surprised that it was long enough for her to see. It was mostly straight, with only a hint of curl. And it was red. A dark, dull red.

Now why did that surprise her?

For the first time, she let herself become aware of what had been crawling in her subconscious, a cold and growing fear she dared not name. She realized she was lying perfectly still now, her arms at her sides, hands clenched into fists, staring at the ceiling as if she would find the answers there.

She was only slightly injured, so why was she there? Because she was ill? What was wrong with her?

Why did her body feel so appallingly weak?

And far, far worse, why couldn't she remember—

"Oh, my God."

The nurse in the doorway came a few steps into the room, moving slowly, her eyes wide with surprise. Then professionalism took over, and she swallowed and said brightly, if a bit unsteadily, "You—you're awake. We were . . . beginning to wonder about you, Fa—Miss Parker."

Parker.

"I'll get the doctor."

She lay there waiting, not daring to think about the fact that she hadn't known her own name, and still didn't beyond that unfamiliar surname. It seemed an eternity that she waited, while cold and wordless terrors clawed through her mind and churned in her stomach, before a doctor appeared. He was tall, on the thin side, with a sensitive mouth and very brilliant, very dark eyes.

"So you're finally awake." His voice was deep and warm, his smile friendly. He grasped her wrist lightly as he stood by the bed, discreetly taking her pulse. "Can you tell me your name?"

She wet her lips and said huskily, "Parker." Her voice sounded rusty and unused, and her throat felt scratchy.

He didn't look surprised; likely the nurse had confessed that she had provided that information. "What about your first name?"

She tried not to cry out in fear. "No. No, I—I don't remember that."

"Do you remember what happened to you?"

"No."

"How about telling me what year this is?"

She concentrated, fought down that icy, crawling panic. There was nothing in her mind but blankness, a dark emptiness that frightened her almost beyond words. No sense of identity or knowledge. Nothing. *Nothing.*

"I don't remember."

"Well, try not to worry about it," he said soothingly. "A traumatic event frequently results in amnesia, but it's seldom permanent. Things will probably start to come back to you now that you're awake."

"Who are you?" she asked, because it was the least troubling question she could think of.

"My name is Dr. Burnett, Nick Burnett. I've been your doctor since you were admitted. *Your* name is Faith Parker."

Faith Parker. It didn't stir even the slightest sense of familiarity. "Is . . . is it?"

He smiled gently. "Yes. You're twenty-eight years old, single, and in pretty good shape physically, though you could stand to gain a few pounds." He paused, then went on in a calm tone completely without judgment. "You were involved in a single-car accident, which the police blame on the fact that you'd had a few drinks on top of prescription muscle relaxants. The combination made you plow your car into an embankment."

She might have been listening to a description of someone else, for all the memory it stirred.

The doctor continued. "It also turned out to be highly toxic to your system. You appear to be unusually sensitive to alcohol, and that, along with the drug, put you into a coma. However, aside from the gash on your head, which we've kept covered to minimize scarring, and a few bruised ribs, which have already healed, you're fine."

There were so many questions swirling through her mind that she could grab only one at random. "Was—was anyone else hurt in the accident?"

"No. You were alone in the car, and all you hit was the embankment."

Something he'd said a minute ago tugged at her. "You said . . . my ribs had healed by now. How long have I been here?"

"Six weeks."

She was shocked. "So long? But . . ." She wasn't sure what she wanted to ask, but her anxiety was growing with every new fact.

"Let's try sitting up a bit, shall we?" Not waiting for her response, he used a control to raise the head of the bed a few inches. When she closed her eyes, he stopped the movement. "The dizziness should pass in a minute."

She opened her eyes slowly, finding that he was

right. But there was little satisfaction in that, with all the questions and worries overwhelming her. And panic. A deep, terrifying panic. "Doctor, I can't remember anything. Not where I live or work. I don't know if I have insurance, and if I don't, I don't know how I'll pay for six weeks in a hospital. I don't even know what address to give the cabdriver when I go—go home."

"Listen to me, Faith." His voice was gentle. "There's no reason for you to worry, especially not about money. Your medical insurance from work hadn't started yet, but arrangements have already been made to pay your hospital bill in full. And I understand that a trust fund has been set up for you when you leave here. There should be plenty of money, certainly enough to live on for several months while you get your life back in order."

That astonishing information made her panic recede somewhat, but she was bewildered. "A trust fund? Set up for me? But who would do that?"

"A friend of yours. A good friend. She came to visit you twice a week until—" Something indefinable crossed his face and then vanished, and he went on quickly. "She wanted to make certain you got the best of care and had no worries when you left here."

"But why? The accident obviously wasn't her fault, since I was alone. . . ." Unless this friend had encouraged her to drink or hadn't taken her car keys away when she had gotten drunk?

"I couldn't tell you why, Faith. Except that she was obviously concerned about you."

Faith felt a rush of pain that she couldn't remember so good a friend. "What's her name?"

"Dinah Leighton."

It meant no more to Faith than her own name.

Dr. Burnett was watching her carefully. "We have the address of your apartment, which I understand is waiting for your return. Miss Leighton seemed less certain that you would want to go back to your job, which I believe is one of the reasons she made it possible for you to have the time to look around, perhaps even return to school or do something you've always wanted to do."

She felt tears prickle and burn. "Something I've always wanted to do. Except I can't remember anything I've always wanted to do. Or anything I've done. Or even what I look like . . ."

He grasped her hand and held it strongly. "It will come back to you, Faith. You may never remember the hours immediately preceding and following the accident, but most of the rest will return in time. Coma does funny things to the body and the mind."

She sniffed, and tried to concentrate, to hold on to facts and avoid thinking of missing memories. "What kinds of things?"

Still holding her hand, he drew a visitor's chair to the bed and sat down. "To the body, what you'd expect after a traumatic accident and weeks of inactivity. Muscle weakness. Unstable blood pressure. Dizziness and digestive upset from lying prone and having no solid food. But all those difficulties should disappear once you've been up and about for a few days, eating regular meals and exercising."

"What about . . . the mind? What other kinds of problems can be caused by coma?" The possibilities lurking in her imagination were terrifying. What if she never regained her memory? What if she found herself unable to do the normal things people did every day, simple things like buttoning a shirt or reading a book? What if whatever skills and knowledge she'd needed in her work were gone forever and she was left with no way to earn a living?

"Sometimes things we don't completely understand," the doctor confessed. "Personality changes are common. Habits and mannerisms are sometimes different. The emotions can be volatile or, conversely, bland. You may find yourself getting confused at times, even after your memory returns, and panic attacks are more likely than not."

She swallowed. "Great."

Dr. Burnett smiled. "On the other hand, you may suffer no aftereffects whatsoever. You're perfectly lucid, and we've done our best to reduce muscle atrophy and other potential problems. Physical therapy should be minimal, I'd say. Once your memory returns, you may well find yourself as good as ever."

He sounded so confident that Faith let herself believe him, because the alternative was unbearable.

Trying not to think about that, she asked, "What about family? Do I have any family?"

"Miss Leighton told us you have no family in Atlanta. There was a sister, I understand, but I believe both she and your parents were killed some years ago."

Faith wished she felt something about that. "And I'm single. Do I—Is there—"

"I'm sure you must have dated," he said kindly, "but evidently there was no one special, at least not in the last few months. You've had no male visitors, no cards or letters, and only Miss Leighton sent flowers, as far as I'm aware."

So she was alone, but for this remarkably good friend.

She felt alone, and considerably frightened.

He saw it. "Everything seems overwhelming right now, I know. It's too much to process, too much to deal with. But you have time, Faith. There's no need to push yourself, and no reason to worry. Take it step by step."

She drew a breath. "All right. What's the first step?"

"We get you up on your feet and moving." He smiled and rose from the chair. "But not too fast. Today, we'll have you gradually sit up, maybe try standing, and monitor your reaction to that. We'll see how your stomach reacts to a bit of solid food. How's that to start?"

She managed a smile. "Okay."

"Good." He squeezed her hand and released it, then hesitated.

Seeing his face, she said warily, "What?"

"Well, since you might want to read the newspapers or watch television to catch up on things, I think I should warn you about something."

"About what?"

"Your friend Miss Leighton. She's been missing for about two weeks."

"Missing? You mean she—she stopped coming to visit me?"

There was sympathy in his dark eyes. "I mean she disappeared. She was reported missing, and though her car was found abandoned some time later, she hasn't been seen since."

Faith was surprised by the rush of emotions she felt.

Confusion. Shock. Disappointment. Regret. And, finally, a terrible pain at the knowledge that she was now completely alone.

Dr. Burnett patted her hand, but seemed to realize that no soothing words would make her feel better. He didn't offer any, just went away quietly.

She lay there staring up at the white, blank ceiling, which was as empty as her mind.

He laughed at her, the sound rich with amusement.

"Well, how was I to know you couldn't boil water without ruining the pot?"

"I just forgot," she defended herself with spirit. "I had more important things on my mind."

He shook his head, fair hair gleaming like spun gold and a wry expression on his handsome face. "To be honest, I'm glad there are a few things you don't do well. If you were perfect, I wouldn't know how to cope."

She reached out a hand and touched his face, the backs of her fingers stroking downward in a quick caress. Her hands were strong and beautiful, well kept, the neat oval nails polished a vivid red. She felt the slight bristle of his evening beard, a scratchiness that was familiar and pleasant, even erotic. It made her breath catch at the back of her throat, and her voice emerged more husky than she had expected. "I may not be perfect, but I'm starving. And since I ruined dinner, I thought maybe we could go out."

"Only if you're buying," he said, still humorous even though his eyes darkened in response to what he heard in her voice. "I refuse to buy dinner for a

woman who ruined three pots and really stunk up my kitchen."

"You needed new pots anyway," she said, and danced away, laughing, when he lunged at her.

But she didn't try too hard to escape, and when his hands were on her, strong and sure and exciting, she let herself melt against him. Their bodies fit together as though they'd been designed to, and his mouth on hers was still a shock of wild, overwhelming pleasure, instantly seductive. But as always, the warning voice in her head told her not to yield completely, to hold back something of herself because she knew how this would end, she knew it. And as always, she ignored the warning and reached eagerly for what he offered.

A burst of heat raced through her and her heart began to pound, and when his hands slid down her back to curve over her bottom and hold her even tighter against him—

Faith woke with a start, shaken yet also exultant.

There was a man in her life. Or had been.

She closed her eyes and tried to recapture the image of his face, pleased when it rose easily and vividly in her mind. That gleaming, spun-gold hair, a little longer than the current fashion, even a bit shaggy—and decidedly sexy. Gray eyes steady and intelligent, going silvery with laughter. Firm, humorous mouth, determined jaw. Deep, strong voice.

And the way he'd looked at her . . .

Faith shivered and opened her eyes, realizing that her cheeks were hot and she was smiling helplessly, that the quiver deep inside her was something other than fear and panic. She swore she could smell the cologne he used, that pleasant scent mixed with the sharper, clean fragrance of soap.

Then that sensory memory abandoned her, leaving only his face distinct in her mind. She held on to it—fiercely.

Her room was quiet but for the murmur of the television, tuned to CNN. She was almost sitting up, the head of the bed raised because she'd been looking through magazines before she'd suddenly fallen asleep. She still did that sometimes, even though it had been almost a week since she'd come out of the coma. Days of painful transition, of moving from a patient who was bedridden and totally dependent on the nursing staff to one slowly and cautiously reclaiming independence.

Small movements had required a great effort at first, and walking even more so. Her muscles were weak and slow to obey her, though daily physical therapy was gradually changing that. Her blood pressure had stabilized, but her stomach still had trouble with solid foods.

The removal of the feeding tube had been surprisingly painless and would leave only a tiny scar, but having the catheter taken out had not been pleasant.

Three days ago she had actually made it into the bathroom on her own, and had spent long minutes staring into the mirror at a face she didn't know. A thin, pale face, framed by mostly straight, dull red hair that fell just below her shoulders. Her green eyes were very clear and strong, but the remainder of her features struck her as less than memorable. Straight nose, generous mouth, determined chin.

Some might call her pretty, perhaps.

She had discovered that she was only a few inches over five feet, very slender, and fine boned. She had small breasts and virtually no hips—minimal curves at best. She thought her legs were okay, or would be once they began to hold her up for more than a few minutes at a time.

Yesterday morning she had taken a long, luxurious bath, and though a nurse had had to help her dry her hair afterward because she'd used up all her strength, the results had been worth it. She felt much better. As for her hair, the dull red had become a rich auburn, which made her pale face look luminous.

It was a face, she thought now, that might attract a handsome man with gleaming blond hair. A man with intelligent gray eyes and a way of leveling them when he spoke that said he was accustomed to getting what he wanted.

What was his name? And if they were so involved that physical intimacy had been very much a part of the relationship, why had he never come to visit her?

That bothered her. A lot.

But the flowers from Dinah Leighton continued to arrive once a week, even after her own disappearance. Faith had gotten up the nerve to call the florist and had found that the order had been paid ahead for another week.

Obviously, no one else cared enough even to acknowledge Faith's presence in the hospital—or her absence from the life she had led before the accident.

Where was that blond man?

How could he be so vivid in her mind—her only

real memory—if he had not been a recent part of her life?

A nurse came in carrying a stack of magazines. "I brought you a few more, honey." She was a motherly woman with a warm voice and gentle hands, and over the last few days she had been the most helpful and encouraging of the nurses.

"Thanks, Kathy." She eyed the short, neat, unpolished nails of the nurse, then looked at her own still-ragged ones. "Kathy, do you happen to have a nail file?"

"I'll get one for you." Kathy put the magazines on the bed and smiled at her with genuine pleasure. "You're looking much better today, honey. And obviously feeling better."

Faith smiled at her. "I am, thanks."

"Dr. Burnett will be pleased. You're one of his favorites, you know."

Faith had to laugh. "Because he wants to write that paper on me, and we both know it. Not too many long-term-coma patients wake up."

"That's true," Kathy said soberly. "And those who do tend to be in much worse shape than you are, honey. With you, it's almost like you were just sleeping."

Faith didn't feel as though she had just been sleeping, but said only, "I know how lucky I am, believe me. And you and the other nurses have been terrific. That makes a difference."

Kathy patted Faith's shoulder, said, "I'll go get that nail file," and left the room.

It was easy enough to say the right words. Faith had been doing that for days now. She had been positive and upbeat. She had listened closely to the psychiatrist on staff and obediently followed her advice to take things one step at a time. She had agreed with the nurses' cheerful predictions that her life would get back on track sooner rather than later. She had read newspapers and magazines and watched television to catch up on current events. She had made herself smile at Dr. Burnett when he visited and had not mentioned the devastating panic that was always with her and how she often woke in the night terrified by the blankness inside herself.

She had some knowledge now, but almost all of it dated from the moment she'd opened her eyes in the hospital. The nurses' faces were familiar, as were the doctors'. The layout of her floor and that of the physical therapy rooms two stories above.

These things she knew.

And there was, absent from her mind until someone asked her a direct question, the sort of knowledge that came from a normal education. She had completed several crossword puzzles, and a game show she had found on television had shown her that she had some awareness of history and science. Facts. Dates. Occurrences.

Fairly useless trivia, for the most part.

But of memories, all she had, all she could claim as her own dating from that otherwise blank part of her life, were the dreams of a blond man she thought she had loved.

There had been two other dreams before today, and they were brief and very similar; just scenes from a relationship, casual and intimate. Each time, the scene had erupted into laughter and ended in lovemaking.

But she still didn't remember his name.

She hadn't mentioned the dreams to anyone. They were something all her own, a piece of herself not given to her by someone else, and she held on to them as to an anchor.

"Here you go, Faith." Kathy returned to the room and handed her the nail file. "Before you start working on those nails, how about a trip around the floor? Doctor's orders."

Faith was more than ready to move. Painful as it still was, at least it allowed her to concentrate on muscles and bones and balance, instead of having to keep thinking and wondering.

"You bet," she said, and threw back the covers.

On November fourteenth, three weeks after waking up from her coma and nine weeks after the accident, Faith went home.

She was not fully recovered. She still got tired very easily, her sleep was erratic and disturbed by dreams she remembered and nightmares she didn't, and her emotional state was, to say the least, fragile.

Dr. Burnett drove her to her apartment, claiming it was on his way home but fooling nobody. He had several times shown himself more than a little protective of Faith.

Faith was more than happy to accept his escort. She was nervous and panicky, afraid the place where she lived would jar memories. Terrified it would not.

She wore her own clothes, thanks to Dinah Leighton's foresight in packing a bag for her and taking it to the hospital just a week after the accident, but though the slacks and sweater fit fairly well, she was uncomfortable in them. Perhaps it was because she had spent so much time in a nightgown.

Her apartment was on the sixth floor of a nice but ordinary building in a suburb of Atlanta. No doorman or guard greeted them, but everything looked clean and in good repair, and the elevator worked smoothly.

Dr. Burnett came in with her, carrying her small overnight bag, which he set down by the door. "Why don't we take a look around?" he suggested, watching her. "I don't want to leave you until you're comfortable here."

Faith accepted the suggestion because she didn't want to be alone.

The apartment was . . . nice. Ordinary. There was one bedroom; the queen-size brass bed had a floral, ruffled comforter set, with lots of pillows tossed against the shams. Curtains at the single window matched the comforter. There was a nightstand and a chair, both white wicker and a white laminated dresser with an oval wicker-framed mirror hanging above it. The color scheme was white and pink.

Faith thought it an odd choice for a redhead, and rather girlish.

The one bathroom was small and standard, with white tiles and plain fixtures. The rugs, towels, and curtains on the window and shower bore another floral pattern, this one with pink and purple predominating.

The kitchen was also standard, white cabinets and a neutral countertop blending perfectly with the vinyl floor. There was a small breakfast table, again of white wicker and glass, with a cheap area rug underneath it. Little attempt had been made to personalize the space as far as Faith could see. There were no place mats on the table, and except for a coffeemaker, nothing cluttered the countertops.

The living room struck her as having been recently decorated, and she had the feeling—certainly not a memory—that some picture in a magazine had been the inspiration. The intended style might have been shabby chic, with distressed wood, lots of texture in materials, and antique-looking accessories.

It didn't quite work, though she couldn't have explained why.

"Nice place," Burnett said.

She nodded, even as she wondered why the little apartment felt stifling to her. Was it the several locks on the door, an indication of someone who had shut the world out—or herself in? Faith didn't know, but it disturbed her.

She shrugged out of her jacket and left it over a chair, then returned to the kitchen and checked the cabinets and the refrigerator. "Sloan was as good as his word," she noted, seeing the stock of foods.

The lawyer had come to see her several days ago, after being notified by Dr. Burnett that she was up to having visitors. He had explained the financial situation, including Dinah Leighton's arrangements to pay the hospital bill and the trust fund she had set up for Faith's use. Her disappearance, he had explained without emotion, changed none of that. In addition, Faith's regular monthly bills had been paid, including recently incurred debts. She wasn't to worry, everything had been taken care of.

Then he had promised to have her apartment cleaned and stocked with food, ready for her return. All per Dinah's careful arrangements.

Faith had been given a generous amount of cash, and her checking account, he told her, had been credited with even more. In addition to that, her rent had been paid for the next six months.

It had been too overwhelming for Faith to think about then, and now she felt a prickle of uneasiness. All this from a friend? *Why?*

"My advice," Burnett said cheerfully, "is to fix yourself something simple for dinner or order in a pizza, and have an early night. Familiarize yourself with where everything is. Make yourself comfortable here." He smiled at her perceptively. "Stop thinking so much, Faith. Give yourself time."

She knew he was right. And she was even able to say goodbye to him calmly, promising to return to the hospital as scheduled in a few days for a checkup and another session with the physical therapist.

Then she was alone.

She locked the door, turned on the television in the living room for company and background noise, and wandered again through the apartment. This time, she looked more closely.

Her initial puzzlement took on a chill of unease.

There was no history here. No photographs, either displayed or tucked away in drawers. And very little to indicate her interests. A few books, mostly recent best-sellers that ran the gamut of genres, and many of those apparently unread.

She found plenty of clothes in the drawers and closet, and the bathroom held the usual supplies of soap and shampoo, moisturizers and bubble bath and disposable razors, and a small toiletry bag of makeup containing the basics, all new or nearly so. A blow dryer and a curling iron were stowed in the cabinet below the sink.

What there was not was evidence that a woman had lived here for more than a few weeks or months. No old lipsticks or dried-up mascaras in the drawers. No unused foundation compacts that had turned out to be the wrong shade. No nearly empty tubes of moisturizer or hand lotion. No fingernail polish or remover. No samples given out at cosmetics counters in practically every store in the world.

Either Faith Parker was the neatest woman alive . . . or she had spent very little time here.

She went into the living room and sat down at the small desk tucked away in a corner. The single drawer held only a few things. A small address book showing meager entries—names, addresses, and phone numbers that meant nothing to her. Her checkbook and a copy of her lease, both of which indicated that she had lived here for nearly eighteen months before the accident. There were regular deposits made on Fridays, obviously her salary, which was enough to live on without living particularly well; some months it appeared that ends had barely met. Checks had been written to the usual places, some of which matched entries in the address book. Grocery stores, department stores, hair salons, dentist, a couple of restaurants, a pharmacy, a women's clinic, a computer store.

A computer store.

Faith looked slowly around the room with a frown. According to the register, she had bought a laptop computer on a payment plan only a few weeks before the accident. It should be here.

It wasn't.

She'd had only a purse with her when she rammed her car into that embankment, they'd told her. So why wasn't the computer here?

On the heels of that question, the phone on the desk rang suddenly, startling her. Faith had to take a deep, steadying breath before she could pick up the receiver.

"Miss Parker, this is Edward Sloan." The lawyer's voice was brisk. "Forgive me for disturbing you on your first day home, but I thought there was something you should know."

"What is it, Mr. Sloan?"

"The service I hired to clean your apartment this week found it in . . . unusual disarray."

"Meaning I'm a slob?" she asked, even though she already knew the answer.

"No, Miss Parker, I think not. Many drawers had been emptied onto the floor, pillows and other things scattered about. It had all the earmarks of a burglary, perhaps interrupted in progress, since nothing appeared to have been taken. This was three days ago. Knowing you were still in the hospital, I took the liberty of acting in your stead. I reported the matter to the police, then met them at your apartment. They took the report, took photos of the place, and questioned others in the building. But since no one saw or heard anything out of the ordinary, and since your television and stereo were still there and nothing had been damaged as far as we could determine, no further action was taken."

"I see," she murmured.

"The cleaning service was allowed to do their job immediately afterward. They were instructed to put things back in place as neatly as possible, and to use their judgment as to where everything belonged. Do you have any complaints on that score, Miss Parker?"

"No."

"Have you discovered anything missing?"

He knew about her amnesia, but it seemed an automatic, lawyer's question.

"No," Faith repeated, looking down at the check-book entry concerning the computer. She did not want to mention it, though she couldn't explain why, even to herself. "Nothing."

"If you do discover anything, you'll let me know?"

"Of course, Mr. Sloan." She hesitated. "There is one thing. You said that all my recently incurred debts had been paid?"

"Yes."

"How did you know about them, Mr. Sloan?"

"Miss Leighton supplied that information, Miss Parker. I believe she took the liberty of going through your desk to get a correct accounting. Other than regular monthly bills such as utilities, rent, a small credit card balance, and so on, there were two recently incurred debts. One for a laptop computer, which Miss Leighton informed me had been in her possession since your accident, and the other for new living-room furniture. Both accounts were paid in full."

"I see." She swallowed. "Thank you, Mr. Sloan."

"My pleasure, Miss Parker." He hung up.

So Dinah Leighton had the laptop that Faith had bought weeks before her accident. Why? And where was it now?

Her thoughts were whirling, confused. Then, to make matters much, much worse, she caught a glimpse of something on the television. She lunged for the remote and turned up the sound.

". . . Kane MacGregor, one of those closest to the missing woman, expressed his trust in the efforts of the police to find her," the off-camera voice intoned solemnly.

The blond man before the cameras looked tired, his face drawn and thin, his gray eyes haunted. Numerous microphones were thrust at him. A question Faith could barely hear was asked, and he replied in a deep voice that made a warm shiver course through her.

"No, I have not given up hope. The police are making every effort to find her, and I believe they will do so. In the meantime, if anyone watching has any information they believe could help locate Dinah"—his calm voice quivered just a bit on the name—"they should call the police and report it as soon as possible."

"Mr. MacGregor, have you called in the FBI?" one reporter shouted out.

"No, the matter is not within their jurisdiction. We have no evidence that Dinah has been kidnapped," he answered.

"Have you hired a private investigator?"

Kane MacGregor smiled thinly. "Of course I have. I'm doing everything in my power to find Dinah."

"Which is why you're offering a million dollars to anyone providing evidence that will locate Miss Leighton alive and well?"

"Exactly." He drew a breath, the strain really beginning to show on his lean face. "Now, if you people don't mind—"

"One last question, Mr. MacGregor. Were you engaged to Miss Leighton?"

For an instant, it seemed Kane MacGregor's face would crack open and all his wild emotions would come spilling out. But it didn't happen, and only his voice, harsh with pain, revealed what he was feeling.

"Yes. We are engaged." Then he pushed his way through the reporters, followed closely by a tall, dark man with a scarred face, and both disappeared into a waiting car.

Faith found herself sitting on the couch, her arms hugging a pillow to her breasts, dazed, no longer hearing the news broadcast.

Kane MacGregor was the man in her dreams. And he was Dinah's fiancé. She was having dreams about Dinah's fiancé? Intimate dreams?

Pain, hot and cold like a knife made of ice, sliced through her. She heard herself breathing in shallow pants, felt her heart thudding, her body trembling.

Had he been her lover first? Had their relationship ended a long time ago, before Dinah came along? Or was Kane MacGregor's haunted, grieving face hiding the knowledge that he'd been involved with her and Dinah at the same time?

Then Faith went even colder.

Dinah was missing. Faith had been in a serious accident.

Did it mean something?

Her apartment had been broken into after her accident, and though she couldn't know for certain if anything had been taken, the lack of personal papers and photographs was decidedly unnatural.

Did it mean something? Anything?

Why couldn't she remember?

"Oh, God," she whispered. "What's happening?"

THE SEARCH

ONE

"Were you?" Bishop asked.

Kane, concentrating on driving, spared him only a quick glance. "Was I what? Engaged to Dinah?"

"Yeah."

"Unofficially."

Bishop thought about that for several beats. "Does *unofficially engaged* mean it was all in your mind or all in hers?"

Kane felt a flicker of grim amusement. "You have to have everything spelled out, don't you, Noah?"

"Just trying to understand."

"Then I guess I'd have to say it was all in my mind. I hadn't asked her yet."

"But you were going to?"

It was Kane's turn to think, and when he answered it was with a weary sigh. "Hell, I don't know. I think so. I mean, I hadn't planned to, but it was in the back of my mind that's where we'd end up. At least . . ."

"Until just before she disappeared?"

Kane nodded. "It's like I told you. Everything was fine. Then she got preoccupied, I assumed by whatever story she was working on. Then there was the accident her friend was in, and she seemed to get even more distant and distracted."

"And she never told you what she was working on?"

"Goddammit, Noah, you know Dinah. She's always been like a clam when it comes to a work in progress. With that amazing memory of hers, she never needs notes. And sure, a story absorbs her, sometimes makes her oblivious to most things. But this time it had gone on long enough to bother me. So I tried to get her to talk about it that last morning, to tell me what she was investigating. She told me practically nothing and ended up mad at me to boot."

"Stop feeling guilty," Bishop said. "You couldn't have known she'd disappear that day."

Since guilt was only a small part of what Kane was feeling, he was able to shrug without comment.

Bishop looked at him thoughtfully. "And you're sure, absolutely sure, that wherever she went, it wasn't willingly?"

"Absolutely positive. And even if I'm wrong about that, she would never stay away this long without letting me know where she is. If she could get to a phone, she'd call me."

Bishop was silent for a couple of miles, then said, "We're reasonably sure that nothing in her personal life would have driven somebody to snatch her."

It wasn't a question, but Kane answered anyway. "Nothing I can imagine. When her father died a few years ago, he was the last of her family, I told you that. Or at least the last she knew of. He left her a huge portfolio of stocks and other investments, but she just turned the management of everything over to someone and more or less ignored the money, as far as I could see."

"You said both you and the police talked to her financial consultant?"

"Sure, early on. Easy enough for me, since he manages my money as well. He said Dinah's business affairs were perfectly in order, that she wasn't being blackmailed or pressured in any way as far as he knew. No large, unexplained deposits or withdrawals to or from any of her accounts. Nothing. Not a single goddamned breadcrumb to follow."

"Still," Bishop said, "maybe it'd be worthwhile to talk to him one more time. Money tends to be at the root of most bad things one way or another. He might know something no one else could tell us, especially now that he's had plenty of time to think about it."

By this point, Kane wasn't willing to discount anything, even going over familiar ground a second time. Dinah had been missing for more than a month, and so far the investigation had led nowhere.

Noah Bishop, special agent for the FBI, had come into the picture only the day before, when he'd arrived in Atlanta. He had been out of the country, whether on Bureau business or his own, Kane hadn't asked. He wasn't formally a part of the investigation, but both his badge and his manner meant that when he asked questions, even of cops jealous of their territory, he usually got answers.

Kane and he had been good friends since college,

when they'd competed in track-and-field events, and had been roommates in their junior and senior years. Their career choices had taken them in different directions after graduation, but Noah always found a long weekend every few months to visit Atlanta.

He had managed three of those visits after Kane had become involved with Dinah, so he had known her fairly well. And since she had been characteristically curious about the FBI and Noah's very specialized abilities and knowledge, and he had a high regard for investigative journalists with integrity and strong ethics, they had found much to talk about.

So, he was almost as upset over her disappearance as Kane was, but only the whitening of the scar down his left cheek bore witness to that emotion. Otherwise, he appeared completely calm and in control, his voice steady and sometimes filled with a dry humor, his powerful body relaxed, pale sentry eyes watchful as always but tranquil.

Kane wasn't fooled.

In response to Bishop's statement, he said, "Okay, we'll talk to Conrad Masterson. I'll call him tonight. In the meantime, there must be something else we can do."

"Between you, the cops, and your private investigator, I'd say everything that could be done has been." As if ticking off the facts on his fingers, Bishop said, "Her movements that last day have been traced as much as possible and every potential lead followed. Everyone she's known to have talked to that last week has been questioned at least once. You've kept a fire burning under the police. Your P.I. has been dogging every step of the investigation and working his own contacts. You've spent days in Dinah's office going through ten years' worth of files, and weeks running down information on anyone she might have pissed off in the course of doing a story. You've talked to her financial manager, her co-workers, and her boss. You've talked to neighbors in her apartment building. You've searched her apartment—twice. You've offered a million-dollar reward for information."

Kane braced himself.

Quietly, reluctantly, Bishop said, "Unless something new comes to light . . . Jesus, Kane. I'm sorry as hell—but the trail is looking awfully goddamned cold."

Kane hadn't wanted to admit that to himself. Not today, when Bishop had kept him from lunging across the desk of a police lieutenant and choking the man. Not yesterday, when the last of Dinah's known enemies had proved to be in prison on the fifth year of a ten-year sentence. Not the day before that, or the days and weeks before that, when useless information had piled up and leads dwindled and hope dissolved.

"I know," he said. "I know."

Conrad Masterson had always amused Kane. He was average in appearance—average height, average weight, an average bald spot atop his head. He didn't care how he dressed, which explained his badly cut suit, and wasn't impressed by impressive surroundings, which was why his small office was filled with aged furniture and worn rugs and smelled vaguely like a wet dog. Or two.

He had no charm, tended to stutter when he got

excited (always about a new stock or other investment opportunity), and had been known to arrive
at the office wearing different colored socks and
unsure where he'd parked his car. But what he
lacked in common sense and personal style, Conrad
more than made up in financial brilliance. In the
investment community, it was well known that he
made money for all his clients, handled their business with scrupulous honesty, and was the absolute
soul of discretion.

Blinking behind his thick glasses, Conrad said miserably, "I want to help, Kane. You know I do. And if
I thought there was anything, anything at all, in
Dinah's financial dealings that might help find her, I
would have said so to you or the police long before
now."

"But you won't show us her file?" It was Bishop
who asked, his voice level.

"I can't do that. As long as there's no proof otherwise, I have to assume she could walk in that door any
minute. And given that, I have to keep her files confidential. I can't give you details—I just can't. And the
judge agreed with me when the police tried to get a
warrant, Kane, you know she did. Unless you or the
police come up with information that indicates Dinah's
disappearance was somehow connected to her financial dealings, my hands are tied."

"Legally tied," Kane noted.

"I have to protect my clients' privacy."

Kane drew a breath and tried to remain patient,
knowing only too well that he would want his own
affairs treated exactly the same way. "Okay, Conrad.
But think. Surely you can tell us if there was anything

unusual, say in the last few months. You've had time to think about it."

"Yes, but . . . unusual how? Dinah left her investments to me for the most part, you know that, Kane. Occasionally she sold stocks against my advice for quick cash, usually because she was trying to help somebody—"

"What do you mean?" Bishop interrupted.

Conrad considered the question and whether he would be breaching confidentiality, then decided to answer frankly. "Just that. She'd do a story on a home for battered women, and then call me to sell some stock so she could give them fifty thousand to remodel or hire a better lawyer, something like that. She'd do a story on a poor congregation losing its church, and right away pour tens of thousands into their rebuilding fund."

He smiled with wistful fondness. "I could always tell. She'd have that note in her voice when she called, so determined you could call it hell-bent, and I'd know she'd found another wounded soul or bird with a broken wing. She's given millions over the years. Even before her father died, she used most of the income from her trust fund to help others."

Kane swallowed. "I . . . never knew that. She never said anything about it."

"No, she wouldn't have. It wasn't something she talked about. She once told me that her father had taught her a lesson she'd never forgotten—that you helped people without shouting about it, because just the act of helping them made you and your own life better. She believed that. She lived up to that."

Bishop glanced at Kane, then said coolly to Conrad, "With that in mind, don't you think she'd want you to help us find her? So she can help more people, if nothing else. The trail is cold, Mr. Masterson. And she's been missing for five weeks."

Conrad bit his bottom lip. "I wish I could help, Agent Bishop. You have no idea how much. But—"

"Had she come to you recently and asked you to sell stocks without any explanation, or without an explanation you considered reasonable?"

"No. She always had a reason, and, after all, it's her money. She's free to spend it however she pleases. Usually, it was her stories and learning about somebody in need that started it for her. Something that got her passionate and made her get involved."

Bishop frowned. "Did she talk about her stories to you before they were written, Mr. Masterson?"

That question surprised Kane; it was not one he would have thought to ask. But the investment manager's answer surprised him even more.

"Sometimes," Conrad said, clearly unaware of having said anything remarkable. "She'd come in here and talk, and days or weeks later I'd read one of her articles and there'd be the things she told me about."

"How about recently?"

It was Masterson's turn to frown. "Let's see. She told me about that murder out in Buckhead about six months ago."

Both Kane and Bishop nodded; that article and its outcome had already been thoroughly checked out.

"And a few weeks after that she was talking about that political scandal she covered, all those goings-on in the lieutenant governor's mansion."

Kane said, "Which, like all good scandals, ended with a miserable whimper instead of a bang." Bishop lifted a brow at him, and Kane explained. "They paid the girl off and she suddenly remembered it was somebody else with his pants down around his ankles. Then she decided she'd rather live elsewhere, and moved out to California."

He looked back at Conrad. "But that was more or less just reporting, and everybody knew what was going on. What else did she talk about?"

Conrad pursed his lips in thought for a moment, then an arrested expression crossed his face.

"What?" Kane demanded instantly.

"Well . . . let's see, it must have been around the first of August or thereabouts when she came in looking really upset. Said she felt rotten and the heat made it worse. It was terribly hot that day, just dreadful. I asked her what was up, and she said she'd just stumbled across what looked like a really big story. She said . . ."

He closed his eyes, the better to concentrate. "She said heads were going to roll, no doubt about that, and what made it worse was that it appeared somebody she liked an awful lot might be involved. I said involved in what, and she shook her head and said it was big, very big. Then she got a look on her face I'd never seen before, sort of cautious and very worried." He opened his eyes and peered at them. "She wasn't—isn't—cautious, you know. Reckless if anything. Always prone to rush in without thinking if somebody's in trouble."

"I know," Kane said.

Bishop looked at him, then at Masterson. "Sounds

like it might be political. Did she tell you anything else?"

He brooded. "No, not that day. And I didn't hear from her again for weeks. She called me about a month later, very . . . subdued. Said she wanted me to free up half a million."

Bishop blinked. "And you didn't find that request unusual?"

"It wasn't the largest amount she'd needed, if that's what you mean. But it was big enough that I asked her if she was sure she wanted to do that, since it'd mean selling a few things better kept awhile longer. She just said somebody had gotten hurt because of her, and she had to take care of the matter." He shrugged. "I did as she asked, freed up the money, and wired it to her bank."

Kane frowned. "There was no deposit that size into her account in the last six months." Dinah's bank had been more cooperative than Conrad in releasing information to the police.

Conrad hesitated, then said, "Well, it wasn't her regular bank. She used another one for this sort of thing. And a lawyer other than her usual one to arrange things, I believe."

"Will you tell us which bank, so we can verify this?" Bishop asked.

After a few moments, Conrad nodded. "I suppose I can do that." He jotted down the name and address of the bank on a piece of paper.

Bishop took it.

"What about this other lawyer, Conrad? Who was it?" Kane asked.

"I'm afraid I don't know. She just mentioned once

that it was sometimes handy to have two attorneys on retainer, one for public stuff and one private."

"And you have no idea exactly what she intended to do with that half million?"

Conrad shook his head. "I never asked how she planned to help this friend of hers. And . . . that was the last time I spoke to her."

A few minutes later, driving away from Conrad's office, Bishop said, "You know, it occurs to me that half a million dollars to help a friend is a bit excessive. Didn't you tell me this friend of Dinah's had been in a car accident and has been in a coma since?"

"Yeah." Kane paused, then muttered, "Oh, shit. I should have gone by to see her. Dinah went twice a week, regular as clockwork." His guilt was obvious.

"Isn't she in a coma?"

"Yes. I looked in on her that first week, when I went to talk to the hospital staff about Dinah's visits. They couldn't tell me or the police much we didn't already know, and Faith Parker certainly couldn't help. I gather they aren't expecting her to come out of it."

"Then," Bishop said, not uncaring but matter of fact, "she wouldn't know if you visited or not."

"I said something like that to Dinah once," Kane confessed. "And she gave me the oddest look. She didn't say anything—but she didn't have to. I kept my mouth shut about it after that."

Bishop looked at him. "Dinah told Masterson this woman had been hurt because of her. Was that true?"

Kane shook his head. "Only in that she was driving to meet Dinah when it happened. But she felt responsible and nothing I could say made any difference. Said if it hadn't been for her, her friend would never have been driving that afternoon, and so would never have run her car into an embankment."

"She lost control of it?"

"According to the police report. I asked about it as a matter of course, after Dinah disappeared. The police couldn't see a connection, and I couldn't either. Just a common traffic accident, caused by carelessness."

"And she was a good friend?"

"It certainly sounds that way, although I can't remember Dinah ever mentioning her before the accident. Not that it's all that unusual for her to have old friends I've never heard of. Especially if they're work related."

"And was Faith Parker work related?"

"Dinah was so upset about the accident, I didn't ask too many questions. All I know for sure is that Faith never appeared in any of Dinah's stories, at least not by name." God knew he was familiar with Dinah's backlog of work; he had spent long hours reading and rereading everything she'd written, looking for clues to her disappearance.

"I don't like coincidences," Bishop said grimly. "A friend of Dinah's, possibly someone related to her work, rams her car into an embankment and ends up in a coma, an accident about which Dinah feels excessively guilty—to the tune of half a million dollars. A few weeks later, Dinah herself disappears. Now, there may be absolutely no connection between the two things, as the police believe. But I think we'd better make sure."

"How? If Faith Parker is in a coma, who do we ask?"

"We'll have to look more closely at the police reports of the accident, maybe take a look at the car, too. Talk to her doctors again, the nursing staff again."

"And ask them what?" Kane was baffled. "According to the staff, Dinah spent her visits in that room talking to her, not to anyone else. And they don't seem to know anything about Faith's background or history."

"Maybe with a different set of questions to ask, we'll get different answers," Bishop assured him.

Kane valued Bishop's intuition as much as he did his investigative training—maybe more so. And he was eager to try anything that might help to point them in a new direction.

"It's worth a try," he agreed. "And maybe Dinah's other lawyer can tell us something as well."

"Maybe. At the very least, we can verify that Dinah really was giving money to worthy causes."

Kane frowned. "You think it could be something else?"

"No, but it never hurts to be sure." He smiled slightly as his friend shot him a look. "Dinah was— is—too smart to pay blackmail money even if she had done something to be blackmailed for, which I very much doubt. But it's possible that someone took advantage of her and she found out about it later, after the money was handed over."

Kane nodded slowly. "Dinah would have been furious, would have wanted to get her money back and punish whoever had deceived her. She wouldn't have been afraid to face up to whoever it was and threaten retaliation, even prosecution. But then—"

He broke off, and Bishop didn't have to hear the words to know how his friend had silently finished that sentence.

In that case, getting Dinah out of the way for some amount of time wouldn't help. Unless she disappeared permanently.

Bishop knew that Kane had been clinging to what was very likely an unrealistic hope. That if she had an unknown enemy, that person had wanted Dinah out of the way only for a while. That she was being held hostage somewhere, undoubtedly furious and bored but safe. That somehow the crisis would be resolved and Dinah would be released unharmed.

Bishop knew better. He didn't want to know it, but he did. Within hours of his arrival in Atlanta, his training and experience told him that it was only a matter of time before Dinah's body was found.

But he wasn't about to offer that cold knowledge to Kane. Stranger things had happened, and there was always a chance, however slim, that Kane was right. Bishop wouldn't take that away from him.

There was time enough for brutal reality if and when it had to be faced.

In the meantime, investigating possibilities was one way of keeping Kane busy. He needed to feel he was doing something to help the woman he loved. And they had to find out what had happened, whether or not the information could help Dinah now; if she was already dead, somebody had killed her, and that somebody was going to pay for it.

Before the silence could grow too large and become filled with paralyzing thoughts and fears, Bishop said, "I still think blackmail is unlikely, but it's something we need to look into. And the connection between Dinah and this friend of hers. Since the police didn't see a connection and moved on, I doubt they'll look again, especially now."

"Why especially now?"

Bishop shrugged. "I have a feeling they're going to have their hands full now that your reward has been announced."

"You still don't think that was a good idea, do you?"

"I think a million dollars is a hell of a lot of money. And I think there are quite a few people willing to make something up if they think there's a hope in hell of getting that money. It could just muddy the water, Kane."

"Or it could inspire whoever might be holding Dinah to tip the police as to where she can be found."

"Yes, it could. Especially since you worded the statement to make it plain the money would be paid only if Dinah is found alive and well."

Kane changed the subject. "Getting back to the second lawyer, do you think he'll be willing to talk to us?"

"I don't know. He'll be bound by attorney-client privilege, but given Dinah's disappearance, he might be willing to set that aside in her best interests. We won't know until we talk to him. Assuming we can find out who he is."

"Well, until the banks open on Monday, we can't pursue that lead anyway. Which leaves us with Faith Parker. The hospital is on our way. Do you think—?"

Bishop did.

But at the hospital, they encountered an unexpected obstacle.

"She was released two days ago." Dr. Burnett, hunted down for them by a somewhat startled nurse, had an air of weariness about him. But he brightened when he talked about Faith, clearly feeling a proprietary pride in his former patient.

"Released?" Kane stared at him. "When I was here a month or so ago, she was in a coma."

"Yes, she was. But she woke up a little more than three weeks ago."

"Isn't that . . . unusual?" Bishop asked.

"Very. I'm writing a paper for the medical journals. It's also unusual that she awakened with minimal aftereffects. No brain damage, good response to physical therapy—she was on her feet and walking within days, and in better emotional shape than most. Even if she did lose her memory—"

"Her memory?" Kane felt a crushing disappointment. "She can't remember anything?"

"No, poor thing. Her life before the accident might as well have been wiped clean. All her language skills are intact, she reads and writes, recalls historical events and even current events right up to the time of the accident—but she has no personal memories. She didn't know her name, didn't even know what she looked like."

"Will her memory come back?" Bishop asked.

"Probably. Though it could take years. She suffered a blow to the head, but we're not sure if the amnesia was caused by the physical trauma or something psychological."

"Meaning the loss of memory could be a defense

mechanism, a way of protecting herself from memories too distressing to recall?"

The doctor frowned at Bishop. "Perhaps."

After exchanging a quick look with his friend, Kane said to the doctor, "I talked to you when I was here before, about Dinah Leighton. Do you remember?"

"Certainly. A very nice lady, Miss Leighton. As I told you before, she and I talked several times—but only about Miss Parker's condition and prognosis. Miss Leighton was most concerned about her." His face changed, and his brilliant eyes narrowed as they fixed on Kane. "I assume there's been no word?"

Kane shook his head. "Agent Bishop and I are gathering information on our own, trying to piece together what Dinah was doing in the weeks before her disappearance." By now, the spiel was automatic.

Burnett frowned. "I wasn't aware the FBI had been called in."

Smoothly, Bishop said, "We don't always alert the media, Doctor. Working quietly behind the scenes often garners faster results."

"I see. Well then, I assume you'll want to talk to the nursing staff again about Miss Leighton's visits?"

"If you could arrange that, we would be most grateful," Bishop said, all but bowing.

"Of course. If you'll wait here, I'll go speak to the floor supervisor and get things started."

"Thank you, Doctor."

Kane watched him stride down the hallway, then looked at Bishop. "You were very polite. Do you dislike him as much as I do?"

"Yes, I believe I do. And I wonder why."

"You shook hands with him—pick up any bad vibes?"

Bishop gave him a look. "None to speak of."

"Then," Kane offered, "it's probably just our natural dislike of human godhood."

"That's an oxymoron."

"No, that's a doctor. I don't like hospitals or doctors as a rule," Kane said, "so maybe that explains my reaction. I couldn't find even a whisper of a reason he might have been involved in Dinah's disappearance. And he appears to have witnesses to his movements that entire last day."

"I didn't seriously suspect him," Bishop said.

Kane sighed and decided not to tell his friend that he had, over these last weeks, suspected virtually everyone he met.

It took them a couple of hours to talk to the staff members who had seen or talked to Dinah. They heard about her friendliness, her quiet charm, her concern for her friend. What they did not hear was any awareness that Dinah had been pursuing a story or any explanation for her excessive guilt over Faith Parker's accident. No one remembered the name of the lawyer who had come to see Faith, and by then Burnett had finished his shift, so they hadn't been able to ask him.

It was late afternoon when they headed to Kane's apartment. "Since we didn't get any information," Bishop said reflectively, "we have good reason to go talk to Faith. Amnesia or no amnesia, she can tell us who the lawyer is."

"You sound doubtful of the amnesia," Kane noted.

"I think it's very convenient, that's all."

"Convenient for whom, dammit? Faith could have answered a lot of my questions, but now . . ."

"Let's wait until we talk to her before we rule her out as a possibly helpful source."

"And we can talk to the rest of the hospital staff on Monday," Kane said, "and see if they have anything helpful to add. I just have an awful feeling we're going to hear more of the same—lovely opinions of Dinah that don't help us one bit."

"That awful feeling is probably an empty stomach," Bishop said prosaically. "We haven't eaten since breakfast. And there's probably nothing in your apartment."

Kane recognized the attempt to take his mind off things, and smiled. They settled on take-out Chinese food, and by seven o'clock, were in the process of putting away the leftovers. When the doorbell rang, Kane assumed it was a delivery boy from the grocery store he'd called. But when he went to the door, he found a woman he didn't recognize standing there.

She was just a bit over five feet tall and too slender by at least a dozen pounds, but she was a knockout. Gleaming dark red hair with golden highlights, luminous pale skin as smooth and without flaw as polished porcelain, full lips—the bottom one currently being worried by small white teeth—rich with natural color, a straight nose, and big eyes the most unusual shade of green he'd ever seen.

After he silently acknowledged her beauty, he realized she was frightened, and that made him speak more gently than usual.

"Can I help you?"

She was staring up at him, an odd series of emotions crossing her face. Disappointment, bewilderment, pain, speculation, frustration, helplessness. She took a step backward.

"No. No, I—I think I have the wrong apartment. I'm sorry I bothered you."

Before she could turn away, he reached out and grasped her arm. It felt very fragile. "Wait. Are you— Do you have any information about Dinah?"

She looked at his hand on her, then up at his face, her own frozen in indecision. "I don't think so," she whispered.

Kane didn't release her. A sudden memory surfaced in his mind, a memory of a still, slight figure in a hospital bed glimpsed briefly as he'd stood in the doorway. Her thin face was so colorless and immobile that it had appeared to him masklike, an inanimate thing holding no life. Eerie and ghostly, especially with the nearby machines audibly counting off the beats of her heart to insist, with a machine's irrefutable logic, that she was, in fact, a living creature.

It was almost impossible to recognize that comatose patient in this woman, whose rioting emotions were the very definition of chaotic life. But suddenly he was sure. "You're Faith, aren't you? Dinah's friend."

Her eyes searched his face, but whatever she was looking for she apparently didn't find. A little sigh escaped her, and she said, "Yes. I'm Faith."

TWO

He didn't know her.

There hadn't been a flicker of recognition in those first seconds.

They hadn't been lovers.

And since they hadn't been lovers, her dreams could not be memories of a relationship.

As Kane MacGregor led her into his apartment, that realization swirled in Faith's mind, baffling, frightening. What could it possibly mean?

He didn't know her, yet her response to him had been immediate and intense. She knew he could feel her shaking, and she was afraid the heat in her skin would also betray her. His voice, his touch, his face, all were utterly, painfully familiar, a small pool of bright, clear certainty in the ocean of blackness all around her, and she feared it would kill her if she had to turn away from that, from him, and plunge alone into the dark unknown.

But she would have to. There was only one explanation she could think of to account for the dreams, one thing that made a certain kind of sense to her, and if what she suspected was true, then those dreams, that connection she felt so vividly between her and Kane MacGregor, were yet another thing someone else had given her. Not hers at all.

She had no sense of herself, and it was terrifying.

He introduced Noah Bishop as his friend, and she vaguely recognized him as the man who had been with Kane on television. The angry scar down his left cheek didn't bother her, but his pale, watchful eyes made her uneasy; they were more silver than gray, and peculiarly reflective. She had the disturbing notion that he could see all the way to her soul.

"Some security building you've got here," Bishop said dryly to Kane.

"It's just electronic security on the front door at night," Kane replied. "Easy enough to get into the building if one of the neighbors is buzzing in a visitor."

"That's how I came in," Faith confessed, not needing to explain that she'd been unsure of her welcome.

Bishop sighed. "An armed guard or two would probably be a good idea."

"I'll add that to my list of things to do," Kane said. "Sit down, Faith."

She did, at one end of the couch, grateful to be off her feet. She still tired easily, and just getting up the nerve to come here had been exhausting.

Kane frowned down at her. "You're frozen. How do you take your coffee?"

She had no idea, and tried to choke back the bubble of hysterical laughter trying to escape her throat. "I—

just any way. It doesn't matter." At least he'd misread her shaking and her flushed cheeks, assuming both to be due to the chilly evening.

"I'll get it," Bishop said, and went around the corner into the kitchen.

Kane joined her on the couch, no more than a foot away and half-turning so he could watch her. "I'm glad you came, Faith." He added almost apologetically, "Do you mind my using your first name? It's the way Dinah spoke of you, and—"

Faith shook her head. "No, I don't mind." *Maybe it'll start to sound familiar.*

"Good. Thank you. I'm Kane. As for my friend, most people call him Bishop."

"Everybody but you," Bishop called from the kitchen, proving that either he had very good ears or the walls were thin.

Kane smiled slightly, then repeated to Faith, "I am glad you came. We wanted to talk to you, even though Dr. Burnett said you couldn't remember anything." There was the faintest questioning lift to the statement.

"Nothing of my life," she confessed. "Nothing . . . personal. Not who I am or where I came from. I'm still not used to the name, the face I see in the mirror. It's . . . disconcerting."

"I'd think it would be scary as hell," he said bluntly.

"That too."

Bishop returned to the room with coffee and handed her a cup. Their hands touched as she accepted it, and she was suddenly conscious of a moment of intense stillness. His eyes seemed to bore into hers, and she was acutely aware of his warm fingers touching hers. The connection was so powerful, it was as if he held her physically in an inescapable grip.

Then, even as she became aware of it, the moment passed. His fingers drew away and he straightened, his gaze calm and cool once more. Shaken, Faith sipped the coffee and tried to think only of the drink. He had fixed it with plenty of cream and sugar, and since it tasted pleasant she assumed this was indeed how she took her coffee. "Thank you."

He nodded and chose a chair across from the couch. Very conscious that he was watching her closely, she turned to Kane.

"I was obviously Dinah's friend," she said to him. "I didn't know you?"

"We never met. I—went to the hospital after Dinah disappeared, to talk to the staff about her visits, and saw you briefly, but that was all."

She was afraid her hands would shake and betray her growing weariness and fear, so she set her cup on the coffee table and laced the fingers together in her lap. "Do you have any idea how long I'd known Dinah, or where we'd met? Anything like that?"

He shook his head. "Dinah and I didn't meet until about seven months ago. I know a lot about her, but certainly not everything. And if you were in any way connected with her work, I'd be even less likely to know about you."

Bishop said quietly, "Were you connected with her work?"

"From what I gathered from news reports, she's a journalist?"

"Right."

"Then I don't see how. According to the pay stubs I found in my apartment," she said wryly, "I worked for the city. I called and spoke to my supervisor. Apparently, I was a small cog in a very big wheel. I did routine office work."

"Which office?" Kane asked.

"Building Inspections and Zoning." She grimaced. "About which I know nothing. Or at least nothing I remember. My job involved typing and filing." She considered for a moment. "I think I know how to type."

There was something forlorn in her voice, and Kane acted instinctively. He reached over and covered her tightly clasped hands with one of his own. "The doctor said your memory will eventually come back to you, Faith. You have to believe that."

She looked down at his hand, her eyes wide; and Bishop, watching her, was reminded of a deer frozen in a car's headlights, paralyzed and unable to save itself from certain death.

In a constricted voice, she said, "Something has been coming to me, but—not my memories. I thought they were at first, but now I see they weren't mine at all."

Kane released her hands and leaned back, frowning. "What do you mean?"

"They started when I was still in the hospital. Just dreams, but maybe memories too, I thought. Dreams like . . . like little vignettes, brief scenes of someone's life."

"Whose life?" Kane asked slowly.

She drew a breath. "Yours. And—and Dinah's."

Out of the coma.

Christ. From everything he'd been able to find out, that was the last thing he'd expected, that she'd wake up. Ever.

He paced for a few minutes, then went to the phone and called a familiar number. Barely waiting for the answer at the other end, he said, "Faith Parker is out of the hospital."

"What?"

"You heard me."

There was a long silence, and then, "It doesn't have to change anything. Even if she remembers what happened before the accident, the drug would've scrambled everything, left her confused at the very least—and possibly psychotic."

"After so many weeks?"

"Look, don't panic, all right?"

"Dammit, I told you we shouldn't have stopped looking. I told you we needed to find it—"

"I said don't panic. The first thing we have to do is find out if she's even a threat."

"And if she is?"

"Then we'll take care of it."

"You dreamed about us?"

Faith winced at the disbelief in Kane's voice. "Oh, I know it sounds absurd. I've told myself that. But the dreams were too vivid, too real, to be something my own imagination conjured up. I think—" She swallowed hard. "The only answer I can think of is that somehow, in some way I can't explain and don't understand, I've . . . tapped in to Dinah's memories."

Coolly matter-of-fact, Bishop said, "How is that possible?"

"I don't know. Maybe I was psychic before the accident." Her hands lifted and fell in a brief, helpless gesture. "Or maybe I am now because of the accident. I went to the library yesterday and looked up coma. According to what I read, a few people have come out of comas demonstrating unusual abilities—especially if there was a head injury involved." She reached up and pushed her hair off her forehead, showing them a small square of adhesive bandage.

Kane remained silent, staring at her. It was Bishop who spoke.

"It's easy enough to claim you've . . . dreamed something. How do we know you really have?"

She bit her lip again. "I don't know how to convince you. What I dreamed were ordinary little scenes. Things anyone could guess would happen between two people. Fixing meals together. Driving in a car." She blushed suddenly and looked down. "Taking a shower together."

"Any birthmarks or distinguishing features?" Bishop asked dryly.

"He has a small scar low down on his left side. It—it's shaped like a triangle," Faith replied, almost inaudibly.

Bishop looked at Kane with lifted brows. "Do you?"

Kane nodded slowly. "I was thrown from a horse a few years ago and landed on a pile of rusty tin pieces torn off an old barn. Took a chunk out of me."

Reflectively, Bishop said, "I suppose someone else could have known about it?"

"My doctor. A few women. Dinah."

Still flushed, Faith said to Kane, "I dreamed about the two of you at a beach house somewhere. It has a screened-in porch with a funny-shaped chair, like something from the sixties. It sticks out from all the wicker furniture out there. The house has a fireplace and a spa tub. Lots of books on built-in shelves. And at the end of the walkway to the beach, there's a flag that says, 'Just one more day, please!' The house is sort of isolated, with dunes all around it."

Again Bishop looked at Kane questioningly.

Kane met his friend's gaze. "All correct. The house has never been photographed, and we never had guests there. It was redecorated a couple of months before Dinah disappeared, the porch screened in, the fireplace installed. She had the flag made our last trip out. It was a joke between us, because we always wanted just one more day there."

Faith looked back and forth between the two men and said, "Maybe I'm psychic. Does that make sense?"

Still looking at Bishop, Kane said, "You can't tell?"

"No."

"Why not?"

Bishop shrugged. "Maybe because of the lack of identity. The lack of self. That sort of emptiness throws up its own barriers. And she's panicked by the memory loss. Trying to protect herself from losing anything else—that's probably blocking me as well. Completely reasonable on her part, but not very helpful."

"I don't understand," Faith said.

"Noah has a knack," Kane explained. "He calls it a bullshit detector. I call it something more."

Before Faith could ask for more clarification, Kane addressed his friend again, and she forgot all about Bishop's knack.

"It has to be Dinah," Kane said, his voice tight.

"We can't know that," Bishop insisted. "It could just as easily be Faith. People *have* come out of comas with new and inexplicable abilities."

"Maybe, but we *know* Dinah is psychic."

"We know." Bishop's voice was patient and careful, the tone of a man unwilling to assume anything or to raise false hopes. "But her abilities worked a different way, Kane. She wasn't a telepath, wasn't able to touch someone else's mind. She was precognitive, able to . . . tune in to future events, to predict the turn of a card or the throw of dice. And it wasn't something she could control with any reliability. Maybe she could tell you the phone was about to ring, even who was calling, but she couldn't project memories into someone else's mind. Even the strongest psychic would find that virtually impossible."

"If she were desperate enough, she might be able to. If it mattered, if it meant the difference between life and—and death. She'd find a way, Noah. Dinah would find a way."

"It isn't that simple. Psychic ability has its own kind of rules, Kane. And a seer doesn't become a telepath. Not one psychic in a thousand has dual abilities."

Listening in fascination, Faith began to understand just what Bishop's "bullshit detector" was.

Kane said, "So tell me where Faith's memories are coming from. Either Dinah is sending them, or Faith is somehow tapping in to them. No matter which way you look at it, it means Dinah's alive, Noah. *Alive.*" His voice was exultant.

At that moment, Faith realized that deep down inside himself, Kane had believed Dinah was dead—and hated himself for giving up hope.

There was a brief silence, and then, with obvious reluctance, Bishop said, "Dinah visited Faith in the hospital a dozen times. Sat by her bed, read to her, talked to her for hours. We can't deny the possibility that she talked about her past with enough detail to plant those images in Faith's mind, even though she was unconscious."

"But—"

"Kane. It's *possible* Dinah is somehow able to transmit images to Faith. It's *possible* Faith came out of the coma with psychic ability, and that, combined with their friendship, is enabling her to reach out to Dinah telepathically. But the *most likely* explanation is that Faith's subconscious retained everything Dinah said to her with unusual vividness and in remarkable detail."

Kane shook his head and opened his mouth to dispute, deny, refuse to believe—but then Bishop cut in, speaking very softly.

"Past, Kane. All those scenes are from the past. If Dinah was in direct communication with Faith, don't you think she'd be trying to tell us where she is?"

His shoulders slumped, but Kane struggled to hold

on to the newfound hope. "Dinah wouldn't have told her about the scar, dammit. How could she know that?"

"It's possible that happened in the hospital. Trying to wake up, and with psychic ability she perhaps didn't know she had, Faith could have reached out telepathically and touched Dinah's mind. She could have gotten all the details and images that way. It's possible."

"*Possible*," Kane said savagely. "Everything is possible—except that Dinah is still alive. Is that what you're telling me?"

"I'm telling you we can't take anything at face value." And then, even softer, "Goddammit, Kane, don't you think I want her to be alive too?"

Faith, watching them in silence, realized with a stab of loneliness and envy that Dinah Leighton must have been a remarkable woman to inspire such strong emotions in these men.

She didn't want to intrude on so naked a moment but was agonizingly aware that she had to. "There's . . . something else," she said as steadily as she could.

Kane turned his head slowly, as if the effort took nearly everything he had. His face was white, his eyes dark. "What?"

She didn't flinch from the harsh question, but her voice began to shake. "It's . . . what made me come looking for you. I fell asleep late this afternoon, and I— I had another dream. Only you weren't in this one. But Dinah was. I'm not sure, but I think it was a basement or . . . or maybe a warehouse. Walls made of cement blocks, and they looked old, damp. It was cold."

Bishop said, "What was happening?"

Faith shivered; she really didn't want to say what

she had to say. "Dinah was in a chair, I think tied to it somehow. She could barely move. There was more than one person in the room with her, she knew that. Somebody was watching, silently, from the shadows or just out of her sight. And somebody else, a man, was asking her questions, over and over. I didn't see his face and I don't remember what the questions were. I've tried, but—but it's like there was a roaring in my ears and I couldn't hear him clearly. Maybe she couldn't either, I don't know. All I know is that he—he hit her. Again and again."

As though her hand were on him, she could feel Kane tense, all his muscles knotting in a blind, instinctive response, and her voice shook even harder as she finished. "Then everything went black . . . and I—woke up."

Bishop drew a breath. "You're saying she is, or was, being tortured?"

"I think so. No. I'm sure. It was too real, too horribly vivid, to be anything but the truth. They . . . want her to tell them something, and whatever it is, she won't tell them." Faith swallowed hard. "And it's gone on a long time. The questions. The . . . punishment. I could feel how exhausted she was. And her pain . . . She's hurting so terribly. . . ."

Kane was staring at her with the expression of a man dealt a mortal blow, and she found it easier at that moment to meet Bishop's clearer—if slightly less human—gaze.

"That entire scene," he said, "could have come from some movie or book."

Faith shook her head. "It didn't. You don't understand. I wasn't observing. I was *there*. I was Dinah, was inside her body, her mind and spirit. I felt her pain and her fear and—and her determination." She lifted her chin and met Bishop's eyes. "There's something I'm absolutely sure of. Dinah won't tell them what they want to know because she's protecting somebody, or believes she is. It's more important to her than her own life."

"And this is happening now?"

Her certainty wavered. "I—I'm not sure. There was no way to tell."

"A basement, maybe a warehouse. But you have no idea where?"

"No, I didn't see anything but that room. And if Dinah knew where she was, it wasn't something she was thinking about or feeling." She paused, then said desperately, "I want to help her. You have to believe me about that. I have to try to help Dinah."

"Why?" Bishop's voice was flat.

Faith felt the burning of tears but refused to shed them before these men. She drew a steadying breath. "Because she's my friend. Because she did everything in her power to make sure I could get my life back on track when I woke up. And because . . . she's all I have."

"I suppose," he said, watching her, "that's a good reason to want to help find her. And maybe gratitude as well. After all, she did settle half a million dollars on you."

Faith shook her head. "Not half a million directly to me. The trust fund she set up is worth a little more than two hundred thousand dollars, according to the lawyer. And there was a fifty-thousand-dollar deposit directly into my checking account. But she arranged to pay my current debts and the hospital bill, and I have no idea how much that was altogether."

"You didn't have insurance?"

"Liability on the car, according to the paperwork I found. But no health insurance. I gather I had changed jobs recently, and the new coverage hadn't begun yet."

"Six weeks in a coma," Bishop mused. "Another three weeks of care and physical therapy. In a good hospital. I'd say that could easily run a quarter million, maybe more."

"One of the things I want to ask her," Faith said, "is why. I don't understand why she would do such a thing."

Kane stirred and spoke, his voice raspy. "Because she felt guilty."

"About what? The accident? They told me it was only my car and my fault. No one else was involved. So why would she feel guilty about that?" Faith was relieved to see that he had regained a bit of color and that he no longer looked so stunned.

"We were wondering the same thing," he told her.

Bishop said, "What caused the accident?"

"Me, apparently." She tried and failed to smile. "The doctor said it was . . . a few drinks on top of a prescription muscle relaxant. He said the combination was toxic and that I don't handle alcohol very well."

"Why were you prescribed muscle relaxants?" Kane asked, making a visible effort to be methodical.

"I don't remember. Obviously."

He frowned. "You didn't have the prescription bottle with you?"

Her purse had been with her other things at the hospital. It had contained the usual items—a billfold, a checkbook, a small, unused spiral-ringed notebook, a couple of pens, and a compact and lipstick.

No prescription bottle of any kind. And there wasn't one in the apartment.

Slowly, she said, "Maybe the police took it as evidence."

Kane was still frowning. "Alcohol. That isn't right. Dinah said you were on your way to meet her for drinks after work. But you never made it. And you'd come straight from work—that's what she said."

"So," Bishop said, "unless you make it a habit to keep a bottle at work in a desk drawer . . ."

She blinked. "I doubt it. There's no alcohol of any kind in my apartment."

Kane saw her swallow convulsively, and when her eyes fixed on his face, there was fear in them. "What?" he demanded.

"Somebody broke into my apartment." She spoke very carefully now. "The funny thing is, nothing was stolen. Not that I have any way of knowing for sure, but the police said the usual things weren't taken. The place was turned upside down, though. Drawers emptied, things tossed about."

"It sounds like a search," Bishop said.

"When did this happen?" Kane asked.

"I'm not sure. I mean, it was discovered early in the week when the lawyer arranged to have a cleaning service come in and get the apartment ready for me."

"When *could* it have happened?" Bishop asked. "Was anyone else in your apartment between the time of your accident and when the cleaning service discovered the break-in?"

Faith thought about it, reaching up to rub her fore-head as though fretful. "I don't think so. Except Dinah."

"Dinah was there?"

"Her lawyer mentioned it. He said she had gone through my desk at home to find out what bills I had so they could be paid. That must have been just after the accident." She was about to mention the missing laptop, but Kane was speaking and her wavering con-centration lost the thought.

"So we have a span of weeks." Kane looked at Bishop. "Great."

Bishop's mind was on something else. "The apart-ment was searched *after* Dinah went there to go through your desk." His pale gaze was intent on her face. "And just a few weeks later, Dinah disap-peared."

Faith tried to make her mind focus on what he meant. "Are you saying that Dinah might have disap-peared because someone thought she—she found something at my place? Something she wasn't sup-posed to find?"

"Maybe." He turned to Kane. "Maybe we've gone about this the wrong way. Maybe there was no direct threat to Dinah, no story someone wanted stopped before she could write it. Maybe it isn't her past we should be looking into."

"But mine," Faith said shakily.

Kane realized suddenly that she was exhausted. It showed in her eyes, darkened with strain, and in the shadows beneath them. She was trying to sit up straight, but her shoulders kept slumping, and her skin was ashen. He was sure that if her hands hadn't been clenched together in her lap, they would have been shaking uncontrollably.

"You need to get some rest," he said.

Apologetic, she said, "I haven't quite got my strength back yet. It hits me all at once and . . . and then I just need to sleep. I'm sorry."

"For God's sake, don't be sorry. You've been through hell, and it's understandable. Besides, you've told us things we didn't know before. And you may be able to help us find Dinah."

Bishop looked at him but said nothing.

"I want to," she said again, then sighed. A shadow of fear crossed her face. "If—if you could call a cab for me . . ."

Kane's hesitation was brief. "Look, I don't think it's a good idea for you to go back to your apartment, at least not tonight. Until we figure out what's going on, until we're sure that what happened to you and what happened to Dinah are unconnected, it's better you stay with us."

Color crept into her face. "I can't stay here."

"Of course you can." He kept his voice matter-of-fact. "There are two bedrooms. Noah's in one, you take mine. I'll bunk down in here." He grimaced. "These days, I'm usually in here most of the night anyway. Might as well get a pillow and blanket and make it official."

She bit her lip in indecision, and Kane thought about how terrified she must be, so alone that even the face in her mirror was unfamiliar to her.

Gently, he said, "We'll take it one day at a time, okay? Tonight, you need to sleep, and I think you'll feel safer here than at your apartment. Tomorrow we'll start trying to figure out what's going on."

Bishop said nothing.

Faith finally nodded. "Thank you."

Kane showed her the way to his bedroom, made sure there were clean towels in the connecting bathroom. He invited her to use Dinah's toilet articles but found one of his own shirts for her to sleep in rather than anything of Dinah's; that was an intimacy he didn't think either of them was ready for.

When he returned to the living room, he found Bishop sitting just where they'd left him, his frowning gaze fixed on the spot where Faith had been sitting.

Silently, Kane fixed drinks for them both, then reclaimed his place on the couch. "Do you believe her?" he asked abruptly.

"I don't know. She could have told us what we wanted to hear."

"I didn't want to hear that Dinah's being hurt." Kane's voice was very steady.

"No. But we might have expected something of the sort, if we're honest about it. And it made for a dramatic telling, didn't it? Virtually guaranteed to create an emotional reaction."

"The details about the beach house—there's no way she could have found those out. Except from Dinah." Kane wasn't ready to give up.

"Or from you."

Kane frowned, then realized what his friend meant. "You mean she could have gotten them out of my mind as we were sitting here?"

"If she's psychic, maybe. Just because she was able

to block me doesn't necessarily mean she can't use her abilities at the same time."

"Another psychic rule?" Kane asked wryly.

"Something like that."

"Okay. I have to admit that's possible. But there has to be a connection between Faith and Dinah, and what happened to both of them. Maybe the threat was against Faith—maybe she was into something dangerous and Dinah just stumbled into the situation. But Dinah clearly felt responsible for Faith's accident, Noah. She felt guilty enough about it to spend a hell of a lot of money trying to fix things for Faith."

Playing devil's advocate, Bishop said, "But she apparently has a history of giving money to people in trouble. So how do we *know* her guilt was excessive? Maybe Faith merely represented . . . one more wounded soul she was trying to help."

"Maybe. But whether Dinah's story got Faith hurt or something in Faith's life became dangerous to Dinah, the answer has to be there, between the two of them. Maybe she won't be able to tell us much, but there are things we can find out. The facts of her accident, for one. What happened to the prescription drug she was supposedly taking and did a doctor actually prescribe it? How did she have a couple of drinks in her just minutes after leaving her job and going to meet Dinah?"

Kane's face was hard with determination. "The police obviously chalked the crash up to a careless, intoxicated driver, so they wouldn't have checked out the details. We can do that. We can do a background check on Faith and find out as much as possible about who she is. We can find out if Faith and Dinah *were* actually friends, if anyone saw them together or knew about the friendship. We can find out what Faith's job involved, and whether it might have provided Dinah with information she was looking for, a story that might have gotten them both hurt. We can look for *facts,* Noah."

After a moment, Bishop said, "So you're convinced both Faith and Dinah were gotten out of the way because of a story Dinah was working on."

"It's possible, isn't it?"

"Yes. It's possible."

"Then we have a lead," Kane said, his voice sharp with anticipation.

"We have a lead," Bishop agreed.

THREE

It was fairly early when Faith woke up, and she stared around the unfamiliar bedroom with absolutely no idea where she was. The panicked confusion was mercifully brief, but it left her feeling shaky.

That was a sensation she was very familiar with.

She took a shower, and it wasn't until she was drying her hair with a blow dryer that she realized she had known exactly where it was in the linen closet, even though Kane hadn't shown her the night before. Then, when she became conscious of her actions, the brush in her right hand suddenly felt clumsy and wrong, and she had to transfer it to her left.

"Left-handed," she murmured. "I'm left-handed." She had been using her left hand consistently since waking up in the hospital. So why had she used her right that morning?

It was probably one of the strange little glitches wrought by her coma, and she forced it from her mind. She got dressed, then made up the bed and neatened the room, leaving everything as she had found it. Finally, unable to postpone the moment any longer, she left the bedroom.

Kane was up. He was freshly shaved, his hair damp and his casual clothing unwrinkled. He was moving restlessly around the living room, and she doubted he had slept much if at all.

He paused near a lovely baby grand piano as soon as she appeared in the doorway, his awareness of her instant and his gaze sharp. "Good morning." His voice, a little abrupt, was softened by a quick smile. "The coffee's hot, and everything's out on the counter. Fruit, bread, cereal. Help yourself."

"Thanks." Faith went into the kitchen and busied herself. She was too aware of him for her peace of mind, especially when he came to the other side of the work island to pick up his coffee cup.

"I hope you slept well," he offered conventionally.

Faith hesitated, then dropped a slice of bread into the toaster and said lightly, "I've slept a lot since coming out of the coma, but I've yet to sleep well. The doctors say it's natural and nothing to worry about."

"Bad dreams?"

"No, not that. Just . . . feelings. It's hard to let myself go, to trust sleep. I'm afraid I won't wake up, or that when I do, weeks or months will have passed. The doctors assure me that such a thing won't happen, but of course the fear isn't rational, and reassurances don't help much. So, because I'm so afraid of not waking up, I tend to wake up often during the night." She didn't go on to describe the rushes of panic, the long minutes of calming herself down enough to sleep again.

"That must be hell," Kane said with sympathy. "No wonder you—"

When he broke off, Faith said, "Jump whenever anyone says boo? Look like hell? Think I'm psychic? Or merely indulge in runaway paranoia?"

"I wasn't going to say anything like that." But instead of explaining, he changed the subject. "Noah and I have been talking, and we think the best thing is for you to stay here at least a few days. We need time to try to find some answers, and until we do that, we won't know if you might be in as much danger as Dinah. So we'll take you to your apartment today and you can pack a bag."

"I can't just take over your bedroom." *I can't force myself into your life. I can't do that. I don't belong here. And you belong to Dinah.* She concentrated on the tasks of spreading jelly on her toast and not looking at him.

"I told you, I'm not using it much anyway. And I'd feel better if you stayed here for a while, Faith." He paused, then added, "Maybe that break-in at your apartment was just that, a random burglary. But maybe it wasn't. Maybe it had something to do with Dinah and why she's missing. I think you can help me find her."

Faith's restless night had done nothing to settle her emotions or clarify the confusion in her mind, and frustration was obvious in her voice. "How? I can't even help myself. God knows I can't remember anything helpful."

"You might get your memory back, or at least some of it. In fact, you probably will."

"But will it be in time to help Dinah?" she murmured, more to herself than to him. Before he could reply, she asked restlessly, "Where's Bishop?"

"On the phone." Kane paused, then added deliberately, "Checking into your background."

That drew her eyes to his face, and she found him watching her intently. "Oh. I guess he can do that, can't he." It wasn't a question.

Kane's eyes narrowed suddenly. "Why do you say that?"

"He's with the FBI, isn't he?"

There was a moment of silence, then Kane said, "Neither of us mentioned that."

"You didn't?" Faith was startled, but quickly realized what the answer must be. "I suppose Dinah told me." She shook her head. "It happens like that—right out of the blue, I just *know* things I can't explain knowing. Either my memories are popping up here and there, or Dinah's are. And since I never met you or Bishop before last night . . ." She returned her attention to her breakfast, unwilling to see disbelief or suspicion in his expression.

But Kane's voice was neutral when he said, "Do you mind that he's checking into your background?"

Faith took the time to chew a bite of toast, then shook her head. "Why should I mind? Maybe he can even find out enough to answer a few of my questions."

"Such as?"

"Such as . . . why there are no photographs in my apartment and almost no evidence of a—a past."

"Some people don't like clutter. Even the clutter of . . . visible memories. Maybe it's only that."

"Wouldn't that be ironic," she said. "If I'd kept out of my life the one thing that might help me *remember* my life."

She drew a breath and looked at him steadily. "I'm

twenty-eight years old, and there should be evidence of that life. Signs that I—that I lived those years. Photographs. A high school yearbook. A sweater my mother knit for me. But there's nothing like that there. It's as if I came from nowhere eighteen months ago when I moved into that apartment."

"Everybody comes from somewhere, Faith. But maybe you chose to walk away from your past for some reason. People do. Go to a new place, start over."

She toyed with the handle of her coffee cup, aware that the gesture betrayed her uneasiness but unable to stop herself. "Maybe that's true. But what could have been so bad that I had to wipe out my past before I could start over?"

It was Bishop, coming into the kitchen at that moment, who replied to her question. "My guess would be murder."

"Amnesia?"

"According to her file, yeah." He scowled at a passerby, sending him on his way without stopping to wait for the phone, then he continued his conversation. "I got a look at the shrink's report. Seems her whole life is a blank, not just the days or weeks before she rammed her car into that embankment."

"Is it temporary or permanent?"

"Beats the hell out of me. And them, apparently. The gist of it is that nobody knows whether she'll ever regain her memory. She could get it all back, some of it—or none of it. And there's no telling how long it might take. She could wake up tomorrow remembering every detail."

"Or it could take years."

"That's what they say." He waited out several minutes of silence, then said, "I don't like it."

"No. Neither do I."

"So?"

"So where is she now?"

He swore. "I don't know."

There was a pause, and then, "I told you to check out her apartment last night."

"I did. She wasn't there."

"And?"

"And I got pissed."

In all her imaginings, Faith had not thought of murder, and a chill raised gooseflesh over her body. "What?" She groped desperately in the darkness of her mind, but there was absolutely nothing, no memory, no knowledge at all. Nothing but the terrifying possibility that she had done something horrible.

Bishop continued to speak as if reciting items on a list. "A little over two years ago, you were living in Seattle with your mother and younger sister. Your sister was still in high school, your mother worked in a library, and you worked as a receptionist at a construction company during the day and waited tables at night." He paused. "I don't have all the details, and I won't until I go up to Quantico and get access to the records. But the facts are simple."

"What facts?" she asked unsteadily.

There might have been a softening of Bishop's steely gaze, but it was difficult to tell. "I'm sorry. Your mother and sister were murdered, and the house was burned to the ground."

Faith felt shock, but it was distant, impersonal, little more than dismay. She could not conjure even a fleeting image of this mother or sister, and the grief that should still have been strong in her was totally absent.

It was Kane who asked quietly, "Who was responsible?"

"The case is still open, that's all I can tell you." Bishop looked at his friend. "And the file is restricted, maybe because it's an ongoing Bureau investigation, something like that."

"Could Faith be a protected witness?"

"Not likely. If that were the case, I would have been warned off the moment I tried to access her file."

She cleared her throat. "Could I—was I a suspect?"

"According to the Seattle P.D., which I called after running into that restricted file, you had an alibi. You were waiting tables in a busy restaurant, in full view of dozens of people, when the murders were committed and the house burned. But the police refused to tell me anything else. It seems their file is off-limits as well."

Kane looked at Faith. "So two years ago, the people closest to you were murdered. No arrests, no convictions. A few months later, you came to Atlanta and started over."

Faith tried to think. "Which would explain the lack of some things in my apartment. Photographs, old clothing. If the house I lived in burned to the ground, I could have lost everything."

Kane frowned at Bishop. "My imagination is probably working overtime trying to figure out how two unsolved murders in Seattle could connect to a traffic accident and a disappearance here in Atlanta two years later. But . . . here's Faith. One very real connection."

"Until we have the details," Bishop said, "there's no way to know if there's any other connection."

"And we get the details only if you go to Quantico."

"We have a *chance* of getting them if I go to Quantico. My clearance might not be high enough, depending on why the file was restricted."

"Weren't you going to have to go back tomorrow anyway? Something about this new unit of yours?"

"I don't have much choice, I'm afraid. And I don't know when I'll be able to get back." He paused. "If I thought there was anything I could do here that you couldn't do just as well or better—"

"You wouldn't leave. I know that."

Bishop went to pour himself some coffee, and Faith was glad their attention had shifted away from her. She needed time to try to cope with the shock of knowing her family had been murdered.

"I'm not too crazy about leaving here just now," Bishop said. "With no solid evidence surfacing, the search for Dinah was going along pretty much according to standard operating procedure, with very little progress and no real surprises." He looked at Faith. "And then you came out of a coma and walked out of that hospital."

Kane frowned again. "Meaning?"

"Meaning the balance has been upset, the status quo disturbed. If anybody is paying attention, now would be the time I'd expect them to make a move."

Faith was puzzled. "You mean . . . whoever has Dinah would have to change their plans because of me?"

"If you figure into this at all—yes. Think about it. If you are or were a threat to someone, that coma kept you safely out of the picture. The fact that you're up and about again has to give them pause. Even if they find out that your memory is gone, chances are they won't feel secure enough to just ignore you. Not for long, at any rate."

"My apartment was probably searched," Faith said slowly. "Maybe they found whatever it is they were looking for." Then a sudden memory made her look at Kane. "Does Dinah have a laptop?"

"Yes. Her briefcase was missing when her Jeep was found abandoned near her office, though, and she always carries the laptop in it."

Faith hesitated. "According to what she told the lawyer, she also had my laptop. Did you ever see it?"

Kane didn't have to think long. "No. I mean, I never pay particular attention when she uses it, so I suppose it could have been yours. But I never saw two of them. And we didn't find one in her apartment when we went through the place after she disappeared. No disks either."

Bishop said to Faith, "I don't suppose you have any idea of what was on yours?"

"No. All I know is that I hadn't had it long before the accident."

"Another dead end." Kane sighed. "Last night I thought we had a lead, but now it looks even more murky than before."

"I don't believe in coincidence," Bishop said.

"Somewhere in all this there's a single thread, one fact or occurrence that ties everything together and makes sense of all of it."

"Even the murders of my mother and sister?" Faith asked.

"That might have been the beginning of it," he answered. "Everything that's happened since could date back to two people being murdered in Seattle two years ago. Or they might turn out to be—pardon the expression—incidental to everything else, important in this instance only because they were the catalyst that brought you to Atlanta."

Faith was beginning to get a headache. She wondered how a mind so empty of anything useful could feel so crowded with questions and facts.

"First things first," Kane said, watching her. "We need to get you to your apartment so you can pack a bag."

Bishop opened his mouth to say something, then apparently thought better of it, and said instead, "It's Sunday, so there won't be much traffic."

Faith occupied herself with trying to figure out what was on Bishop's mind, an exercise which at least kept her thoughts focused on something specific during the trip to her apartment. The answer didn't occur to her until they got out of Kane's car at her building and she saw the agent and Kane look around them with an attention that was far from casual.

Somebody could be watching this place. That's what he thinks. Maybe my cab last night was impossible to follow in Saturday-evening traffic, so they might not know where I went. There might have been no connection between me and Kane until today.

Have I put him in danger by going to him, by being with him? Was I the one who put Dinah in danger?

They went into the building and up to Faith's apartment, meeting no one along the way. The door was closed, but Faith was suddenly even more uneasy than she had been. It was an actual physical sensation, as if something cold had brushed against her skin.

"What?" Kane asked, reading her body language.

"I—It's nothing. Nothing I can explain." She dug into her shoulder bag and produced the door key.

Kane took it from her. "Then it's probably best if we're careful. You wait out here."

Faith stepped to the side of the door, and watched as the two men unlocked and opened it very cautiously and slipped inside the apartment. She was conscious of her heart pounding, of a sick queasiness she recognized as fear, and silently called herself a coward. It did no good to remind herself that she had every right to be frightened, adrift in a life she didn't remember, a life that held the potential of danger.

It seemed hours before Kane reappeared in the doorway. "It's clear," he said. "But someone's been here."

With that warning, Faith braced herself for the chaos waiting inside her apartment.

This time, the search had been far more vicious and destructive. Sofa cushions were cut open, the stuffing bulging half out of them. Prints were torn off the walls and from their frames, the glass broken. Shelves were pulled away from the walls, tables overturned. In the kitchen, the cabinet doors were open, the counters and sink littered with boxes and cans, and both the refrigerator and the freezer had been searched. In the bedroom, her clothing lay heaped on the floor, along with the bedding. The mattress had been slashed open.

Faith stood looking at the mess, her skin crawling with the sensation of having been violated.

"I should call the police," she said.

Kane and Bishop exchanged glances, then Kane said, "I have a friend in the department. Let me call him. I think we'll be better off if we can avoid a media circus." When Faith looked at him, he added, "So far, there's no public connection between you and me, or even you and Dinah. I say we keep it that way as long as possible."

Faith agreed, even as she asked herself if she was deferring to Kane because he was right, or because it was easier to let him make the decisions.

I don't even know that about myself.

Not even that.

Kane's police detective friend was Guy Richardson, a tall, beefy man with thinning brown hair and deceptively mild brown eyes. He arrived with a disinterested police photographer who took pictures of the apartment, spoke briefly and quietly to Kane—filling him in on the lack of progress in the search for Dinah, perhaps?—and then looked around the place thoroughly before asking Faith if she knew for sure if anything had been taken.

Faith had already thought about that and was able to offer an answer. "As far as I can tell, nothing that was here when I left yesterday evening is missing." They were sitting at the small kitchen table, and her hands were tightly clasped before her.

"Kane explained about the amnesia. So you have

no idea why your apartment was searched twice in the last few weeks?"

"No."

"I looked at the report of the previous break-in. Your neighbors were questioned, but no one saw a stranger hanging around or heard anything suspicious. There was no sign of forced entry, but an open window was found." He paused. "This time, there was no open window and the lock was picked. Which tells me a pro got in here, and he did it without leaving much evidence. I can dust for prints, but I'd bet my pension he wore gloves."

There didn't seem to be anything to say, so Faith remained silent, her gaze flickering from her clasped hands to the men around the table.

Kane said, "Assuming he didn't find what he was looking for, do you think he'll be back?"

"I think the man is very serious about his work," Richardson said. "Whatever he wants is important, either because he was hired to find it or because he wants it badly himself. My guess is that he won't stop looking."

"Then Faith isn't safe here."

Richardson agreed. "I'd advise her to stay somewhere else until we get this figured out."

Faith couldn't help wondering if Kane had asked his friend to make that statement—then chided herself for being so suspicious. Still, she had to protest. "But after searching twice, he must know that whatever he's looking for isn't here."

Richardson didn't hesitate. "I'm sure he does. But what he doesn't know is whether you have what he's looking for in your possession or have hidden it somewhere outside this apartment."

Bishop spoke then, his voice cool. "There is another possibility. This second break-in might have been less a search and more a tactic used to intimidate. His aim could be to frighten Faith enough that she either leads him to what he's looking for, or is too afraid to make use of it herself."

"But *what is it* he's looking for?" Faith asked, feeling more desperate than she wanted to admit. "I don't know. I don't remember. Was it something I took from him? Something I found? Something given to me for safekeeping?"

Slowly, Kane said, "Whatever it is, we don't even have a clue as to its size. The way this apartment was turned upside down, it could be anything from papers or a computer disk all the way up to something as big as a bread box."

"Computer disk." Faith looked at Kane. "If Dinah got my laptop just after the accident, then it wasn't here the first time the apartment was searched. Could that be it?"

"Sure it could. But unless you hid backups of your data somewhere safe—and unless you remember where they are—we have no way of knowing for sure."

"And," Richardson pointed out, "if he was looking for a computer he didn't find here, he'll figure you have it with you or stashed someplace."

"So you're a target," Kane finished.

Faith was aware of that queasy feeling in the pit of her stomach once again. Fear. "Until I get my memory back? What if I never do? The doctors say I may never remember the days or even weeks right before the accident."

Apparently regretting his blunt statement, Kane

said more positively, "This may be a jigsaw puzzle, and the largest missing piece may be your memory, but there are other pieces, Faith. We'll find them. We'll put the pieces together and figure out what's going on."

"Whatever I can do to help," Richardson said, "just ask."

Kane didn't hesitate to take him up on the offer. "All right. The car accident that put Faith in the hospital—we need to see the actual police report."

"No problem. I'll have a copy sent over to you by the end of the day."

"We could also use any information you can find on Faith since she moved to Atlanta about a year and a half ago. Did she ever report anything unusual to the police? Was she involved in any kind of accident prior to the one that put her in the hospital? Are there any reports at all concerning her?" Kane paused. "Faith, tomorrow we'll check your bank, find out if you rented a safe deposit box. And we need to find out as much as we can about your friendship with Dinah."

Richardson lifted an eyebrow at Bishop, who said, "He should've been a cop."

The photographer approached Richardson to report that he was finished with his work, and the detective got to his feet. His gaze traveled between Faith and Kane. "Be careful. I don't yet know what's going on, but all the signs here point to somebody who's very determined, and very, very dangerous. For God's sake, watch your step. And watch your backs."

"We will," Kane told him.

When the detective and the photographer had gone, Kane said, "We can get a cleaning service in here tomorrow and have the damaged furniture replaced or repaired. In the meantime, Faith, why don't you pack enough to last a week or so, just in case, and we'll get out of here."

She went off without a word to do as he suggested, and when they were alone, Bishop said, "She could have trashed this place yesterday before she came looking for you. It's possible."

"She could have. I don't believe she did. Do you?"

Bishop's reply was somewhere between a shrug and a shake of his head, not open distrust of Faith but certainly ambivalence. "You do realize that it won't take a public connection between you and Faith to draw the wrong sort of attention if somebody happens to be watching this place."

"I realize that. I also realize somebody could have followed her to my place last night, so the connection between us might already be made." Kane shrugged. "My building's a hell of a lot more secure than this one even with a part-time doorman. And I'll be there. Any way you look at it, she'll be safer with me."

"I wasn't thinking only of her. Kane, have you considered the possibility that Faith might be responsible—directly or indirectly—for Dinah's disappearance? That she might have brought trouble with her from Seattle, trouble that Dinah got caught up in?"

"After hearing about the murder of her family, of course I've considered it." Kane leaned back in his chair with a sigh. "So what should I do differently? She can't remember, Noah. Her past is a blank. Did you see her face when you told her about the murders? Shock, yes, but you might as well have been telling her about

two people she'd never met before. She's the most lost
soul I've ever known, completely helpless to protect
herself from whatever trouble might have followed her
here. Whether she remembers anything to help me or
not, I can't turn my back on her."

"I didn't say you should. But Richardson was right
to warn you to be careful."

"And I intend to be."

"Sure you do. If that lost soul in the next room leads
you right into the lion's den, you'll be careful as hell."

Kane was silent for a moment, then said, "She can
help me find Dinah. I know she can. I can't see further
than that, Noah."

"I know," Bishop said.

*It was dark when she turned off the Jeep's headlights,
dark as pitch, and cold for early October. Dinah shivered a bit even though she was wearing a sweater, and
hesitated as she got out, her gaze going to the nylon
windbreaker in the backseat. But in the end, she
decided the sweater was enough. If she needed to move
fast, the fewer layers that got in her way, the better.*

*She stood beside the Jeep until her eyes began to
adjust to the darkness, then moved forward cautiously.*

Dumb. This was so dumb.

*The building loomed ahead, virtually impossible to
identify, and she felt a moment's qualm as she asked
herself if this was even the right place. The directions
had been maddeningly vague, and she might easily
have been mistaken in the conclusions she'd drawn
from what little information she could trust. She was
probably not even in the right section of the city—*

What was that? A sound . . . from over there. A whimper?

Dinah crept forward, her heart thudding in excitement, trying very hard to keep her breathing soft and even, not to betray her presence. Straining to listen.

No other sound now, if there had been one.

Her overwrought imagination, probably.

God knew she had reason to imagine monsters.

Dinah stopped moving, standing still to better see and hear whatever lay around her. She had good senses usually, and there was also that little bit of something extra Bishop called a "spider sense"; it was a sharpened awareness of her surroundings, as though her five senses were somehow magnified by danger or the possibility of it.

Her eyes having adjusted quickly to the darkness, she was now able to make out more details of the building. Windows were high and dark, offering no clue as to what lay behind them. There didn't seem to be a door of any kind. Somewhere was a loose shutter or piece of tin on the roof; she heard it rattling faintly in the breeze. And she smelled wood, lumber.

Something else as well.

Dinah stood utterly still, her chin raised, sniffing the night air that was teasing her with an odor she knew she should recognize but which lurked just beyond reach.

Primal. Animal.

The hair on the nape of her neck was stirring.

She needed to leave.

She needed to leave right now.

When it came at her there was no warning. No sound. Just a dark shape hurtling from its darker surroundings, and then the blow that knocked her off her feet.

And then the hot, tearing pain . . .

FOUR

Faith jerked awake to find herself sitting up in bed, her arms raised as if to protect her throat and face. Her heart was pounding, her breathing ragged, and her skin clammy, as though she had just raced in from the damp, chilly night.

It took several minutes for her to reassure herself that she was not out in the dark, lying on the cold ground with an animal tearing brutally at her flesh. That she was inside, and safe.

That she was not Dinah.

She was in Kane's bedroom, which was still filled with afternoon light, as it had been when she had retreated there after lunch, when the sudden need to sleep had overwhelmed her. The clock on the nightstand told her a little more than an hour had passed, but when she slid from the bed, she felt slow and clumsy and stiff, as though she had slept heavily for hours. She was also unnerved.

She could still feel those teeth tearing at her.

Shaking off the nightmare memory as best she could, Faith decided she didn't want to be alone a minute longer. When she reached the living room, she paused in the doorway, unnoticed by the two men. Kane was on the couch, Bishop in the chair on the other side of the coffee table, and both were leaning forward as they studied the papers spread out before them.

"No sign another car was involved," Bishop said. "In fact, there were several witnesses, and all confirmed she was driving erratically before losing control and plowing into that embankment."

They were reading the police reports of her accident, Faith realized.

"No mention of a prescription bottle," Kane said, frowning. "And no mention that anyone checked afterward to confirm that a doctor prescribed muscle relaxants. Just the notation that EMS reported alcohol on her breath, then the emergency room doctor's report and the test results." He paused. "Christ, her blood alcohol level was three times the legal limit."

"How could that be?" Faith came into the room and sat on the couch, staring at the report. "I had just left work. There hadn't been time to—to drink so much."

"We don't think it happened that way," Kane told her, and picked up a legal pad covered with notes. "I talked to your supervisor. Listen to this. At five thirty-five that day, she reports that you handed in some paperwork you'd stayed a bit over to complete. The two of you talked for, she says, about five minutes, then you got your purse and left. That building has underground parking for employees, with a gate that requires a keycard. The gate receipt for your car was time-stamped at five-fifty." He paused again. "At six-thirty, you plowed your car into an embankment—six miles from your office building."

Faith thought about that for a moment, frowning. "Maybe it's not so unusual to take forty minutes to drive six miles in rush-hour traffic, but—"

"But it would take a good chunk of that time to drink enough to screw up your reflexes and boost your blood alcohol level to three times the legal limit. And you would have had to be throwing back hundred-proof scotch straight out of the bottle while you were driving."

"Then, if it wasn't possible . . ."

Bishop said, "Possible, maybe. Likely? No. First of all, there was no bar along the route you must have taken, and we can assume you didn't drink in your car because there wasn't a bottle found in it."

"I could have thrown it out along the way," Faith offered, playing devil's advocate.

"You could have, but since you were on your way to meet Dinah for drinks, why on earth would you have drunk so much before?"

Kane said, "And then there's the famous prescription for muscle relaxants, which from all evidence doesn't seem to exist. There was no bottle in your apartment or your desk at work, and none was found in your purse or anywhere in the car. We used the entries in the checkbook you brought from your apartment and called the pharmacy you normally go to. The only prescription they filled for you during the six weeks preceding the accident was the regular one for birth control pills."

Birth control pills. Was there a man in my life after all? Or was I merely prepared for the possibility?

"Faith?"

She looked at Kane and forced her mind to focus on more important matters. "I can check with my regular doctor at that clinic tomorrow just to make sure, but it does sound like those muscle relaxants weren't mine. So how could I have gotten them into my system?"

"The obvious answer," Kane said, "is that someone slipped them to you without your awareness."

"While they were getting me drunk in about half an hour?" Faith shook her head. "That's the part I just don't get. To drink so much at all doesn't feel right to me. To drink that much in so short a time . . ."

"Unless someone's lying and you had nothing at all to drink," Kane suggested. "Maybe it was a setup from the get-go. I'm willing to bet there are drugs that mimic a combination of alcohol and some kind of prescription med, resulting in death— or coma. Maybe someone drugged you, gave it a few minutes to take effect, then splashed a little alcohol in your mouth and on your clothes and put you behind the wheel, knowing damned well you couldn't drive a block without wrecking the car. In downtown Atlanta traffic, chances were good you'd be killed or seriously injured. And when you survived the crash, how hard could it have been in a busy emergency room for someone to get at the paperwork and make sure it tells the right story?"

"Are we talking about one person here, one enemy?" Faith asked. "Somebody who influenced everything from the wreck and my hospital records to Dinah's disappearance? Maybe even what happened in Seattle?"

Bishop said, "There may be one person behind everything—always assuming it's all connected—but there'd have to be more than one person involved."

"Aren't you the man who told me once that true conspiracies are almost as rare as hen's teeth?" Kane asked.

"Yeah. But note that I said *almost*. They do happen. And if Dinah was telling you the truth when she said she was working on a story involving business, politics, and something criminal, then I'd say that's probably what we have here."

"How could a story like that have any connection to me?" Faith asked.

"That," Kane said, looking at her broodingly, "is the question. And we have to find the answer."

Bishop checked his watch and got to his feet. "There's a flight out just after six. I'll head for home tonight, and if they don't put me on another plane before I can unpack, I'll see what I can find out about that restricted file tomorrow."

Faith was a little surprised. "Didn't I hear you say you weren't leaving until tomorrow?"

"That was the plan. But something came up." He didn't explain further.

Faith suddenly heard the whisper of a not-quite-alien voice in her mind. *He wouldn't leave if he thought I was still alive.*

She went absolutely still, conscious of a deep chill

as she tried desperately to listen to whatever else that quiet voice might tell her. But there was nothing else. Just silence.

"Faith?" Kane's voice now.

She blinked and focused on Bishop. He was staring at her, his sentry eyes narrowed and an arrested expression on his face. As if he knew, as if he'd heard it too.

Faith drew a breath to steady herself and give herself a moment to think. Could she reach Dinah consciously, gain some information that might point them to her or her captors? Until she knew for sure, there was no reason to tell Kane about the voice in her head, no reason to baffle or unnerve anyone else, to try to explain the unexplainable.

"Is anything wrong?" Kane asked her.

"It was nothing," she said, so calm that she nearly convinced herself. "I thought I remembered something, but it slipped away."

Bishop didn't contradict her, but she wondered if he could have.

Faith debated telling Kane about her latest "dream" but decided not to, simply because she could see nothing helpful in it either to his search for Dinah or her own search for knowledge of her past. The dream had revealed virtually no detailed information; the area had been too dark and unfamiliar for her to recognize, so she couldn't even provide a location from which Dinah might possibly have disappeared.

Always assuming it had been more than a dream.

That was what worried her most about the dreams

and flashes of knowledge—that they might well be no more than her imagination coupled with a few lucky guesses. It seemed so incredible that there could be some kind of psychic connection between her and another woman, one so strong that she was actually reliving the other woman's experiences and memories, feeling emotions not her own.

Hearing a voice in her head that belonged to someone else.

How could she believe such a thing?

And yet she did. Despite her worry and nagging uncertainty, she believed that a connection between her and Dinah did exist. She didn't know how or why that bond had formed, but she believed it was very real. If she could only figure out a way to use it to find Dinah . . .

But she seemed as unable to control that as she was to find memories of her own in the blankness of her mind. The helplessness was maddening. And sitting around doing nothing wasn't helping.

She could use her brain, though, couldn't she?

When Kane returned from seeing Bishop off in a cab to the airport, Faith was sitting on the couch with a legal pad and the small address book she had brought from her apartment.

Before Kane could ask what she was doing, she picked up the phone and placed a call to the women's clinic. It took several minutes of talking her way patiently past a couple of staff members and then her personal doctor's answering service, but she finally reached her doctor. She made an office appointment for the following day.

Kane said when she hung up, "So she'll see you tomorrow?"

Faith nodded. "And have all my records ready so she can fill me in on my life—the medical part of it, at least. She wasn't surprised about the accident, although she didn't say how she'd heard about it."

Kane nodded and gathered up all the notes and the police report they had been going over earlier. He saw her turn another few pages of the address book and frown down at an entry. "Find something?"

She shook her head half-consciously. "I'm not sure. In the 'in case of emergency' section, there's an address and a phone number, but nothing to identify who or what it is."

"Local number?"

"There's no area code." She met his gaze, then picked up the phone. "One way to find out."

It rang three times before a brisk, female voice on the other end announced, "Haven House."

The name meant nothing to her, but given where she'd found the number, Faith thought surely someone there would recognize her name. So, tentatively, she said, "This is Faith Parker."

There was a moment of silence, then the woman exclaimed in surprise, "Faith? The last we heard, you were still in a coma."

Faith didn't state the obvious. Instead, she said, "I just came home this past week."

"And you're okay? I mean—"

Faith barely hesitated. "I'm fine physically, but I seem to be having some memory problems. Forgive me, but I don't remember who you are."

"This is Karen." The answer came readily enough, but wariness had crept into that brisk tone.

Faith jotted the name down on her legal pad. "So we knew—know—each other?"

"Of course. You probably spent more time here than in your own apartment up until the last few months. We always kept a bed ready for you, in case you wanted to stay."

Puzzled, Faith said, "I'm afraid I don't understand. Just what is Haven House?" She was thinking that perhaps it was a bed-and-breakfast, something like that. The truth came as a definite surprise.

"It's a shelter," Karen replied, even more wary now. "A shelter for abused women."

Faith added that information to her notes automatically, and it was only as she watched her pen moving across the page that she realized she was writing with her right hand. She transferred the pen to her left hand, confused both by her actions and by what she was hearing.

"A shelter. Did I—did I work there? As a volunteer?"

"You helped out when and how you could, same as the rest of us." Karen's voice hardened slightly. "Look, if you really are Faith and what you've told me is the truth, I'm sorry—but I can't tell you anything else over the phone. We have to be careful here. Too many of us are in hiding."

"I understand." Faith wished that she did. "May I—is it all right if I come over there? I have the address." She recited it, just to make sure what was in her book was correct.

"Our doors are always open to women," Karen

said. "But in case you've forgotten the rules—no men. No exceptions."

"I'll remember. Thank you, Karen."

"Don't mention it."

Faith cradled the receiver slowly.

"What kind of shelter?" Kane asked immediately.

"For abused women. And—they know me there." Faith felt peculiar just saying the words.

"But she wouldn't tell you anything else over the phone?"

"No. Understandable, I suppose. I need to go over there and talk to them. Now, today. I don't know if there's a connection to Dinah, but—"

"She did a story on a women's shelter," Kane remembered suddenly. "And Conrad, her financial manager, said she donated money." He paused. "If she donated her time as well, or went there at all, she never mentioned it."

"I don't think she would have. Judging by what Karen said to me, being secretive about the shelter was encouraged." She looked down at the entry in her address book. "I didn't even name it in my book."

Kane nodded, accepting that, then looked at his watch. "Let's go, then. They might not let me in, but I can make sure you get there and back safely."

Faith didn't argue. But when they reached the shelter—which turned out to be a large, pleasant old house in a quiet suburban neighborhood—she realized her visit might take some time and doubted Kane's patience to sit and wait for her.

"You said you wanted to talk to Richardson about that police report," she reminded him. "Why don't you go do that while I see the people here? If we divide the work, we're more likely to find out something useful quickly." She thought she hardly needed to tell him that, but did anyway because she knew he was reluctant to leave her there.

Kane jotted down the number of his cell phone and gave it to her. "If I'm not waiting out here when you get ready to leave, call me."

Faith nodded. She got out of the car and went to the front door of the house, conscious, as she rang the bell, of the closed-circuit security camera positioned near the entrance.

The door was opened by a tall, very thin woman of about thirty-five, with dark hair already going gray. When she spoke after a long, steady look, it was with the brisk voice she had used on the phone.

"So it is you. Good to see you, Faith."

Faith went in, wondering, now that she was there, just what she was going to ask this woman or anyone else there—besides a wistful "Who am I? Do you know?"

The house was fairly quiet, even for a Sunday afternoon. She heard, somewhere upstairs, the faint sounds of children laughing and talking, and someone softly—and inexpertly—playing a piano nearby.

"Let's talk in my office before you see any of the others," Karen suggested, obviously still feeling protective of the shelter and its inhabitants.

Faith was agreeable, and moments later found herself sitting in a small, cluttered, windowless office that had probably once been little more than a closet. The gracious old home showed plenty of signs of recent renovation, but it was clear the money had been spent where it would do the most good, the comfort of the director obviously far down on the list.

"I've been thinking about it," Faith said as Karen went around the desk and sat behind it, "and if you need someone to verify what I claim about the memory loss, I'm sure my doctor will explain everything."

Karen's sharp brown eyes softened. "That won't be necessary. I believe you. Besides, I've known you more than a year, Faith, and one thing I'm sure of is that you'd never do anything to harm this shelter or the women and children who depend on it."

"How did I . . . get involved here?" Faith wasn't sure she wanted the answer, but knew she had to ask.

"The same as the rest of us." Karen's smile was faint and brief. "In your case, an ex-husband."

Faith swallowed, aware of a chill but no memories—still no memories. "Do you know his name? What happened between us?"

Karen shook her head. "Those are the kinds of questions we don't ask around here. And you never offered to talk about it, beyond saying you'd divorced him and that he worked somewhere out on the West Coast."

"Did I come here because I was afraid of him?"

"I think you came here initially because your doctor believed you needed to know there was some place in Atlanta where you'd be safe. That's common among abuse victims, the need to have a safe place. Also, I think, because you'd been at a shelter where you used to live, and it helps to spend time with people who understand what you've been through."

Faith wished she understood—or felt what she thought she should feel. But she didn't remember being frightened or hurt by anyone, much less a husband.

Though that would explain several small scars she had found on her body, she realized.

Trying to concentrate, she said, "So you don't know much about my past?"

"We try to live in the present here. You may have talked more to the others, but this is considered a temporary shelter, and we have a fairly high turnover rate. I'm afraid there aren't many still here who'd know you. Andrea and Katie, maybe Eve. I can't think of anyone else."

"I suppose you wouldn't consider giving me the names and current addresses of any of the women I might have confided in months ago?"

"Against the rules. I'm sorry, Faith."

"No, I understand." She sighed. "If I could talk to the women who did know me, I'd be very grateful. But I also wanted to ask you about Dinah Leighton."

Karen's thin face tightened. "God, that's just awful, her disappearing like that. When it first happened we all wondered about that guy she was involved with—but then we would, wouldn't we? Not exactly an unbiased group here."

It was the first time it had occurred to Faith that Kane might have been suspected of involvement in Dinah's disappearance. Slowly, she said, "Did the police think he might have . . . hurt her?"

"The usual speculation from the media, as I recall, but I don't believe the police ever considered him a serious suspect. According to the newspapers, his movements were pretty well accounted for during the time they think she vanished, and nobody could offer

even the whisper of a motive why he might have
wanted to get rid of her. She wasn't afraid of him; I
knew that and so did everyone else."

"How did you know?"

"She didn't have that look in her eyes." Karen's
smile was a little sad. "The one we all see in the
mirror and recognize instantly in another abused
woman. The one you don't have anymore."

That startled her. "I don't?"

"It's how I knew you really had lost your memory.
You don't remember being hurt, Faith. You don't
remember the fear, the humiliation, the shame. You
don't remember cowering the way we've all cowered
while a man used his strength and his rage as
weapons."

Faith had another realization—that there were
some things in her past she hoped she never remembered. But before she could comment, Karen continued.

"Dinah had never experienced that either. And
though she didn't talk much about Kane MacGregor,
what she did say was pretty clear evidence that she
cared about him."

Faith wanted to stay on that subject, but she knew
all too well hers was a personal curiosity, that it
wouldn't help them to find Dinah. And they had to
find Dinah, they *had* to.

Soon. Before it was too late.

"How well do you know Dinah?" she asked, consciously using the present tense.

The director considered the question. "In some
ways, I knew—know—her quite well. In other ways,
I'm not so sure. She was intelligent, compassionate,

unusually generous. She was easy to confide in and kept other people's secrets as well as she kept her own. But I couldn't tell you anything about her past, or about what she did or where she went when she wasn't here." Karen paused. "She came here to do a story on the shelter months ago, and after her job was done she kept coming, volunteering her time, donating money. She met you here."

Faith stiffened. "She did?"

"Yeah. And it was very unusual, the way you took to each other right off. An instant bond. I remember that first day, you sat on the front steps and talked for hours. I asked you about it later, and you said that for the first time in your life you were beginning to believe in reincarnation, because Dinah *must* have been very close to you at some point in your existence, and yet you two had never met before. You said she was the only person you could ever remember trusting instantly and totally."

Faith thought about that for a moment. "Was I— did I claim to be psychic in any way?"

Karen's eyebrows shot up. "You never did to me. You were always very down-to-earth, even laughed at yourself for considering that reincarnation might be possible."

"What about Dinah?"

"Never heard anything like that from her, either."

Which, Faith thought, meant nothing. Dinah had clearly kept the "sections" of her life separate as far as she was able. What Faith was still unsure of was which section of Dinah's life she had belonged in: the humanitarian section where a shelter held abused women whom Dinah had clearly felt sympathy for, or the work section where there had been a story that might have endangered them both.

"Did she spend much time here right before she disappeared?" she asked finally.

"No, we hadn't seen her in weeks. In fact, we hadn't seen her until just after your accident, when she came to tell us what had happened. We wanted to send flowers or visit, but she discouraged us from doing either."

"She did?"

Karen nodded. "Said you were in a coma and the doctor thought more visitors wouldn't be advisable, that she'd keep us informed. She came by a few times, and then . . . we never saw her again. Things got hectic here, the way they usually do, and . . . time passed."

And Faith had been forgotten. She understood that, even though it caused her a pang, and managed a smile. "I see."

"I'm sorry, Faith. You and I weren't close, but I should have been a better friend."

"Don't worry about it. One good thing about having no memory is that the slings and arrows hardly hurt at all. Karen, may I see those women who might have talked to me?"

"Katie's the only one here today, I'm afraid. That's her trying to play the piano. Her mother, Andrea, made the mistake of letting her ex get too close a couple of days ago, and now she's in the hospital. As for Eve, she's out of town visiting relatives. Should be back any day now, though."

Faith was getting used to disappointment. She listened for a moment to the distant, inexpert piano notes. "I gather Katie is a child. How old?"

"Seven, though she seems older." Karen's sad smile returned. "They all grow up too fast in this house. But you can talk to her. She always liked you, as I recall."

"How about Dinah? Did Katie like her?"

"Very much."

The little girl was alone in what appeared to be a communal music-and-games room. She wore white pants and a Barbie T-shirt, and her long blond hair was held back from her face with pink plastic clips. She was more than a little doll-like herself. She was also extremely grave, accepting without a blink Karen's explanation that Faith had been "sick and doesn't remember things as well as she wants to."

Faith felt momentarily deserted when Karen left her with the little girl, then sat down on the bench beside her and said, "Hey, kiddo. What're you playing?"

Katie frowned, wide blue eyes gazing at Faith for a long silent time before she looked back down at the keys and tapped middle C twice. "I can't play much. 'Chopsticks,' but I don't like that. Some of 'Beautiful Dreamer.' You haven't been here to teach me anything new." The last was said with a careful absence of accusation.

"I'm sorry about that, Katie." Without thinking about it, Faith put her fingers on the keys and began playing a few notes. "Would you like to learn this? It's called 'Moonlight Sonata.' Isn't it pretty?" Music. Something else she hadn't remembered knowing until now.

Katie cocked her head, listening critically. "It sounds sad."

Faith stopped playing. "So it does. I'd forgotten that too, I guess. We'll just have to find something else I can teach you. I'll bring some music with me next time, okay?"

"You said you would." Again, the little girl's voice was neutral, the noncommittal tone of someone who had learned early that the wrong words, the wrong inflection, could incite violence.

Faith didn't like the way that made her feel, but all she said was, "I won't forget, Katie."

Katie looked at her. "Where's Dinah?"

Faith hardly knew how to answer. Keeping it simple, she replied, "I don't know, Katie."

"Why don't you ask her?" Katie asked reasonably.

"If I don't know where she is, I can't really do that, can I?"

"Just close your eyes and ask her," the child said, a touch of impatience in her voice now. "You used to. It was a game you two played. You'd close your eyes and say, 'Dinah, call me,' and the phone would ring."

"It would?" Faith said numbly.

"Sure. Don't you remember that?"

"No," Faith said. "I don't remember that."

FIVE

"You haven't said much since we got back," Kane said.

That was true, but Faith was still unwilling to talk about all she had learned at Haven House. She had related only the bare bones—that she and Dinah had met there, that both had spent some time there. She'd told him without emotion that she had been married to an abusive man, was now divorced, and still didn't remember any of it. She hadn't mentioned the conversation with the sad little girl, the revelation that she and Dinah might have been connected more surely than she had previously imagined.

She wasn't sure she believed it herself.

"You haven't said much either." Restlessly, she moved around the living room, ending up at the piano in the corner near the French doors, which opened onto a balcony. It was dark outside, late. Too late to do anything more, to go anywhere or ask questions or get an inch closer to finding Dinah, and if Faith was maddened by that, she could only guess how Kane must be feeling.

Then again, he'd been going through this for weeks, and by now must have learned the futility of driving himself to exhaustion, must have forced himself to accept that sleep and food were necessary, that moments of inactivity had to be endured no matter how desperately he needed to be out searching for Dinah.

"Neither of us had much luck this afternoon," he said. "Guy couldn't tell me any more about your accident, and nobody at the shelter could tell you anything useful."

She sat down on the piano bench and absently picked out a tune with one hand, idly watching her red-polished nails move over the keys. "I hate this," she murmured. "Not being able to do anything." Both hands began playing now. The quiet music kept her from hearing the ticking of the clock on the nearby wall, but it did nothing to muffle the ticking she was conscious of inside herself. The minutes and hours were slipping past so quickly. So quickly.

After a moment, Kane crossed the room to lean against the side of the piano. "You play well."

Made aware of what she was doing, Faith suddenly felt awkward and uncertain. Her fingers tangled, struck a series of sour notes, and went still. She laced them together in her lap. "I didn't even know I played at all until today. Does Dinah?"

"No." He smiled faintly. "She claims to have a tin ear, says music is just a lot of noise to her. So I consider it remarkably generous of her that she usually manages to stay in the same room when I practice."

Faith thought that in Dinah's place she would put up with more than noise if it meant spending time with Kane. But she wasn't the one in love with him, she reminded herself. That was Dinah. Dinah's memories of intimacy she remembered, Dinah's emotions she felt.

Not her own. Of course not her own.

Trying to think about something else, she recalled the afternoon's vivid dream. Abruptly, she said, "Isn't it possible that Dinah's disappearance has little to do with her work or my past, that she was just in the wrong place at the wrong time and got into trouble?"

"Of course it's possible. It's what the police believe, since they've been unable to turn up any evidence to prove otherwise. But I don't believe that. And I don't think you do either."

Faith hesitated. "Did— Was Dinah ever attacked by a dog?"

Surprised, Kane said, "Never, as far as I know. In fact, animals were pretty much crazy about her. Why?"

"I—had another dream today. When I took a nap after lunch. How was she dressed the day she vanished? Was she wearing jeans and a blueish sweater?"

"Yes." He straightened, fingers drumming restlessly on the polished surface of the piano. "What was the dream, Faith? What did you see?"

"Nothing helpful, that's why I didn't mention it sooner. It was too dark to know where she was. She parked the Jeep near a building and—and crept closer. She was very wary, excited, anxious. Maybe even scared. And then a big dog came out of nowhere and attacked her."

"You're sure she was attacked?"

Faith remembered the hot breath of the animal, the tearing teeth and the way its claws had raked her flesh, and swallowed hard. "I'm sure."

His expression was grim. "Yesterday you were sure she was being tortured."

"Kane, all these . . . memories, these flashes from Dinah's life and experiences, are out of sequence. I can't tell what the proper order is supposed to be, if something happened weeks or months ago—or yesterday. But I think it was the night she disappeared because I'm certain she *was* attacked, and you would have known about it if it had happened before that night. I think the attack was a part of whatever led up to her disappearance."

"And the torture?" He bit out the words.

"I still believe she is—or was—being tortured. I believe her captors want some kind of information from her that she isn't willing to give them."

"How can you know that? How can you?"

She didn't flinch from the rough demand, but it took all her resolution to meet his haunted eyes. "I don't know how, not really. They told me at the shelter that Dinah and I seemed like sisters from the moment we first met, that we were instantly and maybe inexplicably close. And I can't explain that any more than I can explain any of the strange things I've experienced since I came out of the coma. But I know, I'm absolutely convinced, that what I'm seeing in these flashes is real. Somehow, there's a connection between me and Dinah, a tangible bond that exists."

"Then why can't you tell me where she is?"

"I . . . don't know. I'm sorry."

"Have you tried?" Kane leaned toward her across the piano, his voice intense. "Have you made any attempt to reach her directly?"

Katie's blithe assertion that she could do just that rose in her mind, but Faith shied away from it. What if she tried and failed? What if the attempt somehow severed the tenuous connection she knew existed?

"Faith?"

She felt trapped, cornered by his force, his need to reach Dinah. "I don't know how," she whispered.

"There must be a way. Concentrate, Faith. Close your eyes and think about Dinah."

She didn't want to. With her eyes closed, the blank darkness of her mind was far more frightening, and gazing into that was not something she willingly faced. But Kane had asked it of her, demanded it of her, and she couldn't refuse him.

So she closed her eyes and tried to concentrate on Dinah, made herself think of nothing except the question of where Dinah was. Nothing else. Nothing . . .

"There's no proof," Dinah said.

"Then we'll have to get proof," Faith retorted. She chewed on a thumbnail for a moment. "But carefully. These guys play for keeps, Dinah."

"You don't have to tell me that. If what we suspect is true, they've already killed to protect their secret. They won't hesitate to kill again."

"Oh, it's true all right. I'm positive of that. So we need insurance, something we can use for bargaining power if we find ourselves in a corner."

"Faith . . ." Dinah hesitated, but only briefly. "Look, I know how much you've lost. I know how angry you are—"

"No, you don't. You don't know." Her voice was harsh, clipped. "They took everything away from me, Dinah. Everything. And they got away with it. The goddamned bastards got away with it." ·

"Which is all the more reason why we have to be careful now. We have to be sure, Faith. We have to get proof, and it has to stand up in court. Otherwise, you'll never get your justice."

"Justice?" Faith looked at her with an odd little smile. "Yes, of course. Justice."

"Faith—"

The scene shifted dizzily, and she found herself back in that dark, damp room, her wrists bound to the arms of the chair. Her hands were numb, and when she looked down at them through blurred eyes, she saw that the wires had cut into her flesh almost to the bone. Scarlet blood dripped steadily onto the floor.

Idly, she wondered how much she had left.

"Tell me." The man's voice was astonishingly quiet, almost mild. She tried to peer up at him, but the dimness and her swollen eyelids made it impossible to see anything but a shadow looming over her. "All you have to do to stop the pain is tell me what I want to know, Dinah."

Mute, she shook her head wearily.

The closed fist swung at her, the blow so brutal it rocked her head back with almost enough force to break her neck. One more like that, she thought dizzily, and he'll never get his damned answer.

An oath out of the darkness was evidence that the unseen watcher agreed with her. "Careful!" he growled. "She can't tell me what I want to know if she's dead."

She wanted to point out that it was just a matter of time, that her life was dripping out onto the cold concrete floor, but couldn't allow herself to speak because if she opened her mouth, she would scream. She couldn't scream. Wouldn't scream.

"Just answer the question, Dinah. Just tell us where to find it, and we'll let you go."

If she'd been able to summon the energy, she would have laughed. Let her go? She was never going to leave this cold, damp room, not on her own two feet. She would never see the sunlight again. Never see Kane again.

Didn't they realize that she knew that?

Another blow, possibly less brutal but at the moment she was no judge of degree; the pain was constant, radiating throughout her body in hot waves. What they had already done to her was killing her; these sadistic blows were merely finishing the job.

"This isn't working," the man doing the actual beating said unemotionally to the watcher. "I told you it wouldn't."

"Then start breaking her fingers."

"She won't feel it. Her hands are numb."

"Then start breaking something she will feel."

The shadow loomed over her, reaching, and Dinah tried desperately to think of something else, anything else. . . .

Kane. Oh, God, Kane, I wish—

Again the scene shifted, and this time she found herself hurrying down a vaguely familiar hallway.

"Faith?" Dinah caught up with Faith, her frown clear evidence of worry. "Did you find anything?"

"No," Faith replied. "Nothing. But there'll be another chance to look, sooner or later."

Both women kept their voices low, and neither relaxed until they reached the stairwell and hurried down.

"We're running out of time," Dinah said.

"Something else," Faith said. "I think my phone's been tapped."

"What?"

"It's just a feeling, but I think so."

Dinah said nothing for several flights, then, as they reached the parking garage, she grasped Faith's arm to halt her. "I've got a feeling too, and it's a bad one. We've gone as far as we can alone, Faith. We need help."

"I don't trust the cops, Dinah, you know that."

"I know that. But there's a federal cop I know I can trust."

"I trust federal cops even less."

"But you trust me. And I trust him," Dinah said.

Faith bit her lip in indecision, then shook her head. "Not yet, please. I want one more chance to find the evidence we need. It's important to me."

It was Dinah's turn to hesitate, but finally she nodded. "Okay, a few more days—"

"A week. I need at least a week."

Obviously against her better judgment, Dinah agreed. "A week then. But after that, I call out the troops. Understand?"

"All right. Now let's get out of here before the wrong person spots us together."

They split up just outside the stairwell, each going to her own vehicle quickly and quietly. Faith started her car and watched Dinah's Jeep pull out of its parking place; she hesitated a few moments to allow the other woman time to leave the garage. The place seemed full of shadows, and, suddenly nervous, she locked her car doors.

Faith glanced at the big purse beside her on the front seat and murmured, "I'm sorry, Dinah. But you'd try to stop me. And I can't let them get away this time. I just can't. . . ."

Faith opened her eyes with a start, bewildered to find herself on a couch. She was half-propped on a pillow and covered with a blanket, and had the confused sense that far too much time had gone by.

"Faith?" Kane sat down on the edge of the couch near her hips and reached to touch her face, his own strained and pale. "Jesus, don't ever do that to me again."

"Do what? What happened?"

"You were out cold," he said. "I asked you to concentrate on trying to reach Dinah, and the next thing I knew you were toppling off the piano bench, limp as a dishrag and completely unresponsive. If it hadn't been for a strong pulse and the fact that you were breathing with no trouble, I would have called EMS."

"How long was I out?"

"More than an hour. It's nearly midnight." Kane drew a breath and leaned back, his hand falling away from her face. "Noah's told me stories about this. Some of the genuine psychics he's encountered go into a trancelike state in which all the vital signs slow down. As if the body needs to draw on its resources, tap in to whatever energy is available to use those extra senses. That's what seemed to be happening with you, so I didn't interfere. How do you feel?"

Faith took stock of her physical condition and realized she felt all right, just a little tired. Her emotional state, however, was another matter entirely. Going into that "trancelike state" had been like falling into a deep, black hole, and the terror of completely losing her grasp on the here and now was not something she would willingly repeat.

"I'm okay," she said. "But please don't ever ask me to do that again."

Kane nodded, but his eyes were eager. "Did it work? Did you reach Dinah?"

Faith shied away from telling him further details about Dinah being tortured. There was no reason for him to hear that. No reason at all. Instead, she concentrated on the other two scenes.

"Faith?"

She shook her head. "I didn't reach Dinah the way you mean, the way you wanted me to. There were just . . . more flashes, more scenes from the past. But more helpful this time, I think."

"Helpful how? What did you see?"

She told him as much as she could remember about the two memories, which seemed to prove that she and Dinah had indeed been working together on some kind of investigation. She tried to recall all the details, but so much was frustratingly vague, and she was unhappily aware that there were now even more questions. Including the nagging one about what it was she had hidden from Dinah. And how she had been able to hide anything at all if she and Dinah had been able to communicate as easily as Katie claimed.

She's just a little girl, and probably got it only half right. . . .

Faith went still for a moment, wondering if that thought was hers or someone else's. She didn't know, couldn't tell.

"So it must be connected somehow with my past, with what happened in Seattle," she said finally, forcing her mind back. "That must be why I was so determined that *they* wouldn't get away with it again. We were looking for evidence, and I had found something, something small enough to hide in my purse—and I didn't tell Dinah about it, at least not then."

"And you have no idea what that evidence was?"

Faith shook her head. "It was . . . it was almost as if I were watching a movie, just looking on and listening in while they—while we—talked. I don't know what she was thinking, what I was thinking. All I know is that I had found something, and for some reason I didn't want her to know I'd found it, at least not until I could . . ."

"Could what?"

She groped for the elusive knowledge, and finally sighed in defeat. "I don't know. I just don't know. I'm sorry."

"Think carefully, Faith. Was there anything at all that could help us figure out where Dinah is?"

Unwillingly, she thought of that cold, damp place with its concrete floors and shadowy walls, thought of the two men interrogating Dinah, one unemotionally efficient in dealing out agony and the other urgently insistent on getting information from her before she died.

She's dying. I know that. How can I tell him?

And like a distant answering whisper in her mind came the words, *You can't tell him.*

"Faith?"

Steadily, she said, "I don't think so. There was something vaguely familiar about the hallway of that building where I was looking for evidence, but I have no idea what or where it is. In fact, I have no real sense of where either of those two memories took place."

"Do you think you'd recognize either place if you saw it again?"

"That hallway, yes. The other . . . I don't know. But the hallway, that building, seems more important. If I was looking for evidence there—and if I found something—then it has to help us find Dinah. Doesn't it?"

"I wish I knew."

"We can look for it. Begin with places that seem likely—the building where I worked, others in the area. It's a start, isn't it?"

"Yes. Of course it is."

She gazed at his face, feeling a strong pang of loneliness. He was entirely focused on Dinah, thinking of nothing except possible ways of finding her. It reminded Faith yet again of how unconnected she was, to anything or anyone.

"I wish I could be more help," she said. "I'm sorry."

Kane looked at her. "You are helping, Faith. You've given me more pieces of the puzzle than I've been able to find in all the weeks since Dinah disappeared."

"But we still don't know what the puzzle is supposed to look like."

"We'll figure it out," Kane said.

Faith hoped he was right. But all she could do at the moment was wonder wretchedly if it was all her fault that Dinah was dying.

And wonder what Kane would do when he found out.

"There's really nothing more I can tell you, Miss Parker." Dr. Murphy closed the folder and gazed across her desk. "Your visits here during the time you've been my patient have all been unexceptional, regular checkups or very minor complaints. I continued the prescription for contraceptives you'd been using before you came to Atlanta, but the only other medication I prescribed was a course of antibiotics for a mild infection."

Faith wasn't sure how to phrase the questions she wanted to ask. Finally, she chose bluntness.

"So I was sexually active?"

The doctor's brows rose slightly, and a flicker of sympathy showed in her eyes. "You don't even remember that?"

"I don't remember anything before waking up in the hospital."

"That's . . . quite unusual. Amnesia tends to center around the traumatic incident. The patient seldom recalls the events just before the trauma occurred. But in virtually every case I know of, the missing time is only a matter of hours or days."

"In my case, years are missing. A lifetime, in fact." Faith managed a smile. "And I'm trying desperately to—to collect the pieces of my life and put them back together. So anything you can tell me, Doctor . . ."

Dr. Murphy laced her fingers together atop the file on her blotter and gazed at Faith steadily. "I see. I hadn't realized your amnesia was so extensive. That would, however, explain the changes I see in you."

"Changes?"

"In your manner and bearing, your eyes. You said you visited Haven House yesterday. They told you there was abuse in your background?"

"Yes. Though Karen didn't know any details. I gather my ex-husband was . . . physically abusive?"

"Physically and emotionally. You told me you had warned this man to stay away from you, and that you had some confidence that he would because you had medical evidence of past injuries that could ruin his career and put him behind bars."

"Is he the reason I came to Atlanta? Did I want to get three thousand miles away from him?"

"I couldn't say, Miss Parker. You never said as much to me. And I honestly don't know if you were afraid he'd follow you here. I referred you to Haven House because you displayed many of the aftereffects of abuse. You had tension headaches and a low resistance to infection, a poor appetite. Your sleep was disturbed more often than not, and you were reluctant to make friends or form emotional attachments. I thought it would be healthier for you to spend time with other women who had suffered abuse, especially since you had done so the last few months you'd lived in Seattle."

"And did it appear to you that Haven House and the women there helped me?" Faith had no idea where her dispassionate voice was coming from; all she knew was that they were discussing what seemed to be the life of a stranger.

"I believe so. I saw steady improvement."

"And yet you say that I'm more different now?"

"Yes. There's a certain look many abuse victims share, a certain tension in their bearing and actions. That was evident the last time I saw you. It isn't today. If I didn't know, I would never guess you'd been abused."

Questions about that abusive ex-husband rose in her mind, but Faith was all too aware that the doctor could not answer them.

"I wish there was more I could tell you," Dr. Murphy said with obvious sympathy. "But you were reluctant even to confide in me as much as you did, and probably wouldn't have except that you said your doctor back in Seattle had urged you to make me aware of the history of abuse for medical reasons."

"Medical reasons?"

"The effects of abuse can last for years, Miss Parker, both physically and emotionally, and it's always wise to make your doctor aware of the background in such cases. You had no lingering problems from physical injuries, but knowing your history would make me more apt to spot complications in the future."

Faith decided not to ask what those complications might be. Instead, she said, "I see. Thank you, Doctor. For the information, and for taking time out of a busy morning to talk to me."

"You are my patient, Miss Parker." For the first time, Dr. Murphy smiled. "I only wish there was more I could tell you."

"You've . . . told me a lot," Faith said.

"You were a long time," Kane said when she got into his car outside the clinic. "Did you have to wait for the doctor?"

"No, she saw me right away."

"So? Did she prescribe muscle relaxants?"

Faith shook her head. "No."

Kane had his hand on the gearshift, but paused before putting the car into motion and gazed at her questioningly. "What else did she tell you?"

Impossible to keep the information to herself, no matter how much she wanted to; for all Faith knew, that violent ex-husband might lie behind all the violent things that had happened. So she told Kane, staring through the windshield all the while because she couldn't meet his eyes.

"That gives us another possibility, I suppose," she finished, her voice very steady. "It doesn't seem to fit with what I've been remembering, but it's conceivable that he's somehow involved. But the doctor didn't know his name, and I can't remember it. Easy enough to find out, I suppose."

"Faith." Kane put a hand on her shoulder and turned her until she looked at him. "I'm sorry."

She wondered if the return of her memory would mean she'd be unable to bear a man's hands on her. It seemed an alien possibility at the moment. "There's no reason to be sorry, not about this. I don't remember him hurting me, I've told you that. I don't remember anything about him."

She thought she sounded indifferent, and she even managed to smile, but apparently something betrayed the misery she felt, because Kane's fingers tightened on her shoulder.

"I'm sorry there's been so much pain in your life. If I could do anything to . . ."

"To make it better?" This time, her smile felt more natural. "You can't. But my amnesia might turn out to be a blessing when all's said and done. I don't remember the pain or the grief. Honestly, it's like it all happened to somebody else. But at least the facts are coming together. With a little luck, if I finally do remember, at least I'll be prepared."

Kane nodded. "Still, it's a hell of a way to find out about yourself and your past."

"I don't seem to have a choice." She fought a sudden and almost overpowering urge to throw herself into his arms and cling with all her strength. Afraid that showed as well, she went on hastily. "So we add my ex to the list of things we need to investigate further. And go on. Where to now?"

He didn't answer immediately; his eyes searched her face as though looking for something, but in the end he didn't voice whatever it was that disturbed him. He released her and put the car into gear.

"The emergency room where you were first brought after the crash."

That made sense; he was still looking for something to connect her accident with what had happened to Dinah weeks afterward.

"You said Dinah visited me the day she disappeared?"

"She did. And since the police traced her movements of that day very carefully, we know she spent little more than half an hour with you in the morning."

"And then?"

"She went to her office and was in and out several times until early afternoon. Doing routine things, according to her editor. Sometime between noon and one P.M., she left her office—and hasn't been seen since. Except by her captors, of course."

Faith didn't want to think about Dinah's captors, about what was taking place in that cellar. She was agonizingly aware of the minutes ticking away. Of Dinah's life energy fading away.

There's so little time left . . .

Her realization? Or Dinah's?

She forced herself to think. "Between noon and one. But it was night when that dog attacked her, I'm sure of it. So if what I saw actually took place, and took place that day, where was Dinah during the hours before dark?"

"So far, nobody's come forward to admit having been with her. She walked out of her office building and might as well have been swallowed up by a black hole."

Faith thought of that hallway in her dream, and of

the shadowy, lonely parking garage. Had that been Dinah's office building? "Can we go by Dinah's office later?"

"Of course." He shot her a quick glance. "But why?"

"Hallways. I'm looking for one I can recognize from my dream. It probably wasn't in Dinah's office building—why would I have been creeping around a place she had to have been far more familiar with?— but it's something else to check, just to be sure."

"We also need to go to the building where you worked. Talk to your supervisor again, co-workers."

"Yes."

Kane patted the inner pocket of his jacket, where he carried his cell phone—a restless gesture he had repeated several times that morning. "With a little luck Noah will call later today to tell us what he found out about that restricted file."

More appalling and mystifying facts about her past? Faith tried not to shiver. Despite her brave words to Kane, she wasn't sure she could take many more such revelations.

Not many at all.

Faith pretty much stayed out of the way in the busy emergency room while Kane pursued the answers he wanted. He appeared to have a knack for getting people to talk to him despite the rules and issues of legality, and as she watched him patiently work his way through the tangle of red tape, she could only admire both his persistence and his self-control.

It had to be hell for him, this endless, tedious piecing together of one tiny fact or bit of information after another, and yet he had been at it now for weeks. The strain of the search showed in his face and haunted his eyes, but despite the exhaustion he had to feel, he showed no sign of willingness to slow down or give up. He was utterly determined to find his Dinah.

I can't tell him. I can't tell him she's dying.

He wouldn't believe her anyway, that's what she told herself. Wouldn't believe such a horrible truth unless or until the proof was undeniable.

Like a body.

SIX

Faith shivered and crossed her arms over her breasts, rubbing her hands up and down in an effort to find warmth. Or comfort. But there was little of either in the cold desolation of her thoughts. Dinah was dying, and Faith was desperately afraid they wouldn't be able to find her in time.

"Excuse me—are you a patient?"

She jumped when a hand touched her arm, then gazed up at a harried young doctor. "No. No, I'm not."

He frowned at her, mild blue eyes puzzled behind the lenses of his glasses. "You look familiar."

Faith got a grip on herself. "A few weeks ago, I was a patient here. They brought me in after a traffic accident."

"That probably explains it then. I never forget a face." He smiled at her. "Well, you look fine now. Was there some reason why you—"

"Faith." Kane was suddenly there, and she was a little surprised when he put an arm around her and drew her toward him—and away from the young doctor—in a gesture that was curiously protective. "I see you found Dr. Blake."

Faith blinked at the name tag on the doctor's green scrubs. "I guess so," she murmured, feeling oddly out-of-sync.

Kane said, "Doctor, if you wouldn't mind answering a few questions about the day Miss Parker was brought in here—"

Sound seemed to be fading in and out. She'd hear a few words of what Kane or Dr. Blake said, then the words would fade and she could hear only a distant rushing sound, like . . . water? Maybe. Like water from a fall, or gushing out of a pipe under great pressure . . .

It was the strangest experience, not frightening but unsettling. She looked around her, seeing people talking, seeing noises she should have heard and yet didn't, like the crash of several boxes falling from a shelf, and the despairing wail of a woman bent over the still body of an injured child.

All she could hear was the rushing water. It went on and on, filling her ears, all her other senses, her mind. She looked at Kane, watching his lips move, saw Dr. Blake respond, his face serious and a bit perplexed.

She realized she was barely aware of Kane's physical nearness; she stood in the shelter of his arm, yet felt as if she were somewhere else, where water rushed and the musty smell of cold earth surrounded her. Where she felt a smothering sense of claustrophobia, the panic of being trapped and helpless. She was alone. And she didn't know which was worse, the awful musty smell and cold or the devastating knowledge that she couldn't . . . that she'd never . . .

Faith groped for knowledge just out of her reach, and found only blackness. She could hear the water, smell the moldy earth all around her, but the emotions had faded once more into silence. Part of her wanted to close her eyes and concentrate, but remembering the abrupt unconsciousness of another such attempt stopped her.

That wasn't all that stopped her. She was afraid and she knew it. Afraid of what she might see if she closed her eyes and really looked at that place she could hear and smell. Afraid of what awaited her there. It was fear of the unknown, of a nightmare, of the darkness that lay just beyond what the mind understood.

She didn't want to look, didn't want to go there. Didn't want to feel those horrible emotions or to see—

"Faith?"

Like a soap bubble popping, the sounds of rushing water were gone, and as she looked up into Kane's concerned eyes, what she heard was the normal activity of a busy emergency room. "Yes?" Her voice sounded absentminded even to her.

"Are you all right?"

"Fine. I'm fine."

Kane frowned at her. "Are you sure?"

She wondered when the doctor had left them. "Quite sure. But I'm afraid I . . . I wasn't listening. Did Dr. Blake tell us anything helpful?"

He looked around and said, "Let's get out of here."

He put her in his car and drove them a few blocks to a restaurant that wasn't crowded; they were given a booth near a window, where the waitress quickly brought them coffee and left them alone.

Still distracted, Faith said, "What did Dr. Blake say about the accident?"

"The way he remembers it, preliminary tests showed some ambiguous results. Maybe there were alcohol and muscle relaxants in your system, and maybe not. All he knew for sure was that your vital signs were strong and your injuries fairly minor—and that something had put you into a coma. He didn't think it was the head injury and suspected something more toxic than alcohol and medication in your system, so he ordered further tests. He went off duty shortly afterward. When he came back the next day, he was told you'd been transferred upstairs. He assumed that happened because you were stable, and that your regular doctor had taken over your case." Kane paused. "Funny thing, though. The paperwork that's supposed to be kept there in the ER seems to be missing."

"Could it have been sent upstairs with me?"

"A copy should have been, and some paperwork was certainly part of the file that ended up with Dr. Burnett. But the admitting records should be on file in the ER. They aren't."

"I don't suppose we have much chance of finding out what happened to them?"

"You saw how busy that place was—and on a Monday morning, hardly their busiest time. My guess is that we'll never be able to trace what happened to those records between the time you were admitted and when you were put under Burnett's care. But we can assume any number of people had access and could have tampered with the test results."

"What about the lab that did the tests?"

"It's there in the hospital. Their procedure is to keep a copy of all results in their own files. But in this case—"

"Let me guess. Missing paperwork."

"Afraid so. And the blood and tissue samples they used for the tests were destroyed afterward, per standard procedure."

"Am I being paranoid in thinking all this missing and misplaced paperwork means something other than simple human error?"

"I don't think so. When there are this many glitches in a normally efficient system, it usually means someone's been tampering."

Faith sipped her coffee, grateful for the warmth because she'd felt chilled ever since her strange experience in the emergency room. "Then it's a safe bet that we'll never know for sure if there was actually alcohol in my blood or I was drugged intentionally."

"Probably not. But I'm willing to put my money on your having been drugged."

"It seems strange to hope that that's what happened, but I really didn't want to find out I'd been stupid enough to drink and get behind the wheel."

Kane's gaze was intent. "No, I doubt you were so reckless."

She wondered what he was basing that doubt on, but didn't ask. Instead, she said, "If I was drugged, the question is, who did it? I guess the why is obvious—they wanted me out of action."

"Yeah. Grabbed you in the parking garage would be my guess. It was a bit after hours, the area likely to be deserted, so it's a good possibility."

"So why didn't I just go for a phone and call the police once they let me go? Why did I attempt to drive?"

"You may have already been disoriented from the drug, not thinking clearly. They probably held on to you long enough to make sure of that. We do have half an hour or so unaccounted for, from the time you left the garage to the crash only six miles away."

"I suppose." But Faith remembered the flash in which she had reminded Dinah that they couldn't trust the police. Had she, even in a drugged and panicked state, felt that the only thing she could do was get to Dinah as soon as possible?

It might have been better if you had. It might have been so different. . . .

"That's the answer then," he said with bitterness rather than relief, calling from another pay phone. "Just like you thought. She's gone to MacGregor. They're in a restaurant right now, heads together and talking up a storm."

"Get back here now."

"But shouldn't I follow—"

"We've found out what we need to know for the moment. She's gone to him, and you can bet he'll keep her close, hoping she can lead him to Dinah."

"What if she can? What if she can lead him to *us*?"

"We'll have to make sure she doesn't, won't we? Get back here now."

"Right."

"Faith?"

She looked at him, shook her head. Whose voice? Not quite alien in her head, it could have been her own, her subconscious, the healed part of her mind trying to nudge the part still unable or unwilling to remember. Or it could have been Dinah's.

"What is it?"

"Nothing." She tried to think clearly, still not sure of that voice in her head. "So somebody wanted me out of the way and arranged an accident. I end up in a coma, presumably no longer a threat. But then— something happened. Something must have changed. Dinah became a threat to them somehow. Maybe they hadn't even connected her to me until she visited me in the hospital. Then they . . . watched her, maybe? Saw her go to my apartment, maybe leave with my laptop?"

"Maybe. And maybe it was just common sense that she would become an enemy sooner or later. She's a journalist, a good one. Once they connected her to you, they might have been convinced you had told her whatever damaging information you had."

"I don't think Dinah became a threat because they realized she knew me. I think she became a threat when they realized something of theirs was missing."

"This evidence you believe you'd found?"

Faith frowned at her cup without seeing it, trying

to make the pieces fit. "They keep asking her where *it* is. Over and over. That's why they didn't just kill her outright. And it has to be whatever I found, don't you see? They never searched Dinah's apartment, but they've searched mine twice—both times since she disappeared."

"So they have to be convinced you have whatever it is they're looking for, but that Dinah knows where it's hidden?"

"It's the only possibility that makes any sense to me." She looked steadily at Kane. "I took something from them, and they either didn't know about it until after the accident or thought they were safe once I was out of the way. Then they realized there was a connection between me and Dinah—a smart journalist with a knack for breaking big stories. So they grabbed her to try to make her talk. Only she's not talking."

"You said she refused to talk because she was protecting someone." Kane's voice was almost as level as hers had been. "You?"

Faith shook her head. "The last time she saw me, I was in a coma. I was . . . safe."

"Maybe they told her you came out of it."

"I suppose they could have, but why would she feel her silence was protecting me? If I was the one she was concerned about, hearing I was out of the coma would make her more likely to tell them what she knew. Wouldn't it? So they wouldn't come after me."

Kane nodded slowly. "Then who does she believe she's protecting?"

Faith rubbed her forehead fretfully. "I don't know. How can we know that until we know what it is I found? And who's threatened by it?"

He grasped her wrist and pulled her hand away from her face. "Maybe you should take a break for a few hours. I can take you back to the apartment—"

We don't have a few hours. Dinah doesn't have a few hours.

"I'm fine." She carefully avoided any glance at the hand still holding her wrist, and even managed a smile. "But we don't seem to have accomplished much, really. Speculation, supposition, guesses. Maybe we're right, but even if we are, it doesn't get us any closer to finding Dinah."

Kane's fingers tightened around her wrist for a moment. Then his gaze went to that connection between them and he frowned slightly. He leaned back, releasing her wrist. "We have to figure out who's got Dinah, and to do that we need to find whatever it is you found once before." His voice was abrupt. "The best possibility is that you'll remember what you found or where you found it. Why don't we visit the office where you worked and see if that jars your memory?"

Faith nodded and rose to her feet. There was a clock near the door, and she could hear it ticking. Or maybe she imagined it.

Ticking.

"You knew your job." Marianne Camp, Faith's supervisor in the department where she had worked, was matter-of-fact. "You had some prior experience working for a construction company, and that gave you a solid base from which to handle your duties here."

Faith wondered if she had done something to annoy the woman, or if her attitude was so chilly with all those she supervised. Then again, maybe she didn't view aftereffects of a coma as a good reason not to return to work.

Kane smiled at her. "And those duties, Mrs. Camp?"

"Secretarial, for the most part." The supervisor shrugged, possibly impatient to leave on her lunch break, since it was nearly noon. "Entering data into the system, filing paperwork, coordinating the schedules of the various inspectors."

"Was I friends with any of my co-workers?" Faith asked.

"Not as far as I was aware," she replied stiffly. "You kept to yourself. Very quiet and dependable."

Kane said, "According to what you told me, Mrs. Camp, you spoke to Miss Parker for about five minutes before she left the office the day of her accident."

"Yes."

"Do you remember what you talked about?"

"After all these weeks? Not really. I should imagine it was something to do with the paperwork she had stayed late to complete."

"I see. Do you always remain late yourself if someone else is working after hours?"

"Usually but not always. I had paperwork of my own to take care of."

Kane glanced at Faith as she shifted slightly in the other visitor's chair, then said to the supervisor, "Were you both working on the same project?"

"No, Mr. MacGregor. No one in my department is

assigned a specific project the way you mean. We take care of work as it comes in, on a rotation basis. As I recall, Miss Parker was transcribing three different field reports and collating inspection forms from at least half a dozen construction sites. It was by no means an unusual workload."

"Would you happen to know which construction sites those were, Mrs. Camp?"

"Not specifically." Her voice was indifferent.

"Could you find out for us?"

"I don't see how, Mr. MacGregor. There's no reason for our files to show which clerk handled the various pieces of paper."

Faith spoke up then. "Why was I late, Mrs. Camp?"

"I beg your pardon?"

"You said I was dependable. So why did I have to stay late to complete that paperwork? Didn't I have time to get it done during regular hours?"

The supervisor frowned at her. "You took a long lunch that day. Two hours."

"Do you know why I did that?"

"You said you had a doctor's appointment." There was the faintest emphasis on the second word.

Slightly dry, Faith said, "I guess I didn't have a note."

"No."

There didn't seem to be much more they could ask, so after thanking the supervisor for her time, Kane and Faith left her tiny office.

"Good question," he said as they stood in the hallway outside the suite of offices that made up the Office of Building Inspections and Zoning. "It never occurred to me to wonder why you stayed late that day."

"The answer doesn't seem to help us much." She shrugged. "I didn't have a doctor's appointment that day, at least not with Dr. Murphy, so I could have been lying to Mrs. Camp about why I took the long lunch. But we don't have a clue what I might have been doing, or where I went, and after so many weeks it's doubtful we'd find anyone who might have seen me and remembered, even if we knew who to ask."

"And you don't recognize this hallway?"

Faith looked around again. The Office of Building Inspections and Zoning was on the fifth floor of the busy downtown office building, and up and down the hall on this floor and others were more city offices. The hallway itself was generic, almost featureless and without charm, and struck no chord of memory within Faith.

"This isn't the hallway I saw in that memory," she told Kane. "At least, not this floor."

"My guess is that they all look virtually alike, but we can check a couple on the way down."

As Kane had predicted, the other floors they checked were all but identical, and by the time they reached the lobby, Faith was certain it was not this building she and Dinah had been in when she had found . . . whatever it was she had found.

A morning filled with questions, and precious few answers.

Faith said, "I think we should talk to Dinah's other lawyer, Mr. Sloan. Especially since you didn't know about him before."

"I definitely want him to explain why he didn't come forward when Dinah disappeared," Kane agreed grimly.

They got into the car, and for a moment he stared through the windshield without moving.

"Kane?"

A muscle tightened in his jaw. "I don't—I can't *feel* her anymore."

The desolation in his voice went through Faith like a knife and left her aching. For him, for Dinah. And for herself.

"She's gone further and further away from me with every day that's passed. I think about it, and I realize I can't remember the sound of her voice. I glimpse a blond woman on a street corner and my heart stops, yet I have to concentrate to remember her face."

"Kane—"

He turned his head and focused on her. "I have to find her," he said. "Before I lose her completely."

There was nothing she could say to that except, "We'll find her, Kane. We will."

After a moment he nodded, accepting that reassurance because, she thought, anything else was simply unbearable.

"Yes," he said.

She kept her voice steady. "I have Mr. Sloan's card, so I know the address of his office."

Kane started the car, his actions automatic. More coolly now, as though he regretted the impulsive, emotional confidence, he said, "I'm willing to bet he won't tell us anything useful."

"Maybe, but it's a base we have to cover."

"Agreed. But I know lawyers. He won't talk."

As it turned out, Kane was only half right.

Edward Sloan was in his early fifties but looked ten years younger. He was trim and athletic, dressed well without ostentation, and had the trained, evenly modulated voice of an orator. And despite visibly restless clients in his outer office, he agreed to see Faith and Kane immediately.

"How can I help you?" he asked when they were seated before his sleek, modern desk. The question might have been directed to both of them, but his eyes were on Faith.

So she was the one who replied. "Mr. Sloan, do you have any idea if Dinah Leighton was working on a particular story when she disappeared?"

"No. She never talked to me about her work."

Kane said, "She used your services whenever she wanted her actions to remain very quiet."

"Is that a question, Mr. MacGregor?" Sloan smiled faintly. "Yes, I was her confidential attorney."

"Did she—does she use you only to arrange financial deals?"

"Almost exclusively. Miss Leighton's family attorneys tended to view her philanthropy with a great deal of unease, from what she told me. I had the virtue of complete personal disinterest in her and in what she chose to do with her money. She told me what she wanted done, I did it."

"Like the financial arrangements for me," Faith said.

"Exactly so, Miss Parker."

"You never asked her why she did it?"

"As I said, my value to Miss Leighton lay in my discretion and my disinterest. It would not have been to my advantage to ask her questions."

Kane tried another tack. "Okay, then tell us this. Did you notice, in the course of performing your duties for Miss Leighton, anything out of the ordinary? Anything that might give us some idea of what happened to her?"

"You must know I can't talk in specifics about Miss Leighton's business affairs," Sloan replied immediately.

"I'm not asking you about her business affairs," Kane said with just enough patience to make the effort noticeable. "I'm asking you if you know anything—if you saw or heard anything—that might help us to find your missing client."

This time, there was a pause. A rather deliberate one, Faith thought. Her heartbeat quickened as she gazed at the lawyer's face. *He knows something. He knows something, and he's just been waiting for somebody to ask him.* But nobody had asked, because his relationship with Dinah had not been a public one—and Sloan was not a man who would ever volunteer information. Which explained why he had not come forward when Dinah had vanished.

"Please, Mr. Sloan." Faith knew her voice was unsteady. "Please help us if you can. Did anything unusual happen in the days before she disappeared?"

"Just one thing." His voice was composed. "Two days before she vanished, Miss Leighton asked me to recommend a good private investigator, one who specialized in missing persons."

Faith looked at Kane in confusion, and it was he who said, "Did she say why?"

"The only thing she said to me, Mr. MacGregor, was a rather cryptic remark to the effect that she needed someone to look for a corpse."

"And that's all he'd tell you?" Bishop asked.

"That's all." Kane wedged the receiver between his ear and shoulder, reached for a legal pad on the coffee table, and scowled at the notes he'd jotted down earlier. "Just that Dinah wanted to hire a P.I. specializing in missing persons because she needed someone to find a corpse."

"Did he know if she actually hired the P.I.?"

"He said that when Dinah disappeared, he called the two people he'd recommended, and neither had heard from her. I'm inclined to believe him. For one thing, news of the reward has been played up heavily in the media, and I doubt very much that a professional investigator would pass up the chance to make a million bucks if he had any knowledge at all about Dinah."

"That is a point." Bishop paused. "Where's Faith?"

"I dropped her off at Haven House. There's a woman there who seems to have known both Faith and Dinah months ago, and Faith wanted to talk to her. Understandably, men aren't welcome there, so I've been checking out a few other things. Faith's bank, where she has no safe deposit box. Dinah's other bank, where the manager was very cooperative and is even now sending Richardson all the records."

"Did you take a look at those records?"

"Yeah. And they verify what Conrad told us, that Dinah used that bank account the way she used Sloan, to handle those bequests and donations she wanted to keep quiet. Guy's team will go over all of it with a fine-tooth comb." He paused. "Since you're still at Quantico, I assume you've been able to look into that restricted file?"

"I'm not still at Quantico," Bishop said, then went on before Kane could ask him anything about that. "But, yeah, I found out why the files on the murders of Faith's mother and sister are restricted."

"Why?"

"Ties in to what you told me about her former husband and the abuse. It seems that he was, and still is, under suspicion for the crimes. The theory is that abuse escalated to open violence when she dared to divorce him, and that she escaped being killed only because she was unexpectedly called in to work that night."

Grim, Kane said, "That doesn't explain why information about the investigation is restricted."

"Yes, well, it makes sense when you learn one more salient fact. Faith's ex-husband, Tony Ellis, is an FBI agent."

Katie was at school, but Faith left new sheet music on the piano for her. Kane hadn't asked any questions when she'd requested the stop at a music store; she'd told him the gift was for a child, and he had made a couple of suggestions as to what might appeal to a budding young pianist.

Eve—last names weren't offered, which Faith assumed was one of Haven House's policies—turned out to be a not very tall, solidly built woman of about twenty-one, with wary brown eyes that had already seen far too much. She was watching over a small group of toddlers when Karen took Faith down to the roomy nursery in the basement of the house to introduce her. The children's mothers, the director had explained, were working, or job hunting, or busy with lawyers or police attempting to divorce, arrest, or prosecute abusive husbands.

But it was late in the day, and even as Faith was introduced to Eve, women of various ages were beginning to arrive to claim their offspring.

Karen suggested she take over the nursery to give Eve a chance to talk to Faith, and they went upstairs to the second-floor sitting room near Eve's bedroom.

"So you've lost your memory." Eve's voice was a little abrupt, but not unsympathetic, a tone explained when she added, "Happened to me once. Got knocked into a wall and out cold. When I came to, more than six months were a total blank."

Faith winced. "Did you eventually remember?"

Eve shook her head. "Not really. But I pieced most of it together, talking to people. I guess that's what you're doing?"

"Trying to. Can you help me?"

"We weren't close," Eve said frankly. "Friendly, just not confiding. So I don't know much, except that you were very angry."

"Angry? Not frightened?"

"I don't think you were as afraid of your ex as some of us were. Maybe because he was so far away, or maybe because you had other things on your mind. I think you and Dinah were up to something."

Faith blinked. "Up to something?"

"Yeah. A story of some kind. I don't know what it was about, but I got the feeling Dinah was trying to hold you back in some way. To keep you from doing something she didn't think you should do. I think she was worried about you."

Faith wondered again if it was her fault that Dinah was in such danger, and was conscious of a cold, sick feeling in the pit of her stomach. But all she said was, "Were you close to Dinah?"

Eve's rather immobile face softened. "She talked to me a lot for her story. And, after, she gave me the money I needed to go back to school. I got my GED, but I wasn't going to do anything else until Dinah convinced me it was the best thing for me to do. I'm studying computers," she finished proudly.

Faith smiled at her. "That's great."

"Yeah, I think so. I have a future now. Dinah said—" She broke off and bit her lip.

"What did she say, Eve?"

The younger woman hesitated, then said slowly, "I've thought about it since she disappeared, and crazy as it sounds, I think she always knew she'd— she didn't have a future of her own. She seemed almost sad when we talked about my plans. Once, she said I had so much to look forward to, and that she wished she'd be here to see it."

"Maybe she was . . . just planning to go away," Faith said.

"I don't think so. You didn't see her face the way I did, hear her voice. I think she could see the future sometimes, that she knew about things before they happened. She never said so, but once she warned me not to go back to a certain club I liked, and later I found out my ex had been there looking for me. I heard her tell Andrea she should go see her mother, and just a couple of weeks later the poor lady died of a heart attack. And there were other things. The way she looked at Katie and the other kids. The way she moved really fast to arrange things whenever she donated money to Haven House or one of us, as if she knew she had to hurry." Eve shook her head. "I think she knew she didn't have much time left."

Faith suddenly remembered what Bishop had said about Dinah. *She was precognitive, able to . . . tune in to future events, to predict the turn of a card or the throw of dice.*

Had Dinah seen her own future?

SEVEN

The sky darkened early with a November storm, one of those weather systems that seemed to circle a place warily, thunder rumbling and lightning flashing, while it decided if it wanted to strike.

Kane wondered if it was an omen, and tried not to let himself believe that. But it was hard not to. The night and the storm had closed in, cutting him off and making it impossible for him to be out *doing* something, anything, that might help him find Dinah. He hated the night.

It was impossible to sit still. He had learned weeks ago that when he was barred from doing anything to help Dinah, he had to keep himself busy with mundane activities. It kept him grounded. Kept him sane. At least, he hoped it did.

He dug into the freezer for one of the homemade meals that were occasional weekend projects for him. Dinah had teased him that he went on cooking jags on weekends only because he wanted to make her look bad, but the truth was that there was a streak of practicality in his nature and a strong sense of self-reliance, and he regularly practiced the skill of cooking just as he regularly practiced his other skills. Because one never knew when such things would come in handy.

It was after seven, and the storm was rumbling closer, when Faith emerged from the bedroom. She had retreated there soon after they returned from the shelter, obviously upset by what she had learned there, although she had told Kane it was "nothing useful."

He suspected she had discovered more details of her own past and personality, but even so it bothered him that she hadn't wanted to discuss it. In the weeks since Dinah had vanished, he had begun to realize just how much of herself she had been unable or unwilling to share with him. That, coupled with his deepening sense of loss, his increasing feeling that Dinah was slipping further and further away from him, made him want to hold on even tighter to the only connection to her he had left: Faith.

"Are you sure you don't want me to move into the guest room now that Bishop's gone?" she asked abruptly, obviously speaking more to fill the silence than for any other reason.

"I'm sure." He didn't offer a reason, not wanting to admit that either bed was useless to him anyway, since he spent his nights pacing the floor until exhaustion finally drove him to close his eyes for an hour or two.

Faith shrugged. "Something smells good."

"Irish stew. My own version, anyway." A boom of thunder interrupted him, and he waited it out before adding, "Perfect night for it, I thought."

"Isn't it a little late in the year for this kind of storm?" Faith wondered, automatically picking up the plates and silverware he had stacked on the counter and going to set the table. She was just as restless and edgy as he was, a fact he had noticed before now.

"Maybe, but it's not so unusual. According to the weather reports, it'll probably storm all night."

"Great."

He checked the bread baking in the oven, then looked across the room at her. "Do storms bother you?"

"Just a bit. More if there's wind."

"Dinah's just the same," he said, keeping his tone casual. "A feline trait, she calls it. Never having owned a cat, I have no idea what she means by that."

"I do. Means we hate change and low-pressure systems." Thunder boomed suddenly, and Faith jumped. "Damn," she murmured a little sheepishly.

"You're wound pretty tight," Kane noted.

"I'll be all right once the storm actually arrives. It's all this rumbling around beforehand that gets on my nerves. The table's set. Can I do anything else?"

"You can pour the wine. I'll have this ready in just a few minutes."

It wasn't until they were sitting at the table with the meal before them that Faith finally said, with obviously forced nonchalance, "Did you hear from Bishop about that restricted file?"

Kane nodded slowly.

"I can see from your face I'm not going to like it. Let me guess. My abusive ex had something to do with the murder of my family?"

"*Is* that a guess?" he asked.

"Educated. I've been talking to the women at the shelter, remember. Been hearing a lot about violent men. So I had to wonder about the violent man in my past." She paused and seemed to brace herself. "Did he kill my mother and sister?"

"He was—and is—suspected. But the police haven't found any evidence, Faith, and he not only passed a couple of lie detector tests but also told the same story under some kind of experimental truth serum."

"Truth serum?"

"Noah said to forget we heard that."

She smiled, but it was an effort. "Okay, so what story did he tell?"

"He claims that after you left him in L.A.—where you two had lived for the ten months of your marriage—he didn't hear from you again until he was served with divorce papers. At which point he says he got calmly on a plane for Seattle, intending to talk to you about the situation. He also says he checked into a hotel in Seattle, called your mother's house, and learned that you were working. So he says he stayed at the hotel and didn't have a clue what had happened until the police rousted him out of bed the next morning.

"The police, on the other hand, believe that blind rage overcame him when he was served with the papers. That even though phone records show he did call your mother's house, he could have driven out there, still enraged, killed your mother and sister, and burned the house to the ground. There wasn't much forensic evidence, nothing to say who'd done it, but Tony Ellis had motive and no real alibi, so—"

"Tony Ellis. Is that his name?"

Kane heard in her voice a loss he could barely comprehend. At least he knew what he had lost; Faith was daily—almost hourly—discovering bits and pieces of her life, good and horrible, that had vanished from her mind.

"Is it his name?" she repeated steadily.

"Yes. I'm sorry, Faith."

She shook her head and looked down at her plate for a moment, then slowly shifted her fork from her right hand to her left. "I'm glad I don't remember him," she said almost absently. "But I'm still confused about why that file is restricted."

"Ellis is an FBI agent."

She looked up swiftly. "Ah. Now it makes more sense. Covering for one of their own?"

"That was apparently your view. But it really does appear that there was no evidence to arrest him. Or even for the FBI to fire him, for that matter. They demoted him, and he's under close observation in L.A., something he's well aware of, apparently. From everything Noah could gather, he's been behaving himself for the last eighteen months."

"I told someone at the shelter that I had medical evidence that could ruin his career."

"Yes. Hospital records showing broken bones and severe bruising." Kane held his voice even and steady, but it took effort. "You turned it over to the police in Seattle. But when they couldn't prosecute him for the murders, you apparently decided that rather than let them prosecute for assault against you, you'd use the evidence to pressure him into signing the divorce papers and getting out of your life for good."

Faith shook her head. "And then what? I crossed the country just to make sure?"

"Maybe."

And maybe not.

Once again, Faith was unsure if that was her voice, her question—or someone else's.

She tried to think, to concentrate. "I was angry. I wanted . . . justice. That's what Dinah said to me, that we had to have proof that would stand up in court or I wouldn't get my justice. But as far as we can tell, up until the accident, everything that happened to me happened before I came to Atlanta. It has to connect, though, it just has to. Whatever Dinah and I were investigating here has to connect to my life before."

"That makes sense."

"Then it is my fault Dinah's in trouble."

"Dinah's a grown woman with a damned good mind," Kane said after a moment. "Whatever was going on, I doubt she was dragged into it unwillingly."

"What if I didn't tell her everything? What if I took whatever it is they want, and I didn't tell Dinah what I did with it?" She grimaced suddenly and set her wineglass on the table. "Dammit, not knowing what the thing is makes it sound so ridiculous when you talk about it."

"We could always call it the MacGuffin," Kane suggested wryly.

"Isn't that a word Hitchcock coined? To name something in a movie that everybody was after?"

He smiled faintly. "Another Hitchcock fan, I see."

"I guess so."

"Well, then, we'll call *it* the MacGuffin until we know what it is."

Faith waited out a long, rolling rumble of thunder. "I just wish we knew."

"We'll find out." *We have to find out.* He didn't speak the last words, but he might as well have.

He wouldn't let her help him clear up, and when he was done in the kitchen, he lit a fire in the fireplace. Faith wandered uneasily to the piano for a few moments and then to a window. The storm was going strong, and the rain was heavy now, blown against the windows by gusty wind in a rattle that told of sleet mixed in. It made her feel very jumpy.

Be careful.

That voice again, almost inaudible to her now.

"I think this is going to go on all night," Kane said, watching her as he stood by the fireplace.

Move . . . now—

"I think you're right." Baffled by the faint whisper in her mind, by her own tension, Faith winced as a bright flash of lightning illuminated the night, then she turned from the window. "And I don't know why I have this compulsion to stand here and watch when it makes me—"

For an instant, Kane thought it was the crash of thunder that cut off her words, but he saw an expression of puzzlement and then shock twist her features.

Her right hand touched the upper part of her left arm just below the shoulder, and Kane saw scarlet bloom around her fingers.

"Faith—"

"Will you look at that?" She was staring at a mirror directly across the room from where she stood. A cobweb of jagged cracks radiated from a small hole in the center of the mirror.

With more haste than gentleness, Kane grabbed her and pulled her away from the windows. "Goddammit, somebody's shooting."

"At me?" She sounded only mildly interested.

He sat her down on the couch and pried her fingers away from her arm. "Let me see."

Her sweatshirt bore two neat, round holes that were clearly entrance and exit points, and made it easy for him to tear the sleeve to expose the wound.

"It's just a scratch. I've always wanted to say that."

Kane had a hunch it was shock rather than courage that kept her voice strong and her words light. But she was right in that the wound was minor, a bloody furrow carved across no more than a couple of inches of the outside of her arm. He had no doubt, however, that it hurt like hell.

He made a pad of his handkerchief and pressed it to the sluggishly bleeding spot, and looked at Faith's pale, calm face. "Can you hold this in place while I call the police?"

"Of course I can." She did so, then looked at him with amazingly clear eyes. "But I won't go to the hospital."

"Faith, this needs to be looked at."

"I can have Dr. Burnett look at it tomorrow when we go to talk to him," she said calmly. "It'll be fine tonight if you can just clean and bandage it."

"Faith—"

"It doesn't even need stitches. I'm all right, Kane, really." She shivered suddenly as thunder boomed again. "I just . . . I don't want to go out there tonight."

"All right."

He got a blanket and covered her with it before he went to call Richardson. He was careful to stay away from the windows, though he doubted there was any danger. Whoever had been out there was long gone now.

That a shot had been taken on a night like this, with blinding rain making precision impossible, told him the act was a scare tactic, not intended to hit a live target; the bullet had found Faith only by sheer dumb luck. Nothing else made sense.

But that hardly made the situation better.

Kane disinfected and bandaged the wound. She never flinched or made a sound, just sat there and watched him, and for some unaccountable reason her gaze made him feel suddenly clumsy.

"I'm sorry," he said, taping the final piece of gauze into place.

"Why? You didn't shoot me."

Still holding her arm gently between his hands, he looked up to find her smiling faintly. "I can't be flip about this, Faith."

"I see that. Kane, I'm fine. My arm hurts, and I won't be lingering near any windows for a while, but I'm all right."

"You must be one of those people who shine in a crisis."

"You didn't do so bad yourself."

He realized he was compulsively smoothing with his thumbs the tape holding the bandage in place, and forced himself to release her and lean back. "Yeah, well, I'll get the shakes later. And speaking of delayed shock—which do you prefer, whiskey or hot tea?"

"Tea, please."

When Richardson arrived a few minutes later, Faith answered the detective's questions with no visible anxiety. Not that there was much she could tell him.

"I saw the cracked mirror first, and thought how odd it was. Then my arm burned suddenly, but it wasn't until I put my hand over it that I felt the blood. Even then, I didn't immediately realize I'd been shot. I never heard it."

"The storm was right overhead," Kane told his friend. "There was so much noise we couldn't hear the shot or the bullet going through the window and smashing the mirror."

Richardson went over to examine the mirror. "It's gone all the way through and into the wall." He took down the mirror, then produced a penknife and dug into the Sheetrock. Within a very few minutes, he held a misshapen slug.

Even across the room Kane read Richardson's expression. "I guess ballistics are out? No chance of tracing it to a particular gun?"

"I can't even tell what caliber it is, and I doubt the lab will be able to either." He eyed the distance to the window, then went to examine that as well. Like the mirror, the windowpane was marred by a small hole surrounded by a web of cracks.

"Too dark to see much now," he said. "I can come back tomorrow and take a stab at the trajectory, try to figure out where the shooter was. But if he was standing more than a few feet away, he couldn't have hoped to hit what he was aiming at, not in this weather."

Kane said, "There's no fire escape, and we're on the fifth floor. Unless he was outside on the balcony—which is possible, if doubtful—he couldn't have been any closer than the apartments on the other side of the courtyard. And that building is a good hundred feet away."

Richardson studied the distance from the hole in the window to the floor, then compared that with the distance between the hole in the wall and the floor. "Well, he sure as hell didn't shoot upward from ground level, or down from a higher spot. Do those apartments across the courtyard have balconies?"

"Yeah."

"Then we'll look for a vacant or currently unused apartment. I'm willing to bet we'll find one matching the trajectory of the shot. Somebody sat over there watching this place, and when they saw Miss Parker at the window . . ."

"But I stood there at least a couple of minutes before I moved away," Faith protested. "And it wasn't until then that I was shot."

"Then he was probably trying to scare you, and just got lucky with the shot."

"Lucky," she murmured.

Richardson smiled. "A figure of speech." He

looked at Kane. "Did you two do anything today that might have gotten somebody's attention?"

"God knows. We talked to some people."

"In other words, you were driving all over Atlanta poking into corners."

"Guy, I'd swear nobody followed us. And as far as I could tell, no one we talked to reacted in any unusual way to our questions." He had filled in the detective on their suppositions and conclusions, and Bishop's discovery about the murder investigation in Seattle.

The detective sighed. "Well, somebody was obviously upset enough to warn you off. Maybe you should pay attention. Get out of Atlanta for a while and let me do the poking around."

"You know I can't do that. But I can hire a couple of security guards to keep a closer eye on this place. And I'll sure as hell have blinds installed on those windows first thing tomorrow."

"Put one of the guards in the garage to keep an eye on your car," Richardson suggested. "And it wouldn't hurt to hire another private cop to follow you whenever you leave and make sure he's the only one doing that."

Kane grimaced slightly, but nodded.

"When's Bishop due back?"

"He isn't. He'll get here when he can, but something's breaking in a case he's on, so there's no way of knowing."

"Have him call me and fill me in on whatever information he digs up." Richardson looked at his friend steadily. "I mean it, Kane. This little stunt, coupled with the break-ins at Miss Parker's apartment, tells me for damn sure that whatever's going on is deadly serious. You get yourself killed, and the paperwork's going to be hell."

"I'll remember that," Kane said dryly.

Richardson put the flattened bullet into a plastic evidence bag. "I'll file a quiet report on this incident. But it's the last time, Kane. Anything else happens, and I won't be able to keep it under my hat."

"Understood."

Kane showed the detective out and when he returned to the couch, Faith said, "He seems a good friend."

"I'm blessed with a few," Kane agreed. He looked at her searchingly. "I know it's a stupid question to ask if you're all right, but I'll ask anyway. Are you?" She looked so small and still under the blanket, her hair dulled by the low lights of the room and her face ashen.

"I'll be fine."

He looked into her big, shadowed green eyes and saw the fear and pain she was determined to deny. "Faith—"

"I know I should probably call it a day, go to bed and sleep, but . . . I'd really rather not do that just yet." She drew the blanket tighter around herself, the strain showing now in the tension of her posture, and fixed her gaze on the fire. "I don't want to be alone right now."

Thinking of her isolated in her limbo of no memory drove him to say, "You aren't alone, Faith. I'm not going anywhere."

"Thank you."

"But my confidence that you'd be safer here with

me was obviously misplaced. I'm sorry. Noah was right; I should have taken better precautions from the beginning."

"You had . . . other things on your mind."

"That's no excuse. I made your safety my responsibility, and I should have followed through. But tomorrow I'll take those steps I mentioned to Guy, make it impossible for anyone to get close or to see inside. I'll make sure we have an escort when we leave here. You'll be safe, I promise."

She nodded, but said, "If I could only *remember*. We'd be ahead of them then. We'd know what it is they want and why they want it so badly. We'd know who they are. Maybe we'd even know where Dinah is."

"You can't force your memory to return."

"I've been out of the coma now for almost a month. I should be remembering *something*. Those dreams are only flashes—I don't *remember* them, not really, I just see them happening. And what do I know about myself? I play the piano, it seems. I'm nervous about storms." She drew a shaky breath. "My mother and sister were horribly murdered, and I can't remember, can't feel anything about it. I married a man who abused me, who terrified me, yet I could pass him tomorrow on the street and never recognize his face."

"Faith—"

"What's my favorite color? My favorite food? Do I like to read? Do I like animals? Flowers? Did I love Tony Ellis before he beat me?"

Kane pulled her into his arms and held her while she cried. He didn't urge her to stop or tell her everything would be all right; crying was obviously something she needed to do. Careful of her injury, he wrapped both arms around her, rested his cheek against her soft hair, and just held her.

It was a long time before she finally quieted, before she said in a muffled voice against his chest, "Oh, God, I'm sorry."

"Don't be ridiculous."

She pulled back a little. "I don't usually cry." Then she laughed shakily. "At least, I don't think I do."

"You're entitled. More than entitled." Since his handkerchief had been employed earlier, he used a corner of the blanket to wipe her cheeks. "And I bet you feel better now, don't you?"

"As a matter of fact, I do."

"Then I count it as a good thing." He brushed a strand of her hair away from her face and smiled at her when she finally met his gaze. His fingers lingered on her face, and he thought how soft and warm her skin was.

He had never before seen eyes that particular shade of green, like seawater. It would be so easy to sink into them and lose himself. So easy to think of nothing but the ache of loneliness and longing he felt, to forget everything else. Everyone . . .

Kane realized he was staring at her mouth, that his hand had moved to cradle the back of her head and was drawing her toward him. And he froze.

Faith blinked as if coming out of a daze, then very slowly pulled away from him and got to her feet. "I think I'll turn in now after all. Good night, Kane."

"Good night." His voice sounded normal, he thought.

He sat there for several minutes staring into the

fire. Then he pulled out his wallet and opened the section where he kept photographs.

She hated posing for pictures and always had, so this was a candid shot. He had surprised her at the beach, catching her in a brief yellow two-piece that showed her splendid body to advantage. The click of the shutter had just missed her scowl; his own glee at finally capturing her on film after several frustrated attempts had amused her, and she had laughed, giving him a wonderful picture.

It was the only picture of Dinah he had.

"Come back to me," he murmured. "Come back before . . ."

He didn't finish the sentence. Even to himself.

"There's no sign of infection," Dr. Burnett said as he finished rebandaging Faith's wound, "so the shot's just a precaution. In the meantime—"

Faith smiled at him as she pulled down the loose sleeve of her sweater. "I know. Don't stand in front of any more windows."

Burnett washed and dried his hands at the small sink in the examination room, then nodded at the nurse, who left silently. When they were alone, he said, "Faith, what's going on? A gunshot wound?"

She wasn't certain how much she should tell him, and with the new tension between her and Kane, she hadn't felt able to seek his advice before they had parted just a few minutes before, he to question the remaining staff members, she to check in with Burnett and get her arm examined. Going on the theory that the least said would probably be best, she replied, "The police are investigating."

"You have no idea why someone shot at you?"

Lightly, she said, "It was the middle of a storm and at night, and for all I know whoever it was never even aimed the gun, much less aimed it at me. It was probably a fluke. Just a fluke."

Burnett looked unconvinced, but nodded and changed the subject. "So how are you doing otherwise? I called your apartment over the weekend but didn't get an answer."

"I'm . . . staying somewhere else." Before he could question that, she went on quickly, "And I'm fine. I get tired a bit too easily, but that's all."

"No headaches? Dizziness?"

"No, nothing like that." *Sometimes I hear the sounds of water rushing, just inside my head, you understand, but that's probably nothing at all to worry about . . .*

"Any unusual muscle weakness or numbness anywhere?"

"No."

Burnett nodded again and studied her soberly. "Any memories come back?"

"Not really." Faith shrugged, wincing when she felt a twinge of pain in her arm. "More knowledge. I found out I play the piano, for instance. I . . . found out some things about my past, my life before I came to Atlanta, but not through remembering. Sometimes I have dreams that might be memory, but it doesn't feel that way."

He frowned. "Faith, I'd like you to talk to Dr. Wilson again."

Wilson was the psychologist on staff.

Faith said, "But she told me last time to expect odd dreams and flashes of knowledge. She said it could go on for months, even years, until my conscious mind felt more stable and . . . grounded in day-to-day experiences. Until I built new memories."

"I still think you should talk to her again."

Giving in, at least to all appearances, Faith nodded. "Okay, I'll make an appointment."

"Good." Burnett's frown still lingered. "I was a bit surprised to see you come in today with Kane MacGregor."

"Oh? Why? Dinah is my friend, after all."

"I know that. And I know you feel you need to hold on to that connection to the past, but—"

Quietly, Faith said, "Dr. Burnett, my friend is missing. I don't remember my life before the accident, but the one thing I have clear evidence of is Dinah's friendship. If there's anything I can do to help her— her fiancé find her, then I'll do it."

"Without your memory, how can you help?"

Well, Doctor, it seems I'm tapped in to Dinah's mind somehow, hearing her voice—maybe—and sometimes I get to watch her being tortured. . . .

Faith sighed. "There isn't much I can do, granted. But we . . . we think Dinah may have vanished because she was investigating something dangerous, something I got her involved in."

"Something dangerous? Faith, without your memory to provide any useful information or guidance, don't you realize what a mistake it would be to probe into a potentially dangerous situation filled with unknowns?"

"Which is why I came in today with Kane. I'm in good hands, Dr. Burnett, I promise you."

His gaze flicked to her bandaged arm. "Are you?"

"I told you, the shot was a fluke."

"And if it wasn't?"

"If it wasn't . . . I'll stay away from windows from now on."

Burnett drew a breath and spoke in a carefully neutral tone of voice. "Faith, it's quite obvious that Kane MacGregor would do anything and everything in his power to find Dinah Leighton. After so many weeks with no sign of her, he must be getting desperate. Desperate enough to be less mindful of his methods than the results he might obtain."

"What are you saying?"

"I'm saying that you aren't his priority, Faith. You aren't his first concern. Dinah Leighton is."

"I realize that," she said steadily.

"Do you? And do you also realize that he might well be willing to sacrifice your safety or even you if that means finding out what happened to Dinah?"

"Yes," Faith replied. "Yes, I also realize that."

EIGHT

"I need to go by the office for a few minutes," Kane said as they left the hospital.

Faith thought he kept talking, thought he was explaining something about a call he'd received about a problem on a job site, but she could no longer hear him. The sounds of rushing water drowned out his words. She stared straight ahead through the windshield, trying not to flinch away from what she heard even though the force of it was almost overwhelming.

And it wasn't just the sound. Panic was crawling around in her head; the sense of being smothered, of not having enough room, not nearly enough room, paralyzed her. The musty smell of damp earth was so strong she kept her breathing shallow, trying desperately not to inhale that moldy dampness, and she had the eerie certainty that if she looked down at herself she'd find her clothing wet, her skin dripping.

I am wide awake. So why does this feel like a nightmare?

Gradually, so gradually that at first Faith hardly noticed, darkness closed around her. She could see nothing. Feel nothing except the sense of heaviness all around her, of walls too close to bear. She was trapped, helpless. The awful smell grew stronger, so much so that she had the urge to cough to get it out of her throat. And now there was a new sound added to the rushing water. A clicking. No—a clinking. Metal on metal? Not rhythmic but erratic, weak, uncertain . . .

If I can just get this loose . . . if I can get my hands free before they come back . . . Oh, damn, why won't my fingers work? It's so dark. I hate the dark. I hate this place. Why did they have to put me here? There's no room, no air to breathe. Too close, the walls are too close, the ceiling . . . I've got to get out of here before I . . . before they . . . Why is this so hard? Why can't I—

"Faith?"

Why can't I move? If there was just a little light. Just a little more room to move. If I only had more time. If only it didn't hurt so much—

"Faith!"

She came back to herself with a jarring abruptness. Light flooded her vision, and the sudden cessation of the sounds of rushing water made the quiet of the stopped car seem almost deafening. And the familiar voice that had been in her head, its vibrant personality still incredibly strong despite distance and despair and suffering, was gone as though it had never been there.

"Faith, for God's sake—"

She blinked at Kane, realizing that he was holding her shoulders and was shaking her. Her arm ached dully beneath his grip, but it was nothing compared to the agony that had been in her mind.

"I'm all right," she murmured.

His fingers tightened painfully, then released her. "You want to tell me what in hell happened? One minute we were talking, and the next you were so far away I couldn't reach you."

Faith realized that he had stopped the car, that they were in an underground parking garage.

"I . . . I'm not quite sure what happened," she said.

"Tell me what you are sure of."

She was still too dazed to attempt any prevarication, so she told him. "I . . . It was Dinah. Her voice in my head. She was trying to get loose, to escape."

Kane reached out again, this time putting a hand over both of hers where they twisted together in her lap. "Where is she, Faith?"

"I don't know. It's dark and damp and smells musty, like dirt—and all I could hear was the sound of rushing water."

"Water?"

"Yes. Like a waterfall, or water coming out of a pipe at high pressure. Just water. Just water and darkness and that awful smell . . ."

"Right here is where we ran into the problem." Max Sanders, owner of the Mayfair Construction Company, jabbed a stubby finger at the blueprints spread out on Kane's drafting table. "Without some kind of correction, and fast, this wall's coming down, Kane. There are already cracks in the foundation."

Kane frowned. "Let's see the materials list again."

"Jed swears it's a design flaw rather than construction or materials."

"He would." The foreman always did.

"Not that I agree with him." Sanders produced the materials list. "But I've looked the stuff over, and it's just what you insisted on, the best quality and well above code."

"So why is the foundation cracking?" Kane mused.

"Exactly. I honestly don't believe the crew fucked up, Kane." Sanders darted a quick, apologetic glance at Faith.

Kane could have told him that she wasn't listening and so wouldn't be offended by the language. She was sitting on the sofa on the far side of the room with a magazine open on her lap, but as far as he could see she hadn't turned a page in more than twenty minutes. She had retreated into herself not long after they had arrived.

He didn't blame her. What she had experienced had upset him, and he'd gotten it second-hand. Or third-hand.

Was it Dinah? Was she trapped somewhere, badly hurt and trying desperately to reach out?

But where? *Where?* So goddamned maddening to know she was out there somewhere and still, after all these weeks, have no clue where to look for her. . . .

"So if it isn't materials or workmanship," Sanders said, "then what? I'm not questioning your design, Kane, but maybe there's something neither of us could have foreseen. A fault in the ground, maybe, or something underneath the foundation that's causing uneven support."

Kane forced his attention back to the job, as difficult as that was. He went over the materials list carefully, then studied the blueprints again. "Until last night, we hadn't had any heavy rain in weeks. The geological survey said we're building on a solid clay base, with no gas pockets or ground water to undermine the foundation."

"We had to dig deeper than planned for the foundation," Sanders reminded him.

"True." Kane opened a file and looked over the report from the geologist. "But the ground should have been checked out far below that level. I still don't see . . ."

"What?" Sanders demanded quickly when Kane obviously did see something in the report that bothered him. "Have you found something?"

Kane looked at him blankly for an instant, then shook off the abstraction and said, "According to this, there should be no problems directly beneath the building. But there are also reports of springs and artesian wells in the general area, and both have caused problems in other buildings."

"But if the ground under ours is okay, would it be affected?"

"No, I took the water into account early on in designing the building." Kane shook his head. "Let me work on the problem, Max. I'd rather find the cause than just design a quick-fix patch to shore up that wall."

Sanders nodded but was clearly unhappy. "It's

your design. But my crew can't do squat until we get this taken care of, and I can't afford to have them sitting around scratching their balls for days. If it looks like this is going to take a while, I'll have to put them to work on another job, Kane."

"I'll let you know something by tomorrow, Max. Don't worry. I'm no more eager than you are to delay work on the building."

"I hear that."

Kane saw Sanders to the door, and when it had closed behind him, Faith said quietly, "Springs and artesian wells. That's what caught your attention, isn't it?"

So she had been listening after all.

He sat down on a chair near the sofa. "According to what you've ... sensed, Dinah could be held underground. Maybe in a basement or cellar. If the sounds of water you're hearing are coming from a natural source, it could be a spring or well."

"I guess." Faith rubbed her temple absently. "But it was ... so loud. Water under tremendous pressure. If it was natural, I don't see how anything could have been built near it, not without having the structure undermined." She blinked, then said softly, "It couldn't be that, could it? She couldn't be there, in your building?"

"I don't see how," Kane said. "The building site has been crawling with people for months, and the foundation is only now being closed in. The structure has been wide open, no hiding places anywhere."

"What about nearby?"

"Are there other buildings nearby? Of course.

Other office buildings, a hotel, a medical clinic, God knows what else."

"And even if we knew for a fact she was in that area, in one of those buildings, how could we possibly guess which one when we still don't know what this is all about? Why can't I *remember*?"

Kane started to reach out, then stopped himself. He was becoming more and more aware of this urge to touch her, to be close to her. Almost as if . . .

No. It wasn't that. Dinah was the one he wanted.

"You can't force it," he said finally. "And whether you remember or not, sooner or later we'll find out the truth."

She looked at him. "Will we? I can't help wondering how much you'll hate me if we find out that I am responsible for Dinah disappearing, for getting us both involved in something dangerous."

Kane wanted to say he wouldn't hate her at all, but he wasn't sure it was true. He wasn't sure he didn't hate her a little bit even now, for tying his emotions into knots. For wrecking his certainties.

The silence had dragged on just one moment too long when the office door opened and Sydney Wilkes strolled in.

"I'm sorry, Kane—Sharon didn't tell me you had a visitor. Hello, Faith."

This time, the silence was filled with a different kind of tension. Kane looked from Faith's expression of surprise to his sister's dawning confusion, and wondered if his own face was such a study in bewilderment.

"Syd, you know Faith?"

"Of course I know her." Sydney frowned as she

looked at Faith. "I had to deal very closely with the Office of Building Inspections and Zoning on that Andrews project, and Faith was the person I worked with. But I guess I'm not so memorable."

Quickly, Faith said, "I was in a car accident a couple of months ago and lost my memory—of practically everything, including the people I knew."

"Really? How terrible for you." Sydney came to sit on the other end of the sofa, her face filled now with compassion. "That must be the loneliest feeling in the world."

Before Faith could respond, Kane said, "What did you mean when you said you guessed *you* weren't so memorable, Syd?"

She laughed. "Injured vanity, I suppose."

He shook his head. "No, the way you said it implied that Faith was unusually memorable to you. Why?"

Sydney looked uncomfortable. "You're reading too much into the comment, Kane."

"I don't think so."

"Kane—"

"Sydney, part of Faith's lost memory might tell us who grabbed Dinah and why. So if you know anything . . ."

His sister looked at Faith, puzzled once again. "I wasn't aware you and Dinah knew each other."

"We were friends," Faith said.

"I see." Sydney shook her head. "Well, I don't, but that hardly matters. Kane, there's nothing I know about Faith that could possibly help you find Dinah. We knew each other on the most superficial, businesslike level, nothing more."

"But she made an impression on you. Why?"

Sydney let out an impatient breath. "If you must know, it was because she somehow misplaced the paperwork of two inspectors on that project, and we had to wait while the inspections were rescheduled. Set us back two weeks."

"I'm sorry," Faith said.

Sydney smiled at her. "Well, I was upset at the time, but you did everything you could to get the second round of inspections done quickly, even worked overtime, so I forgave you. Paperwork does get misplaced, after all, especially in an office whose sole purpose seems to be to generate paper."

Kane wasn't entirely satisfied with Sydney's explanation, but he let it go. Because he couldn't see how the situation could have had anything to do with Dinah's disappearance, not when it happened last spring.

Sydney said to him, "I gather there's been nothing new on Dinah?"

"No, nothing helpful."

"I'm sorry, Kane. I wish there was something I could do."

Lightly, he said, "You're holding the company together, and that's more than enough."

"I couldn't solve Max Sanders's problem," she said with a grimace. "I mean, it looked like a structural failure to me, but I'm no engineer. I had no idea where to look for a cause or a solution."

"I'll deal with Max, Syd. You just keep the other projects on track and the other clients happy, and MacGregor and Payne will be fine."

"I'll do my best. In fact, I have a meeting in ten

minutes to go over plans with a couple of residential clients, so I'd better get back downstairs to my office. I just wanted to see you while you were here and find out if there was any news."

Kane felt a stab of guilt. "I know I haven't been very accessible lately, Syd. I'm sorry."

"Don't be ridiculous." She smiled a little sadly. "No one else can truly understand how you feel, but at least I have some idea. You've put your thoughts and energies where they needed to go, just as you have to keep doing until you find Dinah. Don't apologize for that. And don't worry about me."

"Thanks, Syd."

"Don't mention it. And call me right away if—if anything changes, all right?"

"Of course."

Sydney got to her feet. "Faith, I . . . wish you luck. I hope you get your memory back."

"Thanks."

When they were alone again, Kane said restlessly, "As far as I can see, there's nothing wrong with the design from an engineering standpoint, so the fault has to be either materials or construction. I'll have to go out there."

"I'd like to come along," Faith said. "Didn't you tell me that Dinah had visited the site the day before she vanished?"

"Yeah, she showed up out there looking for me, and Max gave her a quick tour. The police checked out the area, but as far as they could tell she didn't go back there the day she disappeared."

"And they talked to Max?"

"Of course." Kane frowned. "Why?"

Slowly, Faith said, "Probably nothing, but the only thing I can think of that both Dinah and I had some kind of connection to other than the shelter was construction. I worked at a construction company in Seattle, then came here and eventually got a job at the Office of Building Inspections and Zoning. Dinah's engaged to an engineer and architect whose company is involved in a very large project for the city, a building site she toured the day before she disappeared. I'm in what looks like a manufactured accident, she vanishes—and now your project is in trouble." She paused. "I can just hear Bishop say there's no such thing as a string of coincidences that long."

Thinking about that, Kane said, "The building was started shortly before your accident, so it fits loosely within the time frame. But how many other buildings were started in the same period?"

"God knows." Faith got up. "But I'd say we start with this one."

As they neared the construction site, Faith frowned and rubbed her temple. "Damn," she said softly.

"What is it?" Kane asked. "The water sound?"

"Yes. It's been fading in and out, but it's louder now. At least I think it is."

"Do you think Dinah is somewhere nearby?" he asked quickly.

"I don't know. I don't get any sense of direction. Just the sounds, the smells."

"Maybe your senses are trying to guide you."

"It's like this itching in my mind," Faith said, rubbing her temple again. "Deep inside my head. And along with it is the notion that there's something just out of my reach, something that would answer all my questions if I could just touch it."

"I know you said you didn't want to try to reach out to Dinah directly again, Faith, but—"

"It was like falling into a deep well. There was nothing to hold on to."

Kane parked the car by the padlocked gate at the construction site. "According to what I've picked up from Noah over the years, there's a trick to managing any kind of clairvoyance. The first step is to stay grounded, safely connected to the here and now." He turned to face her and extended a hand. "Noah calls it a lifeline. Take my hand, Faith."

She hesitated, then slowly took his hand. It was warm and hard, and for a dizzying moment the whole world seemed to shift around her. Instinctively, she closed her eyes and reached out, toward the sounds—

The cold was bone-chilling. There was a heaviness, an intense weight bearing down on her, smothering her—

No air. There was no air, she couldn't breathe.

She couldn't move.

She couldn't . . .

The sounds and scents vanished, and Faith opened her eyes slowly. "It's gone."

"Gone?"

She looked at her hand clinging to his, and made herself release him. "Gone. No sounds, no smells, no feeling of being trapped. Nothing. For just a moment, I thought I was right there, in the darkness, and then . . . nothing."

He watched his own hand close slowly into a fist. "Nothing," he repeated.

"I'm sorry, Kane."

After a moment, he shook his head and, in a voice that sounded harsh even to himself, said, "Just tell me she's still alive, Faith."

"I—"

I am, you know that. You know.

Faith caught her breath, tried to listen to that whispery voice, but it said no more.

"Faith?"

"I . . . only know what I feel. What I believe. And I believe Dinah is still alive."

He wanted to believe her. He almost did.

"Okay," he said finally.

Faith looked as if she wanted to say something more, but then shook her head and got out of the car.

Kane had the key for the padlocked gate, and since the nighttime security guard had not come on duty yet, there was no one to see them enter the fenced construction site. Kane paused and looked back beyond his car to an unobtrusive sedan parked across the street.

"Your private investigator?" Faith guessed, aware that the man had been nearby since they had left the apartment.

"Yeah. Some of his people are still out looking for leads, so he decided to take this duty himself. His orders are to follow and to stick with the car. But this time—" Kane gestured slightly, and the man immediately left his car and crossed the street to join them.

Faith was briefly introduced to Tim Daniels, a well-built man in his early thirties with something in his shrewd gray eyes that reminded her of the women in the shelter; they were older than his years and didn't look as though they could ever doubt that evil existed in the world. He wore a gun in a shoulder holster beneath his jacket, and she could see the antenna of a cell phone peeking from his shirt pocket.

"I need to take a look at this site," Kane told Daniels. "It should be secure, but I'd rather not take any chances."

Daniels nodded. "I'll watch your back."

He trailed along behind them as Kane took Faith's arm and guided her down the rutted track that led to the building. They stood looking up at the steel skeleton clawing its way nearly a dozen stories in the air so far. Only the underground parking garage had been partially closed in.

Faith eased her arm from Kane's grasp. "I don't think I want to go down inside that."

"Then you stay here with Tim. I'll be right back."

She didn't question his optimistic estimate, just nodded. But when Kane had disappeared around the back of the structure, she glanced at Daniels and said, "Aren't you worried about him being alone down there?"

"He can take care of himself."

"And I can't." She grimaced, and touched the hidden bandage on her left arm. "Well, maybe so."

"You're vulnerable at the moment. No memory means you couldn't tell friend from foe."

"So you know about that," she murmured.

"Kane told me what he thought I needed to know. No more and no less."

Faith decided not to question him on that point. She turned her attention back to the building. "I'd like to wander around a bit. Alone, if you don't mind."

"Any particular reason?" Daniels asked.

Because Dinah was here. Because I have to . . .

Had to what? She didn't know.

"No particular reason," she said.

Daniels glanced around the site, which appeared to be enclosed by a high wood and chain-link fence. "It looks safe enough. But don't go far."

"No, I won't."

She had no idea what she was looking for, if anything. Maybe it was nothing. Maybe the voices in her head, familiar and unfamiliar, didn't know what they were talking about. Maybe she just wanted to have time and space to herself and for a few moments forget—

Except that you can't forget. I won't let you.

This time, Faith made no attempt to focus on that voice, to reach out for it. To catch it. Instead, she merely let her mind drift, trying not to think about anything at all.

That didn't work either.

She walked slowly, wandering without rhyme or reason. She passed the huge earth-moving machines parked on the site, the stacks of construction materials, and the trailer that housed the construction office.

Nothing she saw awoke a spark of memory.

It was, she saw now, absurd to imagine that Dinah might have been held here. The building was only a skeleton, even the underground floors barely enclosed. In fact, here at the back, the building was still open all the way down to the bottommost concrete floor.

Kane was moving around in the shadows of that lowest area, but she wasn't about to join him—mostly because she didn't care for shadowy underground places.

Mostly.

She turned and continued along a few feet inside the fence, picking her way over uneven ground and around the occasional pile of debris. Two giant Dumpsters barred her way at one point, and she chose to go between them and the fence rather than around them.

If she hadn't, she never would have seen the break in the fence.

The wooden slats had been removed or never installed in this section, so it was possible to see through the chain-link to what lay outside.

There was an empty half acre or so, and then the back of a large building. A warehouse, she thought, maybe for industrial use rather than just storage. She saw at least one loading dock, but the place seemed deserted on this Tuesday afternoon.

Then she caught a whiff of something she thought she should recognize, something that made the hair on the back of her neck stand up.

That was the only warning she had before the eighty-pound Rottweiler threw himself at the fence.

NINE

"No judge in his right mind is going to give the police a warrant to search that place just because they have a guard dog," Daniels said matter-of-factly. "Not on the basis of a dream."

"I think it was more than a dream," Kane said.

"I know what you think." Daniels believed in nothing except what he could see, hear, or touch with his hands—but Kane wasn't paying him to scoff, and he saw Daniels send a faintly apologetic glance to Faith as she stood in the kitchen doorway with a cup of coffee.

Faith lifted her cup to Daniels in a grave salute of understanding, and Kane decided she was holding up pretty well after having a monster dog try to eat his way through a fence to get at her.

Kane, on the other hand, was moving restlessly around the living room of the apartment. Daniels watched him. "So let's talk about that warehouse."

And when Kane shot him a quick glance, he added dryly, "Don't think I don't know you're planning to check it out yourself as soon as it gets dark enough."

"Somebody has to."

"That's a hell of a big dog, Kane."

"Even a big dog can be handled—if you have enough sedatives and a hunk of raw meat."

"Unless he's trained not to take food from strangers."

"Well, there's only one way to find out."

Daniels smiled slightly. "True. But before you start doctoring sirloin, let me make a few calls and find out what I can about that warehouse."

Kane went to sit on the piano bench and absently ran his fingers up and down the scales to work out some of the tension in his hands. "The sign said Cochrane's."

"I saw it. And I got the street address, so I should be able to find out what the place is and who owns it."

"I know who owns it." Kane began to play the piano softly, choosing without thought a piece he was very familiar with—and which had always been Dinah's favorite despite her avowed tin ear: Beethoven's "Moonlight Sonata." "Jordan Cochrane and family. Mostly Jordan Cochrane."

"You know him?"

"We've met here and there. Not really surprising, since his family businesses include various aspects of construction. And since he's beginning a run for the governor's mansion."

Faith spoke for the first time since they'd returned. "Construction again."

Kane looked across the room at her. "You noticed that, huh?"

"And politics. Didn't Dinah say—"

"That this story she was into involved business and criminal elements—and possibly politics. Yes." Kane paused. "You told us you were sure Dinah wasn't in that warehouse now."

Carefully, Faith replied, "I'm sure I would have felt something, being that close. But I'm also sure she *was* there, the night she disappeared."

"Then we have to check it out."

Daniels drew a breath. "Breaking and entering, Kane."

"I'm willing to risk it."

"Yeah. I thought you might be."

"You don't have to—"

Daniels didn't let him finish. "Are you kidding? In all these weeks, this feels like the closest we've come to an honest-to-God trail without ice all over it. I'm definitely coming along."

"So am I." Faith kept her gaze on Kane.

He continued to play the piano for several minutes, looking at her rather than the keys, then broke off abruptly and rose to his feet. "Faith . . ."

"If that's where Dinah was held, where they— where they hurt her, I'll be able to recognize the place, I know I will."

He nodded finally. "All right. You'll need a jacket, something dark. I think there's one of Dinah's in my closet, if you want to grab that."

The dog had either never been trained not to take food from strangers, or defied his training in order to sink his teeth into the raw steak. They had to wait a few minutes for the sedatives to take effect, but he was sleeping peacefully by the time Kane picked the padlock on the gate and they crept in.

"I don't think I want to ask who taught you to do that," Daniels said dryly.

A smothered laugh escaped Kane. "It was Dinah. One of her shadier contacts taught her years ago, and she taught me last spring after I got locked out of the apartment once. She made sure we both kept in practice, said you never knew when it might come in handy." He kept his voice low.

Faith, walking silently between the two men, wondered if that was why Dinah's tormentors had bound her wrists with thin, brutal wire. Had they tried something simpler in the early days of her captivity, like handcuffs, only to find that their victim was adept at picking locks?

"Yeah," Daniels said, "but that's a first-class set of burglar's tools you've got there, pal. Should I ask where you got them?"

Kane patted the zippered leather case he had returned to his jacket pocket. "It's amazing what you can get these days if you ask the right person. Dinah knew who to ask."

"Uh-huh. Well, the warehouse is bound to have a security system," Daniels pointed out. "How are you with those?"

"We'll see, won't we?"

Faith heard Daniels swear under his breath but thought he didn't sound all that upset. In fact, it had already occurred to her that both men relished this outing; after all the weeks of sifting through facts and talking to people, taking even a risky action appealed to them.

As for Faith, she felt . . . peculiar. Lost in Dinah's jacket, which was several sizes too large, and dwarfed by the two large men, she had an odd sense of not really being there. Or maybe that was because the sound of the water was back, so distant she caught herself straining to hear it, and that gave her a sense of some other place.

She tried to concentrate on the here and now, gazing warily around through darkness at the hulking shapes of the warehouse and outbuildings, but the feeling of unreality persisted. Her hands felt cold; she jammed them into the pockets of the jacket. In the right pocket, she felt something, and her fingers explored with idle curiosity. A thin, flexible piece of metal. She had no idea what it was, but could not find the concentration to pull it out and look at it.

The warehouse loomed above them, and she tried to focus on it in another attempt to fix her consciousness on the present. But the faint sounds of water rushing grew more distinct inside her head.

"Here." Kane had located a door into the warehouse, and his pencil flashlight examined it inch by inch. "As far as I can see, there's no security system."

"They think the dog's enough," Faith murmured with certainty.

"Could be," Daniels agreed.

Kane shrugged, muttered, "In for a penny," and knelt to work on the door's lock.

Faith watched his agile fingers using the

fine tools. She wondered if there was anything he had tried his hand at only to fail, and doubted it. Men like Kane seldom failed. At anything.

"Got it." Kane rose to his feet, putting away the tools and securing the case in his pocket, then cautiously tried the door. If there was any alarm raised, it was a silent one.

They stood inside a cavernous space illuminated by a few scattered yellow security lights. The place was virtually empty.

Kane glanced at Daniels, who shrugged and said, "Explains the lack of any real security."

Faith was thinking of something else. "There are windows, and the walls don't look right. Is there something below this level? A basement of some kind?"

"Let's find out," Kane said.

Since it was easy to remain within sight of one another, they split up to search, and it was Kane who summoned the other two nearly ten minutes later. He had located a room, adjacent to the main warehouse, that was clearly meant to house an office but currently held only an old slate-top desk and a wooden chair.

And another door.

The door opened onto stairs, and the stairs led down. There was a light switch just inside the door, and Kane hesitated, glancing at Daniels. "What do you think?"

"I think we're alone here."

"I know we are," Faith said, not even aware of her certainty until she spoke.

That was good enough for Kane, so he flipped the switch. Several naked bulbs awoke to provide enough light to see by.

As soon as the three of them started down, Faith felt the damp chill that was so familiar she stopped in her tracks.

"Faith?" Daniels, behind her, didn't touch her.

Three steps below her, Kane turned and looked back. "Is this it?" he asked softly.

She swallowed. "We're close."

He took her hand. "Come on."

Faith didn't know if she would have been able to continue down into that place without his grip. It was more commanding than comforting, but at least it was contact with something warm and alive.

I have to stay grounded, he said, connected to the here and now.

The water sounds were louder inside her head. She hung on to Kane's hand as if to a lifeline.

At the bottom of the long flight of stairs, they found themselves in a square concrete room hardly larger than the office above. There was no sign that it was intended for anything other than extra storage; open metal shelving units lined two of the walls, though all they contained now were a few dusty stacks of paper and other ancient office supplies.

Faith turned immediately toward the bare wall the farthest from the stairs, and realized she was silently counting only when she reached twelve steps—and that rear wall. Her free hand lifted to touch it gently.

"This shouldn't be here," she murmured. "It . . . She was past this, beyond this point."

Daniels took out a penknife and dug into the mortar between two concrete blocks. It crumbled easily, still visibly damp. "This is a new wall. Only a few days old, if that."

It took them a while to find tools that would work—a dull ax and a heavy mallet from upstairs in the warehouse. Kane and Daniels were able to knock several blocks loose and open up the wall.

Standing several feet away, Faith stared at that gaping maw and told herself there was no reason to fear what lay within. Just the other half of this room, that was all. Bare concrete floor and block walls and . . .

Kane and Daniels went through the wall.

The chair wouldn't be in there, she thought. That would have been destroyed, maybe burned. But they must not have been able to get the bloodstains out of the concrete floor, and so they'd walled up the place, concealing all evidence. Everybody knew the police had all kinds of forensic tricks now, chemicals they could spray on surfaces to make bloodstains show up, even when they'd been scrubbed, even when they were invisible to the naked eye, perhaps painted over.

Closing off that part of the room was safest, that's what they would have thought. Move Dinah somewhere else, somewhere even darker and colder, where the sounds of water were loud and constant and maddening, and then build this wall to hide what had been done in this place.

Faith drew a deep breath and went through the hole in the wall to join Kane and Daniels inside.

The more powerful flashlights they had brought for this interior search helped to delineate the shape and size of the small basement, but there was almost nothing to be seen. Walls, ceiling, floor.

Stained floor.

"They tried to clean it up," Daniels said with

detachment. "But concrete is porous and stains below the surface. They might have painted it, but the entire floor would have had to be done in order not to look suspicious, and who would bother painting a floor in a place like this? Easier and simpler to just make the space down here match up with the size of the office above by building a wall to hide this part. Without the original blueprints, it isn't likely that anyone looking down here would have guessed. The new wall would blend once the mortar cured, and their . . . secret would have been safe."

Faith looked down at the rust-colored stains on the floor, then turned her gaze away with a shudder as she remembered blood dripping from mangled wrists.

Kane was staring down at the floor, unmoving.

She wanted so badly to reach out to him that her hand lifted instinctively. And then hung there between them, meaningless and impotent.

He didn't want to be touched. And most especially, she thought, he didn't want to be touched by her.

In that same steady, unemotional voice, Daniels said, "Kane, we have to get out of here. We have what we came here to get—evidence to convince us that something happened here, that Dinah might have been held here."

"The police," Kane said in an odd, still tone.

"There are still no legal grounds for a warrant. We're in here illegally. If the police even listened to us and came in here, they couldn't use anything they found in court. Worse, storming in here openly before we know more could panic whoever's got Dinah, force them to— We have to find a way to uncover other evidence that will lead the police here logically. It will take time, but it has to be done. We won't help Dinah by rushing off to confront Cochrane before we know more. But we have a place to start now. We have somewhere to look."

Faith forced her hand to drop to her side and made herself speak calmly. "Won't they know we were here?"

"Not if we're careful. And lucky. Kane, we have to go. Now. That dog won't be out much longer."

Faith thought it was a toss-up as to whether Kane would listen to the P.I., but in the end he did. Or perhaps he simply had to get away from those terrible stains on the floor.

He and Daniels replaced the blocks they had removed, using the crumbling mortar for the joints. The result would fool no one close-up, but when Daniels loosened the bare lightbulb hanging closest to the wall until it went out, the dimness made their handiwork much less evident.

They were careful to replace the tools and to close and lock the doors they had found that way, but they wasted no time in getting out of the warehouse and back to the gate. The sleeping dog was just beginning to stir as they slipped past him.

Daniels didn't come in when they returned to Kane's apartment; he wanted to do his own checking on Jordan Cochrane and the warehouse, and said he'd return first thing the following morning to report in— sooner if he discovered anything even remotely likely to help them find Dinah.

Kane was pacing.

Faith wasn't sure he was ready to talk, but she needed to. "There's something bothering me."

It was, on the face of it, an absurd thing to say, but Kane merely sat down in the chair across from her and said calmly, "Something in particular? What is it?"

"When I had the—the dream about Dinah being attacked by that dog, she didn't seem sure where she was. Something about the address being vague, and maybe not even being in the right part of the city."

"So how come she didn't know that place backed up to the building site?"

"That's part of it. And what if she was there to meet someone? What if whoever it was took advantage of an unused warehouse, and the only connection to the Cochranes is that building?"

"Cheerful thought," Kane said sourly.

"But possible."

"Oh, yeah, it's possible."

"And if it's true?"

"Then we're back to square one. Unless that building has some tangible connection to whoever held Dinah there . . . But we don't know it's true, not yet."

He gazed at her broodingly, glad she was there because being alone tonight would have been unbearable. At least when he listened to her voice his imagination couldn't re-create Dinah's cries of pain. At least when he looked at her, he no longer saw stained concrete.

"You haven't told me everything," he said abruptly. "You were upset yesterday when you came back from Haven House, for one thing. For another, I've gotten the feeling more than once that you could have offered more details about Dinah."

She hesitated, biting her bottom lip, then said, "Not details you need to hear. Not details that would help us find her."

Kane closed his eyes briefly. "Is she alive, Faith?"

She hesitated for a moment. "Sometimes I . . . think I hear her voice in my head. But I'm not *sure*. I was told by somebody at Haven House that I seemed to be psychic with Dinah, that we clicked somehow from the moment we met."

"Then—"

Faith shook her head. "If it is her voice I'm hearing, she can't or won't tell me where she is—and I can't control what I hear, can't ask her questions or demand answers. It doesn't seem to work that way, no matter what I try. It just . . . comes when it comes. At odd moments, when I least expect it. A voice in my head I'm not even sure isn't my own."

A slight laugh that held no humor was forced from Kane. "That jibes with what Noah's told me. He says concentration and years of practice help but that few psychics are able to do more than open a door. What comes through, and how, is almost always a jumble and is seldom helpful in any real sense. As if even the subconscious can't cope with those extra senses and has to translate using symbolism and imagery. He says if ever a psychic is born who can control his or her abilities a hundred percent, the whole world will change."

"I'm sorry, Kane. Maybe we could try something

that might help me concentrate more or focus. Hypnosis . . ."

"Noah says psychics can't be hypnotized."

After a moment, Faith said, "I guess he'd know."

"Yeah. He'd know." Kane paused. "You learned something else at Haven House, didn't you, Faith?"

Tell him.

She swallowed. "It's nothing that would help—"

"Something about Dinah? What is it?"

Tell him.

Faith couldn't see how the knowledge would help Kane. She was afraid it might even hurt him more, but heard herself say reluctantly, "I have no way of knowing if it's true, but someone at the shelter who spent a lot of time with Dinah is convinced she—she believed she didn't have a future."

"What?"

"Eve could be wrong, Kane. It was just her impression, based on a lot of little things. A remark here and there, a fleeting expression. She thought Dinah was always aware of time, that she had some sense of it running out. For her."

He got up abruptly and moved toward the dark fireplace. He stood there for a moment, frowning, then bent and turned on the gas logs as though he felt a sudden chill. "That . . . would explain a lot," he murmured.

"What do you mean?"

"I always thought—always felt—there was a reason why she never wanted to make plans beyond the next weekend."

"But if you were engaged . . ."

His smile was twisted. "We weren't. I just said

that to the press because . . . because I wanted it to be true, I suppose. But Dinah and I hadn't come close to that kind of commitment. I was hesitating over suggesting that we move in together, not because she was too independent but because I had the feeling it was a corner she just wasn't ready to turn."

"Bishop said she was precognitive."

Kane nodded slowly.

"Then maybe she did see her future. Or at least see enough to believe it wasn't wise of her to make long-term plans. Maybe that's why she moved so fast after my accident, why she was so careful to set things up quickly even though she knew I might be in the coma a long time."

"Maybe." Kane drew a breath. "But even if she did see her future, even if she believed she was running out of time, she could have been wrong, Faith. Psychics get it wrong all the time, even the best of them. She could still be alive."

"Yes."

"I don't—" He shook his head. "I still don't feel her."

"I'm sorry."

"I almost envy you that voice in your head. At least you can tell yourself it's a connection, whether you really believe it is or not. At least you can tell yourself you have a piece of her."

"It's nothing to envy, believe me."

"Isn't it?"

"No. I don't have a piece of her, Kane. I don't even have a piece of me."

There was something forlorn in her voice, and not

for the first time he had a sense of how hard this was for her. It was his turn to say, "I'm sorry."

Faith shook her head but didn't otherwise reply, and when she looked past him, the reflection of the fire made her eyes look vividly alive.

Green eyes, not blue.

Red hair instead of blond. Slender fragility instead of athletic grace. The intelligence was much the same, the occasional dry humor, but physically—

Realizing where his thoughts had wandered, Kane felt a shock. He stared at Faith, conscious of his heart beating faster, of an emotion that was part longing and part guilt, and something else he dared not examine too closely.

"Kane?" She was looking back at him, puzzlement turning into awareness. One of her hands began to lift as if to reach out to him, but then she clasped both of them tightly together in her lap. The neat red nails gleamed darkly.

Red nails.

Kane turned from the fireplace and from her, crossed the room to the piano, and sat down on the bench. "Don't let me keep you up." His voice was much harsher than he had intended.

He had played no more than a few quiet notes when Faith rose from the couch with a murmured good-night and retreated to the bedroom.

Kane continued to play but wholly by rote. He wanted to go after her. But he couldn't.

He couldn't.

.   .   .

Faith woke to bright morning sunlight slanting through the drapes and the sound of the piano being played softly. She had left her bedroom door ajar for no reason she wanted to explain to herself, and each time she had awakened in the night she had heard the quiet notes.

She wondered if he even realized he had played the same song over and over again.

She rose and got ready to face the day. And him. Showered and dressed, she nerved herself up to walk out into the living room and say good morning in a steady voice.

Kane stopped playing but didn't move from the bench. "Good morning." His voice was as steady as hers, damp hair and fresh clothing evidence that he had showered recently, but she didn't know whether or not he had slept.

"I guess there's nothing new from Daniels?"

"No. But he should be here any minute."

Faith nodded, then retreated to the kitchen and poured a glass of orange juice. She wasn't particularly thirsty but needed a moment to collect herself.

Something had changed.

She didn't know how it had happened or why, but at some point last night Kane had looked at her, really *looked* at her. For the first time, she thought, he had seen her clearly as something other than a means to an end. And once he had done that . . .

No. She would not think about it.

But he's thinking about it. He's been thinking about it all night.

She slowly went back out to the living room. "I wish—"

"You wish what?" Kane's voice was almost controlled enough to hide the underlying note of strain.

He doesn't have to hurt like this. Tell him—

Faith tried to concentrate, but the voice had vanished like a soap bubble. Slowly, she said, "I wish I'd had those years of practice Bishop talked about. I wish I could concentrate, or focus, or do whatever it takes to make sense of this." She set her glass on a nearby table. "I'm sorry, Kane. I wanted to be of some help, but—"

"You have helped, believe me." He got up and stepped around the end of the piano so they faced each other.

"Have I?" She had to ask, even though every instinct warned her she was risking too much too soon. "Or have I just . . . complicated the situation?"

Kane took a step closer, as though pulled against his will. His hand lifted to her cheek, but froze before it touched her.

Faith was suddenly conscious of her heart thudding, her breathing quickening—and of that suspended hand. Last night at the warehouse she had been unable to touch him because he'd been utterly unreachable. This time, she thought, he stopped just short of touching her because he suspected it would cause him pain.

"I won't," she murmured.

"You won't what?" He took another step, and his hand gently cupped her cheek.

"I won't hurt you." She wanted to close her eyes and press herself to him, to rub herself against him. She could barely breathe.

"That's a strange thing to say." He sounded puzzled, but his eyes were on her mouth, darkening, growing intent, watching as his thumb brushed across her bottom lip slowly.

"It's important," she whispered, not knowing why it was. "Please believe me. I won't—"

"I don't care," Kane said, and kissed her.

Faith felt herself melt against him, her mouth opening to him, her soul opening to him. For the first time since coming out of the coma, she was completely and joyously sure of who she was and where she belonged.

The doorbell was so loud in the early-morning quiet that it jerked them apart.

Kane was frowning a little and his voice was husky when he said, "Probably Tim. I'd better . . ."

"Yes, of course," Faith managed to say.

He seemed about to touch her again, then swore under his breath and turned away.

Feeling suspended between joy and disappointment, and an odd sense that she had been a heartbeat away from understanding something that was desperately important, Faith watched him walk to the foyer and open the front door.

For an instant, seeing Bishop and Richardson standing there, she allowed herself to hope.

Just for an instant.

Then Bishop spoke, his voice hard with control. "I'm sorry, Kane. They've found Dinah."

TEN

"She wanted to be cremated." Kane stood staring out the apartment window, through the recently installed blinds. "She wasn't claustrophobic in the conventional sense, but she told me once that she'd always had an absolute horror of being trapped in a small space, especially . . . underground. I don't know why. Something in her childhood, I suppose."

Richardson watched him the way an expert watched a ticking bomb; without fear, but with the certain knowledge that the next second could bring destruction. "It'll be a while yet, Kane. The M.E.'s office has had a busy week, and they're backed up. They might get it done in a week, but the lab is so far behind that the toxicology report will take at least three or four."

Just in time for Christmas, Faith thought.

She sat, silent and still, on the couch where she could see Kane. She thought of the refrigerated storage drawers at the morgue and shuddered. Which was worse? she wondered miserably. That chilled waiting, or the stainless steel table and sharp scalpels that would come eventually?

Not that Dinah would be aware of either, of course. She was out of pain now.

"They did a preliminary exam?" Bishop asked in the flat, almost disinterested voice that might have convinced a stranger he felt nothing about the matter.

"The usual one, at the scene," Richardson replied. "Given where she was found, the M.E. says establishing time of death will be even more tricky than usual, but his initial estimate is thirty-six to forty-eight hours, maybe longer."

Dinah's body had been discovered by two city workers searching an abandoned, condemned apartment building for the source of a water leak. They had found the leak in the dark, dank basement, which smelled of mold and ancient earth and the refuse of people who had stopped caring long before they had left the place. There in that grave of a building, where a pipe had rusted through and water gushed out, one of the men, more curious than his partner, had opened a barred door to an airtight space originally constructed as a bomb shelter.

The tiny concrete room hadn't protected Dinah in life, but the cold temperature and dry airless conditions had, in a sense, shielded her, delaying decomposition of the body that had been so maimed and savaged in its final days.

"You'll need a positive identification." Kane turned suddenly from the window, a last flicker of hope showing in his eyes.

Reluctantly, the detective shook his head. "Her prints are on file, and the dental records are good. I checked both myself. It's Dinah, Kane. There's no mistake."

"I want to see her."

"No," Richardson said. "You don't."

"I—"

Bishop interrupted, deliberately Faith thought, to say, "Is there an obvious cause of death?"

"Didn't find one in the preliminary exam. No gunshot or knife wound, or blow to the head severe enough to kill. The M.E. thinks she probably bled to death, partly from internal injuries. Or if she was alive when they put her in that airtight room, she could have—could have suffocated." Richardson paused, cleared his throat, then went on stolidly. "There was severe bruising of the body, possibly caused by a fall but more likely deliberately inflicted. Broken bones, including several ribs, one of which probably punctured a lung. And both wrists were cut deeply by the wire they used to restrain her."

"Was she raped?" Kane asked, a harsh note creeping into his voice.

"We'll know after the autopsy."

Kane turned back to stare out the window once again.

Faith saw Bishop send Richardson a quick, questioning look, saw the detective nod almost imperceptibly, and a wave of sickness washed over her. Richardson was sure of the rape even if he wasn't willing to tell Kane.

Tim Daniels, who had been silent until then, asked,

"Anything where she was found that might help us catch the bastards who did it?"

"Very little at the scene, though we did get a few fibers from her clothing. The forensics lab should be able to tell us more in a day or two, if there's anything to tell. We've got people canvassing the area in case anybody saw or heard anything suspicious in the last few days, but I'm not expecting results. That area is pretty deserted, and anybody who was around would have been carefully minding his own business."

Faith spoke up for the first time, asking quietly, "What about the dog bites?"

Richardson frowned. "How did you know she'd been bitten by a dog?"

"She dreamed it," Kane said.

Faith winced at the bitter note in his voice but didn't blame him for his hostility. A lot of help her "dreams" had been; last night and even this morning, she had believed Dinah was still alive. She knew only too well her belief had encouraged Kane's, had convinced him they could find Dinah alive if not unharmed.

"What else did you dream?" Richardson asked, with none of the skepticism she'd expected.

"Tell him," Bishop instructed.

So she did, relating as many details of the flashes and dreams as she could recall, including the dog attack. But she didn't mention the voice in her head, which had probably just been her subconscious anyway. . . .

Richardson looked more grim than before. "So you and Dinah were investigating something on your own, and whatever it was got her killed."

Holding her voice steady, Faith said, "That's what we think. Unfortunately, I can't remember whatever it was. And all I really got from these—these flashes of mine was that whoever had Dinah wanted something they thought she—or we—had."

Then she added, "I think I took whatever it is, but I have no idea what I did with it—or even where I found it. But it must be important, because they— they tortured Dinah trying to make her tell them where it was."

Kane moved almost convulsively but didn't turn. Bishop, his gaze on his friend, said to Richardson, "All this has to tie together. Did you find out anything about who took a shot at Faith night before last?"

Was it only then, only night before last? Faith felt as though years had passed.

"The apartment directly across from here is vacant. The door was found unlocked, and there were indications that someone had been using the place at least for a few hours. From that balcony, it would have been a fairly easy shot, even in a storm. Whether they aimed at a lighted window or actually at Faith, I can't say for certain."

"Isn't that supposed to be a security building?"

"Supposed to be. You'd never know it, though. The fire door on the ground floor was unlocked. In fact, the wind from the storm had practically blown it off its hinges. As far as I can tell, anybody could have gotten inside and up to that apartment." Richardson sighed heavily. "And I figure we've got about another hour before the news breaks that Dinah's body was found. We sealed up the scene fairly well, but there were news crews on to it about the time I left. It'll make the noon news, I'd say."

"And we'll have a media circus," Bishop said.

"Bound to." The detective looked at Kane. "That million-dollar bounty caught their interest, and now that there's no chance of earning it—"

Kane turned from the window with more animation than he'd yet shown. "There's every chance of earning it. I'll pay every dime to anyone who points the way to the men who held Dinah captive." His voice was sharp.

Richardson frowned. "I hope you don't mean to word the announcement that way, Kane. You can't reward someone for just pointing the way. They have to provide concrete evidence we can use in court."

"Evidence leading to the arrest and conviction," Bishop murmured.

"It's my money," Kane said. "I'll promise it to anyone I goddamn please."

Very polite now, Richardson said, "That could be construed as reckless endangerment. These bastards have shown all too clearly they'll do their best to remove anyone who gets in their way. Would you put someone else in the line of fire, Kane?"

Kane didn't reply, and the hard expression on his face didn't change. He said again, "I want to see Dinah."

"That isn't a good idea."

"I want to see her."

"Kane—"

"Are you going to take me down there, or do I have to call the chief of police?"

Richardson glanced at Bishop, but the agent

showed no inclination to protest what was such an obviously bad idea. The detective sighed again. "Okay, okay, I'll take you. Grab a jacket and we'll go now, before the media camps out on your doorstep."

Kane left the room.

Richardson glared at Bishop. "You were a lot of help."

"He needs to see her."

"Bishop, do you have any idea what she looks like?"

The agent nodded, his expression bleak. "A pretty good idea, yeah. But he needs to see her."

"Shit. Look, call down to the morgue and tell Conners we're on our way. Tell him to—to do what he can to make her look human."

Faith was numb, but not even that could protect her from the horrible image of Dinah's damaged body. A sound of pain escaped her, and she closed her eyes for a moment.

Richardson seemed about to apologize, then threw up his hands and went to meet Kane by the front door.

Kane didn't say goodbye.

After the door closed behind them, the silence stretched for several minutes, then Faith said, "Why didn't you stop him? You could have if you'd tried. Why didn't you?"

Bishop's face was set, the scar down his cheek white and angry-looking. "You heard me. He needs to see her."

"Why? Why does he have to have that horrible memory of her forever?"

"Because her death won't be real to him until he

sees her lying lifeless and mangled on a slab," Bishop answered, the words brutal but his voice very soft. "The first stage of grief is denial. Until he gets past that, he can't go on."

Part of Faith understood, but another part wanted to spare Kane. She nodded and tried to think about something else. "Were you nearby when Richardson called you? I didn't think you'd come back to Atlanta yet."

"I hadn't. I was in Tennessee."

When he didn't explain, Faith said, "I guess you caught a fast plane."

"Fast enough."

Faith gave up. "Look, I—I need to go to Haven House. They knew Dinah. They should hear about it from someone before they see it on the news. But I promised Kane I wouldn't go anywhere unescorted, especially after the shooting. Tim, would you—"

"Of course," the private investigator answered.

She looked at Bishop. "When Kane gets back . . . I don't think he should be here alone. Do you?"

"No more than he already is," Bishop said bleakly.

Unlike several of the adults in the shelter, Katie didn't cry when Faith told her about Dinah. Instead, the solemn little girl retreated to the music room and began picking her way through one of the songs Faith had brought her to learn.

"Will she be all right?" Faith asked Karen.

"I don't know," the director said wearily. "She wasn't in great shape before, especially since she saw her bastard of a father take a baseball bat to her mother. He was crazy enough this time to go after Andrea in a mall, of all places, so at least he's locked up, but Katie saw more than ever before and she's been awfully quiet since then." Karen frowned. "She talked more to you when you were here Sunday than she has to anybody else since it happened."

Faith had intended to stay only long enough to break the news about Dinah; she was worried about Kane and wanted to get back to his apartment. But now she was worried about Katie as well and couldn't leave without trying to make sure the little girl was all right.

"Hey, kiddo." She sat down on the bench beside Katie. "Do you like the new music?"

Katie nodded and looked up at Faith gravely. "You didn't forget. Thank you."

"Of course I didn't forget." Faith hesitated. "I thought you might want to talk about Dinah."

"Why? She's dead, that's what you told us."

Faith wasn't deceived by the callous words; she had seen Katie's bottom lip quiver. "When people die," she said carefully, "we keep them alive inside us. By thinking about them. Talking about them. I just wanted you to know it's okay to do that. You can talk to Karen, and you can talk to me."

Katie looked down at the piano as she picked out the first few notes of "Beautiful Dreamer." After a moment, she said, "Can I ask you something?"

"Of course you can, kiddo."

"Can you—can you talk to Dinah now? In your head, the way you used to could?"

Out of the mouths of babes.

Oh, God, can I? Can I talk to her?

"No," Faith said, "not that way." It was true, wasn't it? If nothing else was true, at least it was true that nothing was the way it had been before.

"I just wondered," Katie mumbled.

Guessing, Faith said, "Is there something you wanted to tell Dinah? Something you wanted to ask her? Is that it?"

"No. Except . . ."

"Except what?"

"Nothing. I want to practice now."

Faith watched that little face close up and felt frustrated and anxious. But her instincts told her not to force the issue, so she just said she'd see Katie later and quietly went away.

"I'll keep an eye on her," Karen reassured her in the foyer a few minutes later. "She probably just needs time. And her mama out of the hospital, of course."

"Yeah, I guess." Faith gave her the number at Kane's apartment and said, "Call me if—if there's anything I can do to help."

"Sure. Try not to worry, Faith."

That, Faith thought, was easier said than done. Far easier.

"Of course they caught him coming out of the morgue," Bishop said savagely, watching the TV.

As before, microphones were shoved in front of Kane and questions shouted at him, but this time he wore the look of a man barely conscious of those around him—until one reporter demanded to know how he'd felt upon learning of the brutal murder of his fiancée.

Kane gave the reporter a stare of such incredulity that the others were silenced, and into that silence he spoke with cold precision.

"The million-dollar reward I offered for information leading to Dinah's safe return will now be paid to the person or persons providing information that leads me to her killers."

"That's torn it," Bishop said softly.

"Can't Richardson stop him?" Faith asked.

"Obviously not."

The detective was speaking urgently into Kane's ear, but he was totally ignored. Kane repeated his offer, allowing the words to fall like separate chips of ice, and only after he was absolutely sure that every reporter had written down or taped his offer did he allow Richardson to hustle him into a car.

When the TV reporter began breathlessly to relate the gruesome facts of the discovery of Dinah's body, Bishop muted the set and looked at Faith. "Here we go," he said.

"What do you expect to happen?"

"A feeding frenzy. Every reporter in town will be trying to solve the murder, to say nothing of way too many private investigators and amateur sleuths."

"Couldn't that be good? I mean, with so many trying . . ."

"It'll just muddy the water. And Richardson wasn't kidding when he warned Kane he could be charged with reckless endangerment if somebody gets hurt or killed trying to earn that reward."

"He isn't thinking clearly."

"No. And he'll regret it later. But for now—"

"The damage is done?"

"I'm afraid so. Worst of all, Dinah's killers could be spooked into taking actions they might not otherwise have taken."

"They won't go after Kane?"

"Probably not. There's a very bright spotlight on him right now." Bishop looked at her steadily. "But they could very well go after you. With Dinah gone, you're the key, Faith."

"A key with no memory."

"If I were them," he said, "with a city full of people trying to figure out who I am, and a million-dollar bounty on my head, I wouldn't take any chances by presuming the validity of amnesia."

"No," Faith said reluctantly. "Neither would I."

It was called the witching hour, Faith knew. Three A.M., when all the world seemed quiet and still, and nothing was lonelier to listen to than the beating of your own heart.

Except maybe "Moonlight Sonata."

He was playing it so quietly it wouldn't have awakened her if she had been asleep. But she hadn't been. She'd lain there in his bed for hours, staring at the ceiling, and soon after midnight he had begun playing.

The soft sound got into her head somehow, throbbed inside her like the echo of feelings, the wordless rendering of instincts. It made her heart ache.

She thought he was grieving with the music, allowing the notes to express the pain and longing he couldn't yet release in any other way.

He had returned to the apartment so controlled

and withdrawn there had been no way to reach him, to touch him, even if Faith had dared try.

She hadn't dared.

To her he was formal, indifferent. She might have been a total stranger, a guest he suffered in his home and his life out of courtesy and nothing else. More than once, she had the impression he didn't even see her when he looked at her.

And now it was the witching hour, and Faith lay in the bed in which he had coolly insisted she continue to sleep, listening to him play the piano with such grinding emotion she wanted to cry.

She turned over and pulled the pillow around her ears, trying to shut out the aching sound, but even the muffled notes had the power to hurt her. She didn't want to hear them, didn't want to listen to his pain and grief.

She wondered if Dinah had known how lucky she was.

Had she reveled in Kane's love, or had it been a burden to her because she had known they would have no future together? The scenes Faith had witnessed between them, those dreams and flashes of knowledge, had been playful and sexy and filled with intimacy, but had they been filled with love? She didn't know. Couldn't know.

And couldn't ask, not now . . .

The beach was wonderfully peaceful and soothing, as it always was. It fed her soul. The waves were like music, or what Dinah imagined music must sound like to people who enjoyed it, rhythmic, like a pulse, and altogether pleasant.

The sand was warm beneath her bare feet, damp at first, then wet as the waves lapped around her. She walked and walked.

There was a man up ahead, a familiar figure, and she smiled when she saw him. If she walked a bit faster, she could catch up to him.

But no matter how fast she walked, he remained the same distance ahead of her. She began to run. Her heart pounded and her breath came raggedly, and still he was distant and out of her reach.

Beyond her ability to touch.

She finally stopped running and paused to catch her breath, and when she did she was puzzled to find that the beach was gone. She could still hear the waves, the rhythmic pulsing that was so soothing, but now she was at the construction site where Kane's building was going up.

Only it wasn't quite right somehow.

She walked around the steel skeleton to the back, and frowned because on this side it was a solid office building, windows gleaming in the sunlight. That was very odd, she thought. Only half a building. Why would Kane build half a building?

"He must have a reason," she said aloud.

The words were no sooner out of her mouth than she was in her apartment, and she walked through it curiously, looking at familiar things, touching them. But everything was curiously insubstantial, and she was puzzled again.

"You're dead," Faith told her.

"Don't be ridiculous."

"You are."

Dinah shook her head and continued through the

*apartment, searching now, her expression deter-
mined.* "I'll find it, and then everything will be all
right again," *she said.*

"But you're dead," *Faith insisted, miserable.* "It's
too late, because you're dead."

"When I find it, I won't be dead anymore," *Dinah
explained reasonably.*

"How do you know that?"

"I just know, that's all. Why are you here?"

"I tried to reach you," *Faith explained, following
her.* "I tried and tried. But it was so dark, and all I
could hear was the water."

"You're reaching me now."

"Yes, but I think it's because you're dead."

"How you do harp on that," *Dinah said, shaking
her head.*

"Well, I'm sorry, but it's the truth. What is it you're
looking for, anyway?"

"The MacGuffin, I think somebody called it."

"That's what we're looking for."

"Yes, I know. But you're looking in the wrong
place."

"Then tell me where to look."

Dinah made a sound of exasperation. "If I did, it
wouldn't be a treasure hunt, now would it?"

"I guess not. But—"

*They were in the bedroom, and Dinah turned to
her suddenly.* "Faith, you have to wake up."

"But I want to talk to you."

"Listen to me. You have to wake up."

"But—"

"Faith, someone's trying to get in your window."

ELEVEN

Faith opened her eyes and was instantly wide awake. The music from the living room had ceased, and the apartment was filled with a predawn quiet that was peculiarly heavy.

Almost still. Almost, but not quite, silent.

Something was scratching at one of the bedroom windows.

Someone.

Feeling her heart thudding against her ribs, Faith turned her head slowly on the pillow and stared across the room. She could make out the dark square of the window against the pale walls, but the drapes made it impossible for her to see anything else.

We're on the fifth floor, and there's no balcony.

A sudden, distinct click from the window made her stop worrying about how someone could be out there.

Obviously, someone was. And it was unlikely to be a friendly visit.

Moving as quietly as possible, Faith pushed back the covers and slid from the bed. She worked her way cautiously across the room, her eyes fixed on the window, terrified she'd see the drapes move and a black-gloved hand reach in. She eased open the door and slipped through, leaving it ajar. Only then did she watch where she was going as she hurried to the living room.

The room was dark except for the low fire burning in the gas fireplace, but Kane was still awake. He sat in a chair, slumped, his unseeing gaze fixed on the flames, and Faith had to say his name twice before he stirred and looked at her.

"What is it?" he asked, terribly polite. He didn't seem at all surprised to see her standing there shivering in a sheer green nightgown.

"Kane—"

"You should go back to bed. It's late."

She glanced over her shoulder toward the bedroom, wondering only then why she hadn't knocked on Bishop's door and awakened the agent, who probably had a gun. And who was not locked away in some private hell of grief, unreachable and untouchable. Keeping her voice low, she said, "Someone's trying to get in my window."

Strange how calm she sounded, when her every sense seemed to be quivering in alarm.

"You were dreaming," he said.

I certainly was. But Faith wasn't about to tell him about that. "Kane, someone is trying to get in. I swear to you, I didn't dream this. I didn't imagine it. Someone is outside the window trying to get in. I could hear him."

Kane rose and moved unhurriedly toward the hallway. He had, either deliberately or unconsciously, chosen the route that would take him past her at the greatest possible distance, but Faith told herself that didn't matter. Not now. Not until she could think about it.

"Be careful," she urged.

He paused and looked back at her with lifeless eyes. "There's no one out there, Faith. There are two security guards posted front and back of the building. And we're on the fifth floor."

Steadily, she said, "Someone is out there. Please be careful." This time she made no attempt to lower her voice, even raised it. She hoped she woke Bishop, hoped the intruder had his head inside the window and heard her. She was far less concerned with catching whoever it was than in making sure Kane didn't walk uncaringly into a bullet.

He shook his head and took a step into the hallway.

The force of the explosion knocked him back into the living room; he landed almost at her feet.

"The only real point in the bomb's favor is that the blast was contained pretty much in the bedroom." Detective Nolan, in charge of the bomb squad, continued to describe the explosion. "Not much fire to speak of and actually very little structural damage. In fact, even though it blew the hall door almost into the living room, it didn't even breach the closet door. Your bed's only a memory though, I'm afraid."

Richardson, who had arrived with Nolan, didn't wait for Kane to respond. "So it was a focused blast?" He was bright-eyed despite the early hour, and only the colorful hem of pajama bottoms visible under his pants indicated he'd been pulled from his own bed by Kane's phone call.

For some reason, Faith was surprised the detective wore pajamas.

"Oh, very focused," Nolan answered. "I'd say the guy knew he would catch his target in bed, and aimed to get just that."

"Why?" Richardson demanded. "Wouldn't it have been more certain if he'd tried to gut the entire room?"

"Maybe, but if Mr. MacGregor and Miss Parker are right about how little time passed between the time he gained entry and the explosion—"

"It couldn't have been more than a minute or two," Faith insisted. "I don't think he'd gotten the window open when I slipped out of the room, or just barely."

Nolan nodded. "Then I'd say he had two problems to consider in planning. First, to deliver the device quietly and carefully enough so his target didn't awaken before it could go off, and second to get his ass back up the rope to the roof before it blew."

"He definitely came down from the roof?" Bishop asked.

Richardson said, "One of my people found a rope mark on the edge of the roof, and it looks like the rope was fastened to a pipe up there. In fact, we found a smear of blood on a rusty bolt, so I'd say the guy cut or scraped himself because he was in such a hurry to get the rope unfastened. The roof access door was open, so we're pretty sure he got out through that service stairwell. Probably the same way he got up to the roof."

Bishop nodded.

Nolan resumed his report. "From what we found, the explosive looks like a fairly simple sort with a plain burning fuse, a short one. I'd guess he made a little bomb rather than a big one so he'd still be able to get to the roof if it blew prematurely, as homemade bombs frequently do. Anything more powerful and he ran the risk it would have taken him out as well."

"Amateur night," Bishop muttered.

Nolan nodded again, this time enthusiastically. "I'd say. No timer, nothing fancy. A bit of dynamite in some kind of metal container to concentrate the blast is my guess. I have to say, the M.O. doesn't match up with any of our known arsonists or weekend bombers, and since he kept it simple I'm betting we won't be able to trace him through what's left of the bomb. Maybe we'll get lucky and pick up a finger-print—"

"He wore gloves," Faith murmured.

Richardson turned to her. "I thought you never saw him."

"I didn't. Not really, I mean." She avoided Nolan's interested stare and shrugged at Richardson. "You know."

A look of enlightenment dawned. "Ah. Another of your dreams?"

"Something like that. I think he wore gloves. Black gloves. That he was dressed all in black."

"They mostly are," Nolan said practically. "At night, I mean. Helps them disappear."

Richardson asked, "When will you know for sure if this bastard is in our files?"

"Probably by afternoon. Nothing much going on right now, so I can give this priority."

"Thanks." As soon as Nolan left, Richardson looked at Kane. "Dandy idea, your reward," he said sourly.

Kane returned the stare but said nothing. He had said very little since the police and fire department had arrived, and hardly more before that. Picking himself up from the floor, asking Faith if she was all right, making sure Bishop was okay, calling the police—he had done it all as if by rote and without visible emotion.

Faith said, "That couldn't be the cause, surely? I mean so quickly? Besides, how could the bomber have known I was in that particular bedroom?"

"Maybe he didn't," Richardson suggested. "Maybe the intent was to remove Kane—and the threat of that reward. I doubt his estate would have paid it."

That hadn't occurred to Faith. She looked at Kane, sitting so still and silent, his face pale, and she swallowed hard. She felt very cold suddenly. The blanket he had found for her before the police came was around her shoulders, and she drew it a bit tighter.

Bishop said, "Either way, I'd like to know where those expensive security guards were."

"Out cold. Neither one remembers a damned thing before all the lights went out. And the regular building night security guard was at his station off the lobby watching an infomercial with his feet up, so there's no luck there."

Kane said, "So this guy was good enough to take out two experienced security guards without raising an alarm, good enough to rappel down from the roof and climb back up again, and good enough to gain access through a bedroom window wired with a security system without setting it off. But rather than use a gun or something high-tech, he just tossed a pipe bomb in through the window?"

Faith was surprised. She hadn't been sure Kane had been aware of what was going on around him, much less what had been said.

"That makes no more sense than the rest," Richardson said. "And the problem as I see it is knowing where to focus our attention. Was Dinah on to something big and all this is the result? Did she and Faith step in something nasty while they were poking into corners? Did Faith bring trouble with her when she came to Atlanta? Which is it?"

"Maybe all three," Kane replied.

"Shit." It wasn't said in disbelief, but weariness and frustration. Richardson shook his head. "I need more than four hours of sleep to think about this. In the meantime, Kane, are you planning to stay here? I know there was hardly any damage outside that one bedroom, but—"

"This is probably the safest place we could be now," Kane answered calmly. "Especially once I hire a few more guards—this time with dogs—to surround the building very visibly. And a new security company to close up all the goddamned holes in the electronic security net. If we have to live in a fortress until we get to the bottom of this and find Dinah's killers, so be it."

Faith looked at him but said nothing.

Richardson was clearly not pleased, but he didn't argue. "I can step up patrols in the area. The mayor frowns on bombs and so does the chief. But I want all of you to be careful. Damned careful. If the bomber was after Kane to stop that reward, he's obviously panicked and moving fast enough to be careless. And if he was after Faith, failure to get her may just make him more desperate."

"We'll be careful," Kane said.

Nobody in the room believed he meant it.

"Shit," Richardson said again, unhappily this time.

Bishop's cell phone rang, and he retreated to his bedroom to answer it.

"I won't seal the room," Richardson said, "but I'm asking you to stay out of there as much as possible until the damage is repaired. The fire department covered the hole in the wall with heavy-duty plastic to keep out the worst of the weather, and we believe the floor is safe enough, but don't waste any time getting a crew in there, Kane."

"No. I won't."

Richardson looked at him restlessly, seemed about to say something else, then swore. "Hell. I'm going. Call me if anything—and I mean anything—else happens. Understand?"

Kane nodded.

When the detective had gone, Kane said formally, "We'll have to see what's salvageable in the way of clothing for both of us. The closet is mostly intact, and I think the chest of drawers as well. Some things may have to be cleaned, but since there was virtually no fire, we probably won't have to worry about everything smelling of smoke."

Faith wasn't looking forward to going back into that blackened shell of a room, but said steadily, "I'll do that if you like. Go through everything and see what has to be sent to the cleaners, what's usable."

"Thank you."

She wondered how long she'd be able to bear his politeness.

Bishop came back into the room, drawing their attention easily. He was scowling, an expression made more savage by the scar on his face and so unusual for him it was almost shocking.

"What's up?" Kane asked.

"It looks like I am," his friend replied tersely. "Back up to Quantico."

"Your breaking case?"

"Just broke wide open."

"Then go. And good luck."

"I don't like leaving, Kane—not with all this going on."

"We'll be fine. I'll ring this place with security, so don't worry about us. We'll be safe and sound here."

"Listen to Richardson. Don't make yourself a bigger target than you already have."

"Noted. Go pack, Noah."

It seemed for a moment that Bishop had more to say, but finally he shook his head and went to pack.

When they were alone once again, Faith took a long breath and said, "So he's not infallible. I had wondered about that."

"I don't know what you mean."

"Sure you do. But if you have to have it spelled out—I mean that this time Bishop's famous bullshit detector failed him. Or does it work only when he touches somebody? Anyway, he believed you."

"And you don't."

"No. I don't. I think you have no intention of sitting here surrounded by security while other people look for answers. You intend to find out who killed Dinah, even if that means standing in the line of fire."

His voice remote, Kane said, "You'll be safe here, I promise you that. No more bombs. No more intruders. You can move your things into the spare bedroom, stay there until we get the other room repaired. No one will hurt you, Faith."

Too late.

But all she said was, "So you expect me to stay in a nice, safe cocoon while you go after them alone? That is not going to happen, Kane."

"No?"

"No."

He shook his head. "Don't try to fight me on this, Faith. I'll win."

She drew a breath. "My memory may be nothing but shadows, my legs may be shaky, and I may scare easily these days—but I have just as much right as you to go looking for the people who destroyed my life."

She rose to her feet, holding the blanket tightly around her, and added, "I'll get changed and see what can be salvaged in the bedroom."

She passed Bishop in the hall, and Kane heard her bid him a simple farewell. The agent came into the living room carrying his luggage.

"I always forget how quickly you pack," Kane commented.

"Years of experience. I've called a cab, so I should be on my way shortly. I'll check in with Richardson to keep abreast of the investigation. But if I *am* stuck at Quantico or elsewhere longer than I expect, I'll still fly down for the funeral or memorial service."

Kane didn't want to think about that. "I'll let you know. When it's set, I mean."

"Good." Betraying an unusual restiveness, Bishop said, "I wouldn't leave if it were anything else. You know that."

"I know that. You've been looking a long time, God knows. Maybe this time . . ."

"Maybe. And maybe it'll be another dead end." He let out a short laugh.

Conscious of all his own regrets, Kane said abruptly, "Don't give up. Don't stop looking, Noah."

"I'm the ruthless, coldhearted bastard of a federal agent, remember? I'll use anything and anyone I have to in order to achieve my ends."

Kane was silent for a moment, then said, "That still rankles after all these years? From what you told me, she was so distraught she would have said anything right then. You were the closest target, so you got the blame."

"I deserved the blame."

"You were doing your job."

"No." Bishop looked at him with a hard sheen in his eyes. "I went way beyond doing my job."

"You were trying to stop a killer."

"And instead, I allowed him to kill again."

"Allowed him? Noah—"

"Never mind. It's the past, dead and buried. I don't know why the hell I brought it up. Right now, I'm worried about the present." Bishop hesitated, reluctant to interfere but unable not to. "You can say it's none of my business, but I would have to be blind and stupid not to notice how things are between you and Faith. And I'm neither."

"I don't know what you mean." Kane heard the echo of his earlier denial to Faith, and wondered if everything he felt was branded on his forehead like neon. "And you're right. It's none of your business."

Bishop was no more warned off than Faith had been. "She got under your skin—and you're angry at her for making you betray Dinah."

"You're full of shit."

Bishop smiled. "Am I? Maybe about some things, but not this. All I'm saying is that you can't beat up yourself or Faith because of what you feel, especially now. I can't believe Dinah would consider it a betrayal that the friend she tried so hard to help might find a place for herself in your life."

"There's no question of that."

"No?"

"No. I don't feel anything for her. Not anything like that. She's just . . . a tool I can use to help me find out who killed Dinah. Nothing more."

Deliberately, Bishop said, "It's hell having a guilty conscience, isn't it?"

"You don't know what you're talking about, Noah."

"I'm sure you'd like to think so."

"Leave it alone, all right? Just—leave it alone." Kane didn't want to talk about it. He didn't want to think about it. And most of all, he didn't want to have Noah's probing spider sense focused on him.

"I can't do that, Kane. It goes against the grain with me to walk away and let a friend tear himself to pieces just because he's human. And that's all it is, you know. You're human. Dinah's gone. She's been gone for weeks, and if you're honest with yourself you'll have to admit that deep down inside you knew she wasn't coming back."

"Just shut up, all right?"

"It's the truth and you know it. You gave up on Dinah, Kane, even though you kept going through the motions, kept telling yourself it wasn't true. But it is true. She's gone, and even while you were searching for her, another woman got under your skin."

Kane allowed some of the rage inside him to boil over. He was on his feet before he realized he had moved, hands clenched into fists, so desperate to strike out it was a sick pain in his gut. "What the hell's wrong with you? Christ, Noah, Dinah's barely cold! She's lying on a slab in the morgue, hurt in so many god-awful ways I could hardly recognize her as the woman I loved. Her final days were spent in a hell of agony I can't even imagine, and when those bastards were finished with her, they shut her away in her worst nightmare, leaving her to die alone and terrified, to bleed to death or smother in the dark grave of that tiny room beneath the ground."

"We don't know for sure she died in that room. Maybe she never suffered that final terror," Bishop said quietly.

Kane barely heard him. His voice rose, anguished, as he asked the contemptuous questions that had been whispering in the back of his mind for days now. "What kind of man do you think I am? Do you think it's so easy for me to forget her, to just push her aside because a fresh new piece walks in the door? Do you think any other woman could take Dinah's place? That I could ever feel for anyone else a tenth of what I felt for her?"

"Kane—"

"I loved her. Do you understand that? I loved her."

"I know."

"I wake up every goddamned night aching inside because she's not here. Because she hasn't been here in so long. I hate myself because I gave up on her even before they found her body, even before I *knew* she was gone. I'm furious at her because she kept so much of herself out of my reach, furious at myself because I wasn't able to reach her. And now—now I'll never be able to. She's gone. She's gone."

"And Faith?"

"Faith?" A hard laugh escaped his lips. "I thought she was a connection to Dinah. That's all. For a while, I even thought—even believed—that some part of Dinah was alive in her, had rubbed off on her somehow. I'd see her find Dinah's nail polish without really looking for it, as if she knew just where Dinah kept it, see her eat the same things Dinah did in just the same way. I'd smell Dinah's perfume on her, hear her use the same phrases, the same tone of voice, turn her head the same way . . . and I let myself believe Dinah wasn't really gone."

"Are you so sure that's what it was? All it was?"

"Of course I'm sure. Do you really think I could feel anything else? For *her*?"

"It's all right to feel, Kane."

"No, it's not all right! God damn you, it's never going to be all right!"

In the hallway, unseen by the two men, Faith crept away, into the bathroom where she had been about to shower. She closed the door and turned on the water to shut out even the distant rumble of Kane's raised voice, and stared at her pale face in the mirror.

Odd. She'd never before realized that pain could be a visible, suffering thing in someone's eyes.

She looked away, then focused on her hands lying tense on the vanity top. Dinah's red nail polish coated her neat oval nails. Nearby was a bottle of Dinah's perfume, which she had so unthinkingly used.

The terrible anger in his voice.

She looked at the blouse and slacks on the hamper, the clean clothing she'd found unharmed in the closet and had meant to wear after her shower, and realized she had no idea whether it was her clothing or Dinah's.

"I'll know if it doesn't fit," she murmured to herself. "Her clothing doesn't fit me. At least there's that."

The horrible revulsion in his voice.

She picked up the bottle of perfume and shut it away in the cabinet of the vanity. Then she began to remove her nail polish. She swiped the cotton ball roughly back and forth against her nails, frantic to get the red color off.

There was a queasiness in the pit of her stomach, and she felt light-headed, dizzy.

"I didn't do it deliberately," she murmured, avoiding the reflection of that stricken woman in the mirror. "I didn't even realize I had. . . ."

.   .   .

Kane sat on the couch with his head in his hands for a long time before he was finally able to look at his friend. "Jesus. I'm sorry," he said.

"Don't be. You needed to let it out."

"Maybe." Kane felt exhausted. "But I didn't need to act like it was all your fault."

"It's nobody's fault."

"I'd really like to blame somebody, Noah." Kane knew his smile was twisted.

"Because you've been lucky enough to find two women you could feel so much for? I'd say fate was smiling on you for that, pal."

Kane linked his fingers together and stared at them. He didn't want to say it, but the words seemed forced up from some wellspring of emotion he had finally tapped. "I can't be in love with her, Noah. I can't. I still love Dinah."

"You'll always love Dinah," Bishop said quietly. "It isn't a betrayal of her memory to also love someone else."

"Then why do I hate myself for it?"

After a moment, Bishop said, "Guilt is easier to feel than acceptance."

"Bastard," Kane said.

"It's true. Dinah's gone. You're still here. And life goes on." He smiled. "Clichés, but also truth. You have to go on with your life. Plan her memorial service, Kane. Try to discover who killed her and see to it they're punished for what they did. Then let her go. Say goodbye."

"I don't know if I can do that."

"You've been letting go of her for weeks now." He

watched that truth settle over Kane, saw the slight nod of reluctant agreement, and was satisfied.

The intercom buzzed then, announcing that Bishop's cab had arrived, and Kane got up to see his friend to the door. "Keep in touch," he said.

"Oh, I will. And you do me a favor, okay?"

"If I can."

"Take care of yourself. And take care of Faith."

"I'll do my best."

When Bishop had gone, Kane went to the end of the hallway to the bedrooms and listened. He heard the shower and felt a twinge of relief that Faith had been occupied and had missed his tirade.

He really wasn't ready to face her with his tangle of emotions.

They had already jabbed at her once or twice.

TWELVE

"I came as soon as I heard about the explosion. Kane, what on earth is going on?" Sydney sounded as shaken as she looked. They had spoken the day before by phone, after the discovery of Dinah's body had hit the news, but Kane had warned her not to come to his apartment because of the media camped outside.

This morning, she came despite that.

"The police are still investigating," he told her. "Guy Richardson thinks whoever killed Dinah wasn't happy when I put a bounty on his head, and tossed a bomb into my bedroom to remove the threat of it."

Sydney frowned. "Didn't you say Faith was sleeping in your room?"

"Yeah. She woke up and heard someone at the window. Otherwise she'd be dead too."

Kane had been listening for Faith but she had not yet emerged from the bedroom.

"Then the bomb could have been meant for her?"

"Could have. But with her memory like Swiss cheese, and no real evidence that she was the intended target, it's just as likely I was."

Sydney sipped her coffee for several minutes. "Kane, that reward . . ."

"What about it?"

"Well, maybe Guy is right. Maybe offering that money put a giant target on your back."

"Then it's accomplishing at least one of my goals— it's making somebody very, very nervous. And nervous men make mistakes, Syd. If he's running around trying to kill me, he's not hiding—and I have a better chance of spotting him."

She looked at him searchingly. "Getting yourself killed won't bring Dinah back."

"I know that. I don't have a death wish, if that's what you're thinking. I'm just trying to flush the bastard out into the open."

"Kane . . . I'm so sorry about Dinah. I know I said it yesterday, but I don't think either of us was making much sense, and—"

"I know, Syd." His sister's sympathy was like salt rubbed into a gaping wound, and he felt guilty accepting it from her. He wondered what she'd think of him if she knew that in his heart he'd given up on Dinah weeks ago.

"Will there—Have you thought about a funeral? Made any plans?"

"No, not really. The medical examiner won't release her body until after the autopsy, probably a week or more. She wanted to be cremated, had it in her will, I think. So I guess a memorial service would be better." He heard the detached tone of his voice and wondered if his calm sounded as precarious as it felt.

"I can make the arrangements if you'd like, Kane. You have enough on your plate right now and—and I'd like to do something for Dinah."

His impulse was to accept, but he disliked leaving others to perform the difficult chores he knew he should do himself. "I'll think about it, Syd, thanks. Let's wait a couple of days before we decide anything."

"Probably best," she murmured. "Besides, she may have left specific instructions as to what she wanted. Have you heard from her attorney?"

"No, not yet."

"Are you her executor?"

Kane frowned. "I'd be surprised if I was, since we were involved only about six months before she disappeared. She never said anything about making changes to her will."

"But she didn't have any family still living, did she?"

"No. She had Conrad Masterson, though, and my guess would be that he's her executor, since he handled her money. I know she trusted him."

"Then maybe he'll know what she wanted done."

"Maybe so." More to himself than to her, he said, "I wonder if killers really do show up at the funerals of their victims."

"That's a morbid thought."

He looked at his sister and managed an apologetic smile. "Isn't it. Sorry."

Before Sydney could comment, Faith came into the

kitchen. She looked about fifteen years old, with her hair pulled back with a wide elastic headband and wearing faded jeans and a too-large white sweatshirt. No makeup at all, and Kane noticed immediately that she'd removed the red nail polish.

Even more than young, she looked . . . exposed. Completely vulnerable, stripped of even the few defenses she had managed to erect since waking up with her past a blank page.

"Hi," she said, her voice more subdued than Kane had yet heard it, her gaze fixed on his sister.

"Hello, Faith."

Kane didn't try to approach her, but poured a cup of coffee for her and pushed it across the work island toward her.

She kept her eyes fixed on the cup as she dumped sugar and cream in it, then carried it to the table and sat down across from Sydney.

"I hear you had a close call last night," Sydney said.

Faith's pale lips moved in an imitation smile. "Close enough. If he hadn't made a noise or two getting the window open . . ."

"But you didn't see who it was?"

"No."

"So it really could have been Kane the guy was after."

"I suppose so. Detective Richardson seems to think it's possible."

"Kane, I hope you mean to increase security around here. Those guards of yours have their hands full with the media outside."

"I'm calling the security company right after

breakfast. A dozen more men and a couple of dogs on each shift ought to do the job."

Faith sent him a quick glance. "Won't the other tenants in the building object?"

It was Sydney who replied. "Probably not. Kane's their landlord."

Faith hadn't realized he owned the building. Or perhaps the entire complex.

He said, "I doubt they'd say much anyway if the object is to keep them safer."

Faith thought he had a point.

After breakfast, Faith and Sydney shared the cleaning chores while Kane got on the phone to his security company. They ignored the dishwasher by tacit consent, both needing to be occupied by the simple physical actions of washing, drying, and putting away the dishes. It wasn't until the women were alone together that Sydney asked a quiet question.

"How is he doing, really?"

Faith didn't know how to answer that except by being honest. "He hasn't said much to me. I think . . . he talked to Bishop."

"They've been friends a long time. If anyone could help . . ."

Faith wondered if anyone could, but all she said was, "I don't know what to say to him."

Sydney leaned a hip against the counter and kept her gaze on the plate she was drying. The delicate charm bracelet she wore tinkled softly. "There isn't much you can say, I guess. Me either. All we can do is sympathize with someone else's pain. And be here, in case he needs us."

Faith drew a shaky breath. "Yes, but in my case, I could actually be responsible—directly or indirectly—for the murder of the woman he loves." She used the present tense deliberately.

"You don't know that, Faith."

"That's just it. I don't know. And neither does he."

"Still no luck in remembering, I take it."

"None. And even though we've found out some details of my past, nothing is even vaguely familiar to me."

"So it's still possible that whatever you and Dinah were involved in is something you . . . brought with you when you came to Atlanta?"

"More than possible. Something drove me to cross the country and come live in a strange city. I just wish I knew what that was."

"You have no idea at all?"

They've taken everything away from me, Dinah. Everything.

Faith hesitated, then said, "Apparently, my family was killed, murdered, but I don't know why or by whom. Maybe I came here because of that, but if I did, I still don't remember."

"You have had it rough, haven't you?" Sydney's lovely face mirrored the compassion in her voice. "I'm really sorry, Faith. I wish I could help."

"You said it yourself." Faith smiled. "All we can offer is our sympathy when someone else hurts. Thank you for yours."

"If there's anything I can do to help, I will. Don't forget that, Faith."

With absolutely no forethought, Faith heard herself say, "Well, there is one thing. You can tell me if it would be as difficult to rappel down from the roof of this building as I think it would."

Sydney paused in putting a stack of plates in the cabinet to give Faith a startled look, then smiled. "Oh. I suppose Kane told you I used to do some mountain climbing."

As a matter of fact, he had not, but Faith forced herself to nod noncommittally, even as she wondered how she had known. Maybe a lingering memory from Dinah? Or maybe something she had plucked out of the ether all on her own? This psychic business was very disconcerting.

"It wouldn't be easy for an amateur," Sydney said in answer to the question. "A sheer wall and pitch darkness, the need for silence. But an experienced climber could handle it without much problem, I'd think."

"I see."

Sydney hung her dish towel very neatly on a bar, fixing her attention on the task. "I guess Kane also told you that my husband was killed in a climbing accident."

"I—No, he didn't. I'm so sorry, Sydney. If I'd known, I never would have—"

"Don't worry about it. David was killed more than two years ago. It isn't a . . . fresh wound anymore. In fact—" She laughed suddenly, a sound that was almost convincing. "Never mind. Why don't we finish up in here and go see if Kane's managed to turn this place into a fortress?"

When they emerged from the kitchen, they found that Kane had concluded his business with the security company and was checking with the answering service that had been taking all calls to his main number since the preceding day. He was over by the piano, portable phone in hand, jotting down notes on a legal pad.

"The media, I guess," Sydney murmured.

Faith thought she was probably right, but when Kane got off the phone, he didn't confirm it. Instead, looking at his sister, he said, "The security company had already sent over more people, and the police have made the media move back away from the building, so you should be able to get out of here without too much trouble."

"I should get to the office," Sydney agreed.

"I appreciate your covering for me, Syd."

"It's no trouble. But you should make a decision on the Ludlow building. Max says his foreman has already gone AWOL, and he's going to have to put the crew back to work on Monday no matter what. Either there or on another project."

Kane frowned. "Jed Norris is missing?"

"Well, Max didn't say missing. I mean, he didn't seem worried, just pissed. Said Jed was steady enough when he was kept busy, but apt to vanish if he had too much time on his hands. What do you want to do about the building, Kane? I've already had a couple of calls from the investment group, and they're not happy work has stopped."

In his mind's eye, Kane saw again those cracks in the foundation, and realized that he was no closer now to figuring out the problem. "Let's get an inspector out there to look it over," he suggested. "Maybe he or she can spot something I missed."

"Okay. I'll make the arrangements. Is there anything else I can do?"

"No, thanks."

"What about you two?" Sydney glanced toward Faith, so still and silent by the fireplace.

"We have plenty to keep us busy," Kane said.

But when his sister had gone and they were alone, he found it difficult to speak to Faith. She seemed faraway, and he had the uneasy feeling that one wrong word or gesture would send her completely out of his reach for good.

It reminded him of that last morning with Dinah, when he had weighed each word before speaking it, certain that they were at a dangerous crossroads. He hadn't pushed hard enough then, hadn't been honest about what he was feeling.

And I never saw her again. Except cold and mangled on a slab in the morgue.

Kane pushed that terrible image from his mind.

"I've made arrangements to have the bedroom repaired," he said finally, standing in the center of the room with his hands in his pockets as he watched her. "It'll take several days. The work crew should be here anytime to get started. It'll be pretty noisy in here, I'm afraid. So we should probably go somewhere else for the rest of the day."

She looked at him, finally. "What did you have in mind? Jordan Cochrane?"

Even the name made rage churn inside him like bile, but Kane was able to keep his voice level. "Not today. I called his office and his home. He's out of town on a business trip. Expected back in a day or two."

Establishing his alibi? Faith wondered. "How long has he been gone?"

"A week. They said. But we can check into that."

Faith knew that the last thing he wanted was to find Jordan Cochrane blameless. Kane wanted to blame someone for Dinah's death.

"And in the meantime?" she asked.

"In the meantime, we both need to get out of here for a few hours. I need to go out to the construction site, for one thing, meet with the inspector. And don't you have a physical-therapy appointment?"

"Oh. Yes." It was Thursday. She'd forgotten.

"What time is your appointment?"

Faith looked at her bare wrist, frowned, then looked at the clock on the VCR. Nearly ten. She couldn't believe how much had happened during this eternal morning.

"It's at eleven-thirty, I think."

"Okay. Why don't we plan to leave at eleven? That'll give security enough time to figure out a plan to get us out of here unnoticed. As soon as the crew gets here, I'll put them to work. Until then, we sort through what was left undamaged by the explosion."

"All right," Faith said.

It was nearly one by the time Faith completed her therapy, showered, and dressed. As usual, the treatment energized her, and she hoped that tonight she'd be able to sleep deeply and dreamlessly.

But she wasn't counting on it.

"Faith."

Just outside the physical-therapy rooms, Faith

turned to see Dr. Burnett coming down the hall toward her with a smile. Beyond him, she saw Kane rise from the chair where he had waited for her. Near the elevators, the new bodyguard who had accompanied them today leaned against a wall, seemingly relaxed but entirely watchful. He was dressed in jeans and a sweatshirt, and Faith wondered where he carried his gun.

"Faith?"

She smiled at Burnett. "Hi. What are you doing up on this floor?"

"Checking up on my star patient." The words were light, but his gaze was intent, concerned.

"I'm fine. Even though Tracy tortured me as usual."

"She called me while you were in the shower."

Faith sighed. "I see. And told you what? That I couldn't lift the weight I was able to lift last week? That I lasted only ten minutes on the stair climber?"

"That you'd lost five pounds. Faith, if you aren't taking care of yourself, you're going to wind up right back in here. Is that what you want?"

"No, of course not."

"Then start taking better care of yourself. I can't stand by and watch you lose all the ground you've gained."

"Bullying your former patient, Doctor?" Kane's voice held a distinct warning.

He had walked over and was now standing close to her, and Faith felt trapped, hemmed in between the two tall men. She could feel their dislike of each other as clearly as if it were written on them in neon.

Burnett's face tightened, but he returned Kane's

stare without backing down. "I care what happens to her, Mr. MacGregor. Do you?"

"Of course."

"Indeed? And yet you drag her into a dangerous situation where she's shot at, nearly killed by a bomb according to the news—"

"She'll be safe from now on. I've made certain of that."

"By bringing armed guards into her life? By shutting her away so those who care about her can't even reach her? I tried calling yesterday, and—"

"A service is taking calls." There was a hard sheen to Kane's eyes, an edge to his voice. "To weed out those from the media since Dinah's body was found. Surely you understand that, Doctor?"

"I left a message, Mr. MacGregor. Which Faith clearly never received."

Faith looked up at Kane. He hadn't mentioned a message for her, and she had to wonder why.

"It's been a busy morning," was Kane's only reply.

"I imagine so," Dr. Burnett said. "It's been all over the news about that reward you offered. You've got the whole city stirred up. That's what all this is really about, isn't it, Mr. MacGregor? All you're thinking about is finding the people who killed your fiancée, isn't that true? Nothing else matters to you. And you'll drag Faith along with you, wherever the search takes you, whatever the danger—"

It was suddenly too much, and Faith, feeling smothered, cut him off. "Enough. Doctor, nobody dragged me into this situation—except the people who tried to destroy my life."

"Faith—"

"No. No more. I realize I'm your pet project. I also realize that I appear somewhat frail at the moment. But you're making a very big mistake if you imagine I'm nothing more than a doll with no mind of my own. I am perfectly capable of taking care of myself." She shifted her gaze to Kane and lifted her chin. "It's time I started doing that."

She brushed past them both and walked toward the elevators, leaving them staring after her.

THIRTEEN

Kane caught up with her at the elevators, but since the bodyguard joined them, he didn't say anything to her.

As for Faith, she realized with some surprise that she was angry—and that it felt good.

She was angry at Dr. Burnett for seeing her always as walking wounded in need of his professional advice and concern, angry at Kane for leaping to her defense as if he also believed her in need of his protection, and angry at herself most of all for having apathetically accepted the attitudes from both men.

Maybe her legs were a bit shaky these days, maybe her memory was as blank as a mime's face, and maybe she *was* an emotional mess. But she was also a grown woman who'd had the guts to leave an abusive husband, travel three thousand miles across the country alone, and start her life over again.

It was a realization to hold on to.

Their car and driver were waiting for them, and even though the bodyguard got into the front, leaving Faith and Kane alone in the backseat, there was no partition to give them any privacy.

So Faith kept her voice low and even indifferent when she asked, "When do you have to meet the inspector?"

"Three o'clock."

She felt him looking at her but didn't turn her head to meet his gaze.

He drew an audible breath. "Faith, I'm sorry I didn't tell you about Burnett's message when I called the service this morning."

"All right. You're sorry."

"You don't believe me?"

"Of course I believe you. Why wouldn't I?"

"Faith—"

"If we have time, would you mind going by my apartment today or tomorrow? I want to get my watch." She looked down at her bare wrist. "I didn't even realize I wasn't wearing it until this morning. I suppose I forgot to get it the other day when I packed up my things."

"Of course we'll have time."

"Thank you." Her tone was polite.

Kane glanced at the two men in the front seat and resisted an urge to swear. For this kind of security and safety, privacy had to be sacrificed—and he didn't like it. He also didn't like feeling so raw and touchy; he knew all too well that he had overreacted with Burnett, and in so doing had upset Faith.

But the truth was that he *was* raw, his emotions too close to the surface and all too easily touched.

Most of all, he was angry. Angry at Burnett for his possessive attitude toward Faith. Angry at Faith for getting under his skin. Angry at Dinah for getting herself killed.

"Do you want me to apologize for what I said to Burnett, is that it?" he demanded.

Faith blinked at the anger in his voice, but otherwise remained unruffled. "If you feel you were wrong, say so. But don't do it just to placate me."

For a dizzy moment he wondered if she had any idea how much like Dinah she'd sounded. Dinah, who had hated false repentance and always refused to accept a careless *I'm sorry,* even to pour oil on troubled waters. She had always preferred an honest fight to fake peace, no matter what is cost her.

Slowly, he said, "I don't feel I was wrong, except maybe in presuming that you needed me to interfere. I will apologize for that."

"Thank you. I can fight my own battles, you know."

"You didn't seem to want to fight Burnett."

"Dr. Burnett," she said with great deliberation, "helped me get back on my feet after I came out of the coma. I'll always be grateful to him for that."

"It was his job, Faith."

"I'm aware of that."

"Is he?"

Faith was silent for a moment, then said, "I'm his patient, nothing more. Not that it's any of your business."

Kane knew she was right. It was none of his business. Absolutely none of his business.

Casting about for something casual to say, he asked,

"Did you bring your apartment keys with you? If so, we can drop by on our way out to the construction site."

"I think so." She opened her shoulder bag and checked inside. He heard the clink of keys and then saw her frown.

"What?"

She drew out a folded piece of paper and opened it slowly. Her face went blank as she read whatever was written there, and he saw her fingers tremble.

"Faith?"

She looked at him, and for an instant he thought she was going to crumple the paper or tear it to pieces. Then she held it out to him.

It was half a sheet torn carelessly from a notebook, and the single handwritten sentence on it sprawled across the page as if the author had been in a hurry.

Faith, look in my apartment inside the book.

"It isn't my writing," Faith said.

The words blurred before Kane's eyes. "No. It's Dinah's."

She didn't want to go into Dinah's apartment. Beside her, Kane was still and silent, and she was vividly conscious of his anger and disbelief.

He didn't believe she had never seen the note before or that it had not been in her bag a few days before. Nor did he believe she hadn't written it herself, somehow aping Dinah's handwriting well enough to fool his incredulous eyes.

He didn't believe, because any other explanation chipped away at his sanity. And he was angry with her because . . . what? Because he thought she was playing with his emotions, mocking his grief?

Faith didn't know what she believed. All she knew was that the note had *not* been in her bag before today and that she had *not* written it herself in some inexplicable attempt to deceive Kane—or anyone else. She knew Dinah hadn't written it, because Dinah was dead.

And she knew one last thing, one final stark fact she was absolutely certain of: Wherever the note had come from, the message it contained was from Dinah.

She knew that.

Kane said, "If it takes longer than . . . If it looks like I'll be late in meeting the inspector, I'll call and have him wait." He sounded calm, but she thought it was a precarious calm.

He's angry at everybody because she's gone. And now this has to happen. And I make a handy target for his anger.

She didn't blame him for what he felt, but there was an anger in Faith as well, and she didn't know how much longer she could handle it in silence.

When they reached Dinah's apartment building, the driver went around the block once so they could make certain no media lurked in the area. But since no crime had been committed there, since her apartment was empty and her neighbors had long since stopped responding to questions from the press, the journalists who had camped out there in the days just after Dinah's disappearance had finally gone away.

Even so, the bodyguard insisted on going with

them up to the third floor, insisted on checking the
apartment door carefully with a little electronic
gadget he carried, and, after Kane had disarmed the
security system, insisted he go in first to make certain
there was no danger. It was, after all, what Kane was
paying him for.

Faith was grateful for the few minutes allowed her
before she had to go inside.

"Do you know if I've . . . ever been here before?"
she asked Kane, after the bodyguard closed the door,
leaving them alone.

"She never mentioned it."

Angry. He's so angry.

Faith didn't say anything else. She felt Kane's gaze
on her.

The bodyguard came out and said they could enter.

Faith walked slowly into the living room and
looked around. The apartment smelled of lemon;
Kane had told her that he'd had a cleaning service
come in every week, just as Dinah had, but it had
been vacant for many weeks and there was an air of
emptiness about it.

Faith shivered and wrapped her arms about
herself as she tried to remain detached and study
the room. Plenty of natural light, spacious. The furniture was high quality, the wood pieces gleaming with lemon oil and the upholstery constructed
of expensive material, but the appearance was
casual, the cushions overstuffed and comfortable.

The neatness contributed to the empty feel, with
accent pillows placed precisely, and magazines on the
stone-topped coffee table aligned exactly, and no clutter anywhere.

Looking around, she was sure that she had been here before, and more than once. *I know there are two bedrooms and a bathroom. And even though I can't see it from here, there's a clock near the kitchen table, and the dish towels have apples on them. And she loves plants, but hers are silk because she forgets to water the real ones and they die. . . .*

Shaking off the odd sensations, Faith walked over to a wall between two large windows where a bookcase was filled to bursting.

. . . Inside the book.

Which book? There must have been a hundred on this set of shelves alone, and she didn't have to look down the hallway toward the bedrooms to know that it was lined with bookshelves just as filled as these were.

Conscious of Kane behind her, Faith reached up to a shelf and began running a finger along the spines of the books, stopping on each just long enough to read the titles.

"What are you looking for?" he asked.

"I don't know."

"Don't you?"

She looked back over her shoulder at him. "No, I don't know. I have no idea which book she—which book the note meant. Do you?"

"The note was directed to you," he answered implacably.

"Okay, fine. Why don't you go on to your appointment with the inspector? Leave the guard outside and take the driver with you. I'll stay here and look through these books."

His mouth tightened. "I'm not leaving you alone."

"I'm not alone. The guard can stay."

"It'll take hours to go through all her books," Kane said roughly.

"Then I'll stay here for hours."

"Goddammit, Faith, you know Dinah didn't write that note!"

She didn't flinch. "I don't know who wrote it. But I am absolutely positive the *message* is from Dinah."

"Dinah is dead."

"Yes." Faith made herself go on in the calmest voice she could manage. "And I've known things about her all along, Kane. The flashes of those scenes with you. The dog attacking her. That room in the Cochrane warehouse where they—where they hurt her. And the sound of water near where she was found. I knew all of that, saw it or heard it or felt it. And I'm telling you now that the message in the note is from Dinah."

"Are you channeling the dead now, Faith?"

"I'm just telling you what I know. There is something in one of these books, something Dinah wants me to find. I have to look for it."

Kane stared at her for a long while, then swore and reached for his cell phone. "All right. I'll reschedule with the inspector for tomorrow."

He stepped away to use the phone, and Faith didn't try to talk him out of it. She knew he still didn't believe her about the note, but at least now he was willing to give her the benefit of the doubt.

Faith turned back to the bookshelves and began scanning the titles again. She really had no idea what she was looking for. All the books were novels, rang-ing from mystery, romance, and science fiction to blockbuster best-sellers and literary fiction.

If nothing else, Dinah had certainly ranged widely in her reading.

Faith plucked a few titles off the shelves and flipped through them, feeling helpless and frustrated. Which book? How could she possibly guess what might be important?

"We'll have to go through them one by one," Kane said behind her. "Check every book. That is—if you really don't know what we're supposed to find."

"I really don't know," she said.

He let out a short breath that sounded impatient. "Okay. You start in here, and I'll take the hallway."

"She had a lot of books," Faith murmured.

"There's another wall of shelves in her bedroom," Kane said, then turned and went into the hall.

An awful lot of books.

More than an hour later, Faith had taken down, searched, and replaced on their shelves nearly half the books, without finding anything out of the ordinary. A few bookmarks. A years-old grocery list. Theater ticket stubs.

She sat on the floor, her legs out before her, touching her toes and stretching her sore muscles gingerly. She was tired. And she was frustrated.

Dammit, Dinah, where is it? Where do I look?

She didn't know. And if it had been Dinah trying to help her find some necessary clue, she was being silent and unhelpful now.

Faith got to her feet and went into the hallway, intending to ask Kane if he'd found anything. She assumed he would have told her if he had, but the silence was wearing on her nerves and she wanted to hear the sound of his voice.

He wasn't in the hallway, though books stacked neatly on the floor gave evidence of his efforts. Faith went on down the hall, moving noiselessly, not sure why she felt the need to be silent. At the end of the hallway were the two bedrooms and bathroom.

In the room that had undoubtedly been Dinah's, Kane sat on the bed, his bowed head in his hands, shoulders hunched, utterly still.

Faith had a confused impression of a lovely room decorated in cool shades of blue, of patterns and materials that were feminine without being frilly, of more bookshelves and oil paintings of seascapes and a few figurines that were beautiful and tasteful and didn't clutter up the room.

Then she crept away silently, back to the living room. Mechanically, she continued searching through the books, looking at each one from cover to cover before returning it to its shelf. She didn't realize she was crying until everything got blurry and she saw wet splotches on the page she was staring at.

"Dammit," she whispered. "Dammit."

"Any luck?"

Faith put one last book back on the shelf, got to her feet, and looked at Kane as he stood in the doorway. She thought he was calmer, less angry. Or maybe he was simply as tired as she was. They'd been in Dinah's apartment nearly three hours.

"No. How about you?"

"Not so far." He frowned at her, seemed about to ask something, but in the end didn't.

Faith wondered if her eyes were red. She said, "I thought of something a few minutes ago. My apartment was searched at least a couple of times. Do you think this place might have been searched too?"

"Maybe. Right after Dinah disappeared, I went through here with a fine-tooth comb, and the police searched it as well. The security system has been active, and the only ones who are supposed to come in are the cleaning crew. But there's always a chance somebody else got in. If they did, though, they were neat about it. The cleaning service was under orders to report anything out of the ordinary—and I certainly haven't noticed anything out of place."

Faith went over to sit in an armchair near the fireplace. "I keep thinking I should know just where to look. That note . . . it *assumed* I'd know. 'Inside the book,' it said. As if there were only one book. One important book."

Kane sat on the arm of the couch near her chair. "And you have no idea what book would be important." He didn't say it derisively or accusingly, just matter-of-factly.

She pressed her fingers to her temples and closed her eyes. "No. But I—" Her head lifted abruptly, and she stared at him. "Did Dinah use a day planner? A date book?"

"Two of them. One she kept with her in the Jeep, for business, the other one here for personal stuff." Kane got up and went to the antique desk near one of the windows. He took a black leather book out of the top drawer and came back to hand it to

Faith. "I've been through it a dozen times," he said, sitting on the couch. "So have the police. In the first few weeks, we retraced her steps those last days, trying to find some clue to what happened to her." He paused. "I never saw anything unusual in there, nothing that drew my attention."

But that would have been the point. Not to draw anyone's attention.

Faith examined the book carefully. It was the usual sort of day planner, with an address book and calendar and tabbed sections for appointments and schedules and notes. There was a pocket in the front cover for Dinah's business cards, and several pages of clear plastic sleeves for the cards people had given her.

There was, as far as Faith could see, nothing out of the ordinary.

She looked through the sections one at a time, turning each page slowly. It wasn't until she reached the second-to-last section intended for notes that she looked up at Kane. "There are no pages here. The tab says notes should be in this section, but all the pages are missing."

"I didn't notice that. But it might mean nothing. Dinah could have torn them out one or two at a time, never intending to keep them. People do that."

Faith closed her eyes, thinking. "If I knew somebody might try to get some information I had, that someone could come looking for it, I just might write it down twice. Once in a reasonable place where I could be fairly sure it would be found—and then again somewhere else."

"Where?" Kane asked.

Faith stared down at the planner. "When you're

looking for something and you find it, you stop looking. Right?"

"Right."

She turned the final tab, which was labeled MISC., and discovered several lined pages with a scattering of reminders written in Dinah's hand. Faith ran her finger down them slowly.

Get the Jeep's tires rotated. Find out Sharon's birthday. Have a putting green installed in Conrad's office.

Faith looked up at Kane and repeated that one aloud. "Conrad?"

He smiled slightly. "Conrad Masterson. A financial manager who's also a golfing nut. Dinah was wondering what to get him for Christmas."

"Oh." Faith returned her gaze to the pages. More reminders. To trace the whereabouts of a catalog order that had not arrived. To schedule a routine checkup with her doctor. To return a Stephen King novel to the library.

Faith stopped again at that one. "But she buys his books."

"What?" Kane leaned toward her.

She looked up at him with a frown. "This note says she has to remember to return a Stephen King novel to the library. But she buys his books in hardcover—I found half a dozen."

"I found two," Kane said slowly.

"Does—did she even take novels out of the library?"

Kane had to think about that for a moment. "I don't think so. She used the library for research, but she was always willing to buy a book, even by a new author. Building a personal library was important to her." He indicated the bookshelves throughout the apartment. "Obviously."

"Then I think," Faith said, "we should look for more Stephen King novels."

They found the handwritten list of names in the fourth King novel on the bedroom shelves.

There were six names, all men. Five were prominent Atlanta businessmen, two of whom were politically active. The sixth man, Kane told Faith, had committed suicide a week before Dinah vanished.

The third name on the list was Jordan Cochrane.

But what caused Faith and Kane to look at each other in surprise was the single word Dinah had written and twice circled at the bottom of the page:

Blackmail.

"Blackmail," Tim Daniels said, "is a nasty business, and the kind of dirt men pay to keep under the rug tends to be bad enough to provide a motive for murder."

"Or suicide," Kane said. "One man on the list took care of his apparent problems by blowing his brains out, and it emerged afterward that for about six months before he'd been trying to pay back some money he had *borrowed* from the company he worked for. It was a lot of money. He would have gone to jail for a long time if the company had found out, and his very nice churchgoing wife would have been disgraced."

"I'd call him a likely target for blackmail," Daniels allowed. "Assuming somebody found out what he was up to."

"And if he was paying hush money, it was probably next to impossible for him to also pay back the money he'd embezzled. Which probably explains the suicide. Poor bastard was caught in a no-win situation."

"I'd say," Daniels agreed.

"We can also assume that since his name was lumped in with the five others, all these men were probably being blackmailed. Which begs the question—"

"Who's doing the blackmailing?" Faith supplied.

"Exactly."

"It also," Faith noted, "seems to indicate that Jordan Cochrane is on the victim side of the equation."

"That doesn't mean he wasn't involved in Dinah's murder. Some secrets *are* worth killing to keep."

"True enough. But there are four other names on that list, Kane. And you said all five share one other connection besides apparently being blackmail victims."

"All are in some way involved in the construction business. The man who committed suicide was too. He kept the books for Mayfair Construction."

"Isn't that the company—"

"Working on the Ludlow building, yes. Or will be, when I can put them back to work."

Slowly, Faith said, "Another connection."

"Another connection," Kane agreed.

FOURTEEN

"I don't much like you waltzing around in my dreams," Faith said to Dinah.

"It's not my idea of fun either," Dinah retorted, very busy with what she was doing. "If you'd only get your head on straight, I could get on with my life."

Faith opened her mouth to remind Dinah once again that she had no life to get on with, but finally just shrugged and stepped closer, watching the other woman curiously. "What are you doing now?"

"I'm fixing it, of course." Dinah was carefully gluing together delicate porcelain pieces of a shattered figurine. It was, Faith saw with a shiver, the figurine of a woman.

"Are you trying to say you put me back together?"

Dinah sighed, a bit impatient. "Never mind this. You aren't ready to think about it yet. What you have to do first is understand what that list means."

"The names? It means blackmail, doesn't it?"

Dinah looked at her sympathetically. "This is going to be very hard for the next little while. But you have to get through it. You won't begin to see the truth until you get through it."

"Get through what?"

"There's another body, of course. Once you begin killing, it's so easy to keep doing it. It even seems reasonable to use that means to solve a problem—especially if you've been successful before. And he has. First back in Seattle, and now here."

"Who? Who is he, Dinah?"

"Just remember that the body isn't who it appears to be. Don't let them make that mistake, Faith. You have to be sure who the body is, or you won't have the right answer."

"But—"

"And when you find the bell, make him tell you the truth. He won't want to, but you have to make him. He has pieces of the truth, and you need them."

"Dammit, why do you have to talk in riddles?"

"It's the only way you can hear me."

That made no sense to Faith, and she sighed. "Can't you at least tell me where to look? There has to be a key to all this, and we need it. I don't even know the right questions to ask!"

Dinah returned her attention to the figurine. "Ask yourself this, Faith. Ask yourself how many people you would die to protect. And be careful. Be very careful. He's watching, you know."

· · ·

It was the second time in as many days that Faith
had jerked awake in the darkness just before dawn
but this time no intruder lurked outside the
window.

"Just the one in my mind," she heard herself
murmur.

She remained in bed for as long as she could, but it
wasn't yet six-thirty when she finally got up. She
slipped into the bathroom to take her morning
shower.

*Ask yourself how many people you would die to
protect.*

What frightened Faith about that question was her
certainty that Dinah had done just that, had died
believing her silence was protecting someone she
cared about. And so far, the only person Faith could
imagine the other woman caring for so deeply was
Kane.

Had he been in danger even before the last few
days?

Because he was somehow involved? Viewed objec-
tively, she supposed it was possible—though nothing
she had seen or felt supported the likelihood.

But there was that elusive thing Dinah's torturers
had demanded of her, and Faith's apartment had been
searched at least twice. She doubted the simple list of
names was the cause of all that. Whatever else it was,
its threat against the equally elusive villains had to be
incredibly explosive to justify torture and murder,
gunshots and bombs.

No, it wasn't the list. She thought it was something
she herself had found not long before the accident,
some evidence that not only identified but con-

demned those behind the blackmail, and the murders of her family and Dinah.

The list was a beginning, at least, the beginning where Dinah had started.

Faith made her way to the kitchen. She didn't go near the couch, hoping that Kane was sleeping. He needed to sleep.

She turned on the dim light above the stove and got the coffeemaker started. Then she leaned back against the counter and waited, trying not to think because she felt so weary of her thoughts chasing one another around in her mind.

"You're up early." Kane stood in the doorway, his pale hair tousled and stubble on his jaw.

"Sorry if I woke you," she said.

"You didn't." He came in and busied himself getting the cups. Faith moved away a bit nervously to get the cream from the refrigerator. Kane didn't appear to be watching her, but she thought he noticed.

"You cried out in your sleep," he said suddenly.

That surprised her, and she looked at him uncertainly. "I did?"

"About two-thirty. I opened your door and looked in. You seemed restless, and you'd thrown off most of the covers."

Remembering the thin nightgown she'd slept in, Faith felt heat rise in her face. But Kane was pouring coffee into their cups and didn't notice.

"I went in to straighten the covers, and I thought for a minute you were awake. You said my name. But you were sound asleep."

"I must have been. I don't remember."

"Bad dreams?" He looked at her finally, as he handed her a cup.

"Just the usual. Bits and pieces." Faith dumped sugar and cream into the coffee and took a sip. Kane tasted his and grimaced.

"Sorry," she said wryly. Clearly, he didn't like the way she made it. She sipped her own again; it tasted to her the way coffee always tasted—slightly bitter.

Kane said, "If you don't mind . . ." and poured the entire pot down the drain.

She was not offended. "I suppose there's a knack to it. I don't seem to have it."

He got the second pot started. "Some people don't. I'll shave and shower while this is getting ready. You wanted to go by your apartment for your watch, and I have that appointment with the building inspector. We might as well clear out before the work crew gets here."

"Okay." She thought he was a little abrupt but didn't protest or question his mood. She was still unsettled by his announcement that he had gone into the bedroom while she slept and that she had said his name out loud. She was bothered by the knowledge that some dream or nightmare had caused her to cry out, had caused her to say his name.

There's another body, of course.

"My subconscious doesn't know what it's talking about," she murmured to herself. But she went into the living room and turned on the TV anyway. She wanted to see the news, even though she didn't believe there would be another body. Not really.

The first part of the program was taken up with a rehash of Dinah's disappearance and the discovery of her body, complete with all the gory details the media had been able to obtain through their various sources. There were numerous shots of Kane as he had been in the early days, haggard with worry but determined to find Dinah, saying little except that.

And someone had unearthed a short video clip of Dinah herself, caught unawares about six months before by a news crew as she was working on interviews for her magazine article about Haven House. The news crew had been there because a rather well-known Atlanta wife, supposedly taking shelter there, had called a reporter friend to come and tape her tearful accusations of repeated abuse.

It was, of course, a complete coincidence that their divorce proceedings had turned nasty a few weeks before that.

The only positive note about the situation was that the news crew had been responsible enough not to show any identifying characteristic of Haven House—such as a street number or a long shot that might have placed its location. Even after having been there, it took Faith a couple of minutes to realize it was Haven House she was looking at.

She listened to the society woman's accusations with half an ear, her attention fixed on the background of the shot, where Dinah, notebook in hand, was cradling a sleeping infant.

She had been a beautiful woman, Faith realized. And her lovely face wore compassion and empathy so openly and naturally. It was a face to which even strangers would be drawn to tell their secrets, even their shames, and Faith wondered how many confidences Dinah had carried with her to her death.

Before Faith could do more than ponder that question, her attention was caught by another person moving in the background, someone across whose face an expression of anxiety appeared when she saw the news crew filming the place. And her. Someone who darted through the doorway and disappeared into the shelter.

Herself.

Faith frowned at the set as the news piece continued. What was it about the scene that nagged at her? It wasn't as if she hadn't known she had met Dinah at Haven House when Dinah was researching her article.

What was bugging her?

Kane came into the living room just as a perky weather lady was saying it might rain today, and Faith knew she had to tell him. Whether he believed her or not.

She drew a breath and stared at the television. "I didn't really answer you when you asked if I'd had nightmares last night. I don't remember everything I dreamed, but I do remember one of those . . . those odd dreams. There was a warning. A warning that another body will be found."

Kane sat on the arm of a chair near her. He was gazing at her, not in disbelief but in apprehension. "Whose body, Faith?"

"I don't know."

"Where did the warning come from?"

"I don't know. My subconscious, which seems to know more than I do. Or that psychic ability I might have but can't control. Or even that—that connection with Dinah."

"Dinah is dead."

That's what I keep telling her. Faith felt a bubble of hysterical laughter rise in her throat, but managed to swallow it. "Yeah, well. The last time she warned me, she was right."

"The last time?"

Faith wasn't surprised that his face was masklike in its stillness. "Dinah told me in a dream that somebody was trying to get into my window. When I woke up, someone was."

"You know very well that *had* to be your subconscious, Faith. The noise you heard while you were sleeping found its way into your dreams, that's all."

"Probably," she agreed. "So I have to wonder, Kane. I have to wonder what I've seen or heard that convinced my subconscious there's another body out there somewhere." She returned her gaze to the television screen. "Unless I know there is, of course."

"How could you?"

"Exactly. How could I?"

Like Dinah's, Faith's apartment felt too empty, and Faith wasted no time in searching for her watch. But it was nowhere to be found.

"You know, now that I think about it," she said to Kane, "I don't think there was a watch among my things when they gave them back to me in the hospital."

"It could have been destroyed in the accident," he pointed out.

"Yes . . . But how many people do you know who have only *one* watch? Especially a woman. They're cheap accessories."

Kane helped her search a second time, but there was no watch in the apartment. They found a small trinket box containing a few pairs of earrings, long and jangly with brightly colored stones and crystals. Faith reached up absently to touch her earlobe, finding the simple pearl stud there a far more restrained style.

"Dinah's," Kane said. "She kept a few pairs at my place, in a box in the linen closet."

Faith stared at him, horrified. "You mean I just—took them? God, Kane, I'm sorry. I hadn't even realized—"

"Don't worry about it. I doubt it would bother Dinah, and it doesn't bother me."

But she knew it did bother him, and that she had unconsciously aped Dinah in yet another way definitely bothered her. She brooded about it all the way out to the construction site, even more unnerved when she realized that at some point in the last twenty-four hours, she had, without even noticing her actions, polished her fingernails again.

With Dinah's red polish.

The building inspector was surprised that Faith didn't recognize him; they had, after all, worked in the same city office for months. He was also surprised to learn of her accident, which told Faith he hadn't felt enough interest in her to notice her absence.

Since it appeared that the morning's weather

report had been accurate, and distant rumbles of thunder promised more than just rain, Kane and the inspector wasted no time in going down to the half-finished lower levels of the Ludlow building to look at the foundation.

Faith remained outside. She stood, actually, between the building and the gate, beyond which their car and driver waited, and the restless body-guard paced.

What is his name, anyway? she wondered for the first time. Kane had called him something, but for the life of her she couldn't remember what it was. She supposed bodyguards grew accustomed to being ignored; if they did their job well, they were supposed to be virtually invisible to the people they guarded— or so she assumed.

A sudden gust of wind stirred her hair and chilled her despite her sweater and jacket, and she thrust her hands into her pockets. In the right pocket, she felt a thin, flexible piece of metal, and her fingers probed it curiously. There was some-thing familiar about—

"God, I'm wearing her jacket again," she muttered to herself. "And I didn't even notice."

It scared her, made her feel she wasn't in control.

She turned her back to the building and hunched her shoulders against the growing chill. Richardson was just coming through the gate, apparently having paused to reassure the bodyguard that he was no threat. He came straight down the rutted track toward her.

The grim look on his face made her heart sink.

"Where's Kane?" he asked when he reached her.

"Around back with the inspector, checking out the foundation. What's happened?"

He studied her, seemingly weighing her, then said bluntly, "We've found another body."

Faith thought the world tilted. But the dizzy sensation passed quickly. "Do you know who it is?"

"That's why I'm here." Richardson nodded toward the building. "It's the foreman of the construction crew supposed to be working here. Jed Norris. He was shot. Two bullets to the back of the head. But this one is easy to figure out. We have the gun. It's registered to Jordan Cochrane."

Richardson thought Faith was nuts when she insisted they take further steps to identify the body. He pointed out that there had been a driver's license on the body and that two of his co-workers, including his boss, Max Sanders, had identified the body. Norris had had no family in the city to perform the gruesome duty.

"Fingerprints," she said. They were back in Kane's apartment, and she was walking the floor, more agitated than Kane had ever seen her. "You can check his fingerprints."

Richardson grimaced. "The body's been out in the woods for a couple of days at least, and the animals have gotten to it. Getting fingerprints might not even be possible."

"You have to try. Please. He's not who you think he is."

"I have a victim," Richardson said, counting off on his fingers. "I have a murder weapon. I have a suspect. My job is to gather up all three and present the evidence to the D.A."

Softly, Faith said, "And I'm telling you that neither you nor the D.A. will ever understand why that man was killed until you know who he really was."

Richardson looked at Kane, who said, "Max says Norris worked for him only a little over a year. References were local and he knew his job, so Max never looked deeper. Maybe we'd better."

"What do you expect to find?" Richardson asked them both.

"Somebody else," Faith said.

Kane shrugged. "All I know is that the foreman of my construction crew turning up dead just as a building inspector informs me that somebody deliberately sabotaged the project sounds extremely convenient."

"How far does it put you off schedule?"

"Off schedule?" Kane laughed without amusement. "Guy, the sabotage is in the foundation, and the inspector tells me it sure as hell can't be patched. It was a subtle job but damned thorough. The whole structure is undermined. We'll have to pull it down and start over. That's *if* the project can even continue, and I don't know that it can."

Standing by the piano and staring down at the ivory keys, Faith murmured, "Want to guess who's going to get the blame?"

Kane nodded and told Richardson, "Max got me on my cell phone on the way back here, and he's already covering his ass, saying somebody obviously hired Norris to sabotage the building and then killed him to wipe out tracks. He doesn't know about your suspect yet, but his theory could still hold together.

And if it happened that way, Norris just might be more than he appears to be."

"Who would want to sabotage an office building? Why would Jordan Cochrane, for God's sake?"

"I don't know, but it has to be tied in with the rest of this, Guy. Dinah was out there at the site the day before she vanished. Cochrane's name has already turned up more than once, since he owns the warehouse where we believe Dinah was held. And so far, nearly everything we've found ties in to construction in some way. Including the names on that list." He had told Richardson about that as soon as they had arrived at Kane's apartment.

The detective sighed. "Shit. All right, I'll put the forensics team to work to get us a useable print. But, listen, I meant what I said about you staying away from the men on that list, Kane. If they are being blackmailed it's because they've done something they want to keep secret—so they'd be really pissed if you came stomping into their lives yelling about it. Are we clear on that?"

"We're clear."

"As for Cochrane, his people claim he's out of town, and has been for days, but they don't seem to know just where he is. Sounds to me like he slipped his leash, but we're checking on that. Maybe he'll have an alibi, and maybe the alibi will hold up. But it's my job to figure that out. Let me do my job, all right?"

"Just move fast, Guy." Kane's gaze was on Faith. "I don't know how much more of this we can take."

"I'll be in touch," Richardson said as he left.

When Kane returned from showing the detective out, Faith was sitting on the piano bench. Her fingers rested lightly on the keys, unmoving. He thought she looked bewildered, lost somehow.

"Who *would* want to sabotage an office building?" she asked slowly. "Who'd have something to gain?"

"I don't know. It's intended to be leased mostly by the city, but privately owned. There's a large group of investors, and they stand to lose a bundle if the project stalls too long or gets canceled outright."

She took her fingers off the keys abruptly and turned to face him. "The men on that list—are any of them investors in the project?"

"I didn't recognize any of the names—but there are a lot of investors. Wait." He got on the phone to his office, and within an hour they knew that Jordan Cochrane, through an investment company he partially owned, was in for a substantial sum in the Ludlow project.

Kane said, "It looks like so much of his personal capital is tied up in the project that if it goes bust, so will he."

Faith thought about that, then shook her head. "This doesn't make sense to me. Maybe Cochrane held Dinah captive in his warehouse. But only if he's the blackmailer instead of being blackmailed himself. Maybe he shot Jed Norris after ordering him to sabotage the building. But why? You just said he stands to lose an incredible amount if that building isn't completed on time."

"It doesn't make sense at all," Kane agreed reluctantly.

"We need to talk to him."

"We won't get a chance unless we find him before the police do."

"Do you think he really is out of town?"

"He seems to be out of touch."

Thoughtful, Faith said, "The report Tim left here after he brought me back from Haven House, the one he worked up on Cochrane—I glanced at it last night."

"And?"

Faith went over to sit on the couch and began to leaf through the pages. "I remember reading something about Cochrane that made me wonder. . . ."

Kane joined her on the couch. "What?"

"He has a condo right here in Atlanta with the ownership run through so many holding companies it's sheer luck Tim found out it was his. Now why do you suppose Mr. Cochrane feels the need for a cozy little place with its own private entrance barely five miles from that big mansion of his?"

"Keeping a mistress?" Kane guessed.

Faith sent him a quick smile. "That's what occurred to me. The information here says he's been married for nearly twenty years to a fine, upstanding Catholic woman who's on record as saying in no uncertain terms that divorce is an evil practice of the state and that those whom God hath joined together—"

"Are together forever."

"Exactly. And when she married him, she brought along a very nice little contribution to the family war chest. Something in the neighborhood of five million dollars. Add in a budding political career . . ."

"Maybe he's being blackmailed about a mistress and has to pay up in order to keep his fine upstanding wife from finding out and his political aspirations going up in smoke?"

"It seems possible, doesn't it?"

"I'd say so."

"And I'm willing to bet the police won't have this information for a while. Will Richardson be furious at us if we talk to Cochrane before he does?"

"Furious," Kane said, but in a tone that said he didn't give a damn. He was smiling.

Without thinking, Faith reached out and with the backs of her fingers stroked gently down his cheek.

Kane froze for an instant, then jerked back his head and said something violent under his breath. His eyes were hot and angry and bewildered.

Faith felt a jolt of pain. But then scenes flashed through her mind, countless moments when Dinah had touched him just that way.

"Kane, I—"

He stood up and left the room.

Faith was conscious of her heart beating quickly. She stared at her hand, at the oval nails that were polished red. She hadn't realized she was holding her breath, but now let it go in a ragged sigh.

She had forgotten. In the excitement of fitting puzzle pieces together, she had forgotten what this was really all about. She had forgotten her blank past. She had forgotten blackmail and torture and death.

She had forgotten Dinah.

Consciously, she had forgotten.

Whispering even though she was alone in the room, Faith said, "Dammit, Dinah. It's getting harder and harder to know where you end and I begin."

FIFTEEN

The bodyguard was not happy when he was ordered to stay in the car with the driver once they reached Jordan Cochrane's secret condo.

"Mr. MacGregor, you hired me to protect the two of you and I can't—"

"I know, Sam, but we can hardly take you with us into a private home and then expect the man to talk to us. Don't worry, we'll be all right."

Sam. So that's his name.

"At least take my weapon," Sam said.

"I'm armed. You stay here."

"Yes, sir," Sam replied reluctantly.

The first drops of rain fell as Faith and Kane went up the secluded walkway to the condo. Even though it was only about four o'clock, it was already getting dark.

"I didn't even know you had a gun," Faith murmured.

"I know how to use it, so you don't have to worry about that."

They were, Faith thought, being very polite. Both of them were acting as though nothing had happened between them, as though this tension didn't exist. But it did. And for an instant as Kane rang the doorbell, Faith was tempted to suggest that they leave right now, that they let the police do their jobs and find out whether Jordan Cochrane was villain or victim. But then the door was opening, and it was too late.

"Cochrane. I'd like to talk to you," Kane said.

The man in the doorway was in his forties, handsome in a dark, rather saturnine fashion, and completely unsurprised by their arrival on his doorstep.

"I see." His voice was matter-of-fact, betraying no concern or animosity.

But there was something, Faith thought, something she felt more than heard or saw. Then his gaze focused on her, and she heard Kane introduce her, saw Cochrane's polite nod.

"Come in," he said.

Kane was visibly wary as they stepped into the elegant foyer and watched Cochrane close the door behind them. He led the way to a comfortable living room where a cheerful fire burned in the fireplace. He used a dimmer switch to brighten several lamps, then invited them to sit down and offered drinks or coffee. A wineglass on the coffee table was evidence of what he'd been drinking.

Faith wasn't terribly surprised when both men remained on their feet. Echoing Kane's refusal of refreshments but a bit more politely, she sat down on the long couch where she could see both men.

Watch. Listen.

The abrupt return of the voice in her head was eerie, especially since it had been absent—except in her dreams—since she had learned of Dinah's death. But all Faith could do was obey it, settling back with a pretense of relaxation.

Cochrane said, "Would you mind telling me how you knew I was in town?"

"Lucky guess," Kane answered.

"I see. And how you found out this condo belonged to me?"

"Good research."

Cochrane's slanted brows drew together, lending him a distinctly ominous expression. "May I ask why you were researching me, Mr. MacGregor?"

Faith heard his question echoed by the faraway sound of a bell tinkling, but it was such a fleeting thing she wasn't at all sure of it.

"Because I wanted a few answers." Kane barely waited for that to sink in before going on. "Your company does own the warehouse at 281 Ivy, doesn't it?"

"Yes. But it hasn't been used in months, not since we built a new plant with adequate storage room last April."

"Then why the guard dog?"

"To protect against vandals, of course. Empty buildings are always targets, you must know that. What is this all about?"

Now.

Faith heard herself ask, "Mr. Cochrane, did you ever meet Dinah Leighton?"

"No."

He's lying.

"I don't think you're telling the truth, Mr. Cochrane."

"I can't help what you think, Miss Parker."

I came to see him. Here. October eighth.

Faith felt a chill and was surprised she was able to keep her voice steady. "Here. On the eighth of October. She came to see you, Mr. Cochrane."

Kane said, "That was two days before she disappeared."

Cochrane didn't take his eyes off Faith, and it was to her that he spoke, in the matter-of-fact tone of before. "I suppose she told you."

Had she? Faith didn't know. She just didn't know.

But what she said was, "She asked if you were being blackmailed. What did you tell her, Mr. Cochrane?"

At first it seemed he wouldn't answer, but then he shrugged, accepting something he knew he couldn't change. "I told her I had been approached by someone demanding money. I also told her it was none of her goddamned business."

"And she went away meekly?" Faith smiled slightly, aware of that ghostly bell ringing again.

Cochrane's mouth softened in an answering smile. "Hardly."

"She knew you had a mistress?"

Kane's sharp question drew Cochrane's gaze, and his reply was just as intense. "She knew I was . . . involved outside my marriage. She also knew that my wife would never consent to a divorce—and would make my life a living hell if she found out about the other woman. To say nothing of what would happen to me politically."

The bell rang again, and Faith looked around. What on earth was that?

"Was it a secret you were willing to kill to keep?" Kane demanded harshly.

"I am not a killer."

"I'm sure you told yourself that. But you had so much to lose, didn't you? And there really wasn't another way out for you, was there?"

"It wasn't like that."

"No? Then tell us how it was."

Faith heard Kane's accusations and Cochrane's quiet denials, but she had also heard that bell again. She shifted on the couch, to get a better angle to see more of the room, and as her hand rested over the edges of two cushions she felt something.

It was caught between the cushions, out of sight, but her fingers found it and pulled it out. A tiny silver bell.

Faith stared at it, holding it in such a way that if the men looked at her they would think she was intently studying her fingernails. A tiny silver bell. A tiny silver charm she suddenly remembered having seen before.

Did you know about this, Dinah? Or am I the one who knew somehow?

The dead didn't answer, so Faith said to the living, "What did Dinah want of you, Mr. Cochrane?"

He turned his head quickly to look at her, seeming relieved to face her rather than Kane. "She said she was working on a story, that she suspected other prominent men in Atlanta were being blackmailed. She wanted to know if I'd be willing to come forward when the story broke, to go to the police."

"You told her no."

"I told her I handled my own problems."

"And did you? Handle it?"

"I thought I had."

Faith didn't have to listen to the voice in her head now. "You refused to pay, didn't you? Refused to pay them and told them to go to hell. You were the first not to give in to them. To be willing to see your secret exposed rather than pay hush money."

"The . . . lady involved found out about the threats and agreed I couldn't bow to blackmail. We both knew it would never end, that I'd be bled until I stood up to them. So, yes, I refused to pay. And they backed down. Or so I thought. There were no more demands for money, and my wife never received that envelope of incriminating photographs they'd promised."

"But?" Faith watched him steadily.

"But . . . we began having problems out at the new plant. Mechanical breakdowns, tardy deliveries, mistakes in orders. It looked like sabotage, but there was never enough evidence to point to a culprit. And then problems began cropping up in our other divisions, the same sort of delaying, destructive tactics."

"You were being punished."

"So it seemed. I realized these faceless enemies were out to destroy me, and that I was helpless to stop them."

"You could have paid," Faith noted.

"No," Cochrane said. "I couldn't have done that."

"You could have gone public about the affair, taken that weapon out of their hands and taken your chances politically. Extramarital affairs aren't the political death knell they once were."

"True enough. I could have. The lady was willing, and I was ready to accept the consequences. But they had shown their hand. They meant to destroy me, piece by piece. If I took one weapon out of their hands, they would have found others. Another secret, some stupid mistake I'd made somewhere along the way." Cochrane smiled wryly. "I haven't led a particularly blameless life, Miss Parker. And I have no desire to watch all my mistakes exposed one by one."

"Then what can you do?"

"I'll fight them. Fight their tactics, hold my own until I discover who they are. I may lose. But I won't go down without a fight."

"I see."

Cochrane looked at Kane. "By the time I realized the scope of my problem, Miss Leighton had been missing for several weeks. I hope you believe me when I say that if I'd thought I could help the police find her, I would have come forward."

Before Kane could respond, the sliding doors of the connecting study opened, and a new voice spoke quietly.

"And so would I."

Kane was stunned, and Faith looked at him with sympathy, then stretched out her open hand, the charm lying on the palm.

"I think this came off your bracelet, Sydney."

· · ·

Kane's discomfort was obvious, and even though neither Cochrane nor Sydney seemed to bear him any malice, the next few minutes were very strained. It was left to Faith to keep the discussion going.

"You're absolutely sure you have no clue as to who is trying to ruin you?" she said to Cochrane.

"I've racked my brains." He sat beside Sydney at the other end of the long couch. "The problem is, I have plenty of enemies. I just can't settle on anyone with a grudge big enough to drive them to blackmail and sabotage. Unless it's purely money, of course, and I was chosen because I had a point of vulnerability and the means to make blackmail worth the risk."

"You've got bigger problems than that," she told him after a glance at Kane. "Do you know a man named Jed Norris?"

"No, I don't think so. Why?"

Kane asked, "Do you own a handgun, a .45 automatic?"

"I own several, including two .45s. Why?"

"Because," Faith said, "the body of a man identified as Jed Norris was found this morning. Murdered, execution-style, shot in the head. A gun registered to you was found nearby. And it is the murder weapon."

"Oh, my God," Sydney murmured.

Cochrane reached for her hand and held it. He was a little pale, but composed. "Setting aside that I would hardly be stupid enough to use a gun registered to me in a crime and then leave it at the scene, the last time I can swear all my guns were in the case was months ago. Someone must have stolen one of them."

"The case isn't locked?" Kane asked.

"Of course, but it's hardly more than a childproof lock, a simple precaution. There is a security system, but it's active only at night."

"Who has access during the day?"

"To the room? Quite a few people. The house-keeping staff. My wife's secretary, my own assistant. And my wife has held two charity functions in the house or on the grounds in the last three months. The place has been crawling with people at various times." He paused. "Who was this man apparently killed with my gun?"

Sydney said almost inaudibly, "He was off some-where, Max said, just AWOL because they weren't working. . . ."

Kane looked at Cochrane. "Norris was the con-struction foreman on the Ludlow project. The crew wasn't working this week because there was a prob-lem. Today, I discovered the site has been sabotaged."

"How badly?"

"It's bad enough. Somebody who knew how to do it undermined the foundation. The inspector says it can't be patched. Which means we pull it down and start all over—or cancel the project."

"That," Cochrane said without emotion, "would be the final nail in my financial coffin."

"Maybe that's the idea," Kane said. "Put your back against the wall financially so that taking any action other than paying them would mean total ruin."

"If so," Cochrane said, "it's a smart plan. Too

many of my business interests are largely dependent on my wife's money, and she wouldn't hesitate to sell out her interests to get back at me—no matter how many people were put out of work because of it."

"In the meantime," Faith said, "the police are probably trying to find a motive for you to have killed Norris. They'll want to know where you've been. People at your office and home—"

"Said I was out of town. Yes, it's what I told them to say." Cochrane looked at Sydney. "We hadn't had much time together these last weeks, so I invented a business trip. I've been here at the condo since Sunday night."

"So have I," Sydney said instantly.

"Not all the time," he said, his voice astonishingly gentle and his smile too tender for onlookers. "You've been at the office during the day, Syd."

Her mouth firmed stubbornly. "I slipped out a lot and came here to be with you. Got in late at the office, took long lunches, and left early every day. You know I did."

Cochrane smiled at her again, then said to Kane, "When was this man killed? Do they know?"

"The police say the body's been . . . exposed to the elements . . . for at least a couple of days. My guess is that they won't be able to pinpoint the exact time of death."

"Then I have no verifiable alibi," Cochrane said calmly.

"Jordan—"

"No one was witness to my movements all the time, Syd. It won't help me for you to say you were with me some of the time, and it could only hurt you for no good reason. Don't worry. I had no reason to kill this man."

Faith said, "Somebody's already suggested Norris was hired to sabotage the building, then killed to cover it up. I don't see how you could benefit if the construction is stopped."

"I couldn't. I have a lot of personal money tied up in that project, and the investment only pays off once it's completed and generating income." Cochrane frowned suddenly and looked at Kane. "Why did you ask about the warehouse? What has that to do with any of this?"

Kane's gaze dropped to his clasped hands. "We have . . . reason to believe that warehouse is where Dinah was held at least part of the time she was missing."

"Kane, no." Sydney was staring at him. "Jordan had nothing to do with that. Not Dinah's disappearance or—or her murder."

Faith said, "My guess is that it was yet another way his enemies thought they could chip away at what mattered in his life. Mr. Cochrane, you said the blackmailers threatened to send photographs to your wife?"

"Yes."

"Then they knew it was Sydney you were involved with."

"Yes."

"What better way to drive a stake into the heart of that relationship than to have you suspected of having tortured and murdered her brother's fiancée?"

"I would never have believed that," Sydney said fiercely.

Faith wasn't surprised by the loyalty, having watched them together. But she said, "It wouldn't have been pleasant, though. And for all we know, the real killers might have evidence they mean to plant against him. At the very least, by holding Dinah in the Cochrane warehouse, they've managed to involve him."

"Assuming the police discover that," Kane reminded her.

"Oh, I imagine they'll be led to discover it. Unless we can figure out the truth before then." Faith spoke absently, her mind fully occupied in trying to do just that. She reached into the pocket of her jacket and brought out a copy of the list they had found. "Take a look at these names, Mr. Cochrane. They're the men Dinah suspected were being blackmailed. Do any of the other names mean anything to you?"

He stared down at the list. "Mason is dead, suicide. Carson . . . Hayes . . . Swain . . . Gordon . . ."

"We know they're all involved in construction in some form," Kane said. "Is there anything else you know of that these five men have—or had—in common with you?"

Cochrane looked up, a sudden realization on his grim face. "Just one thing. I wouldn't know in the ordinary way because he's so damned discreet, but I accidentally saw some files in his office one day. Conrad Masterson. We all use him to manage our personal money."

In the darkness of the sedan's backseat, Faith said, "If Dinah had shown the list to Cochrane . . . she might not be dead. She would have known to be wary of Masterson."

"Conrad. Jesus." Kane was still coping with the shock.

"Only someone who thoroughly understood Jordan Cochrane's financial situation could know where and how to strike at him. That makes sense, doesn't it?"

"Yes, but—" With barely suppressed anger, Kane said, "I can't believe Conrad would have hurt Dinah. I always thought he was the least violent man I'd ever met in my life."

"Maybe he didn't. We've always known there was more than one person involved in this. Maybe Conrad works for or with whoever killed Dinah. Or maybe it's just a huge coincidence." She watched his profile, visible only now and again in the streetlights they passed. "Look, we've done all we can tonight. Richardson was right—we have to let him talk to the other men and find out if they can point to Conrad."

She forced a note of humor into her voice. "In fact, we're lucky he didn't throw us both in jail after we told him about finding Cochrane—and all the other bits and pieces we'd kept to ourselves."

The hour or so in Richardson's office had not been easy, but Faith was still glad she had been able to persuade Kane to go that route rather than follow his first instinct—to find Conrad Masterson. Of course, it had helped her cause when a couple of phone calls had found Masterson neither at his home nor his office, and so temporarily out of Kane's reach.

"He'll get over it," Kane said, referring to Richardson. "And sooner rather than later if the information we gave him helps him solve a few crimes."

From the front seat, the bodyguard said, "You folks still want to go by your office, Mr. MacGregor?"

"I know it's getting late, Sam, but—"

"Don't mind me or Steve here," the bodyguard said with a faint gesture toward the driver. "We get time and a half."

"The office it is, then." Kane lowered his voice and said to Faith, "Are you sure you don't mind? I want to pick up the master blueprints for the Ludlow building and see if I can figure out a way to salvage that situation."

"No problem." She knew very well that he'd go crazy unless he had something to fix his mind on while the police plodded along trying to gather evidence. "Cochrane will certainly thank you if you can—if the police don't arrest him for Norris's murder."

"Guy didn't seem too keen to do that just yet," Kane reminded her. "Aside from having no believable motive, he agreed Cochrane would be too smart to use his own gun and drop it at the scene after wiping all the prints off."

"I wish they'd get that report on Norris's fingerprints," Faith said restlessly. "It's important, Kane, I know it is."

"Probably tomorrow, Guy said. He's checking the system for a match *and* sent them up to Noah for good measure. Assuming Noah's at Quantico. One of them will call us as soon as anything turns up."

Faith nodded, but she still felt uneasy. If Norris *had* been involved, why was he dead now? Had Conrad

Masterson killed him? Was Masterson even guilty of anything? And *what* was the thing Dinah was tortured for? Dammit, they still didn't know!

The storm had passed hours ago, but it was still a cold and wet and miserable night to be out. Even so, the driver circled the offices of MacGregor and Payne out of caution, and both he and Sam were alert as the car pulled into the underground garage.

It was mostly empty, and as safe as electronic security and surveillance cameras could make it, so Faith wasn't worried as she, Kane, and Sam rode up in the elevator to the fifth floor, where Kane's office was located.

There was a security guard stationed in the reception area, as there was on every floor, and he reported to Kane that everybody had logged out and all was secure.

"I'll be right back," Kane said, digging for his keys as he headed for his office.

"I'll be here," Faith said. She began wandering along the hallway looking at photographs and paintings of past MacGregor and Payne projects.

Sam leaned against the desk to chat with the guard, one security person to another. "Nice setup," he noted.

"Yeah, cost a fortune. This place is about as secure as technology can make it." Nodding toward Faith as she strolled away, the guard indicated a bank of monitors that showed views of several hallways. "I can track anybody all through the building. Beats me why they're so hot to protect a bunch of offices, but I get paid to watch, not wonder."

"I hear that." Sam looked down the corridor to

find Faith as she neared another hallway, then looked at the monitors. "Which one's she headed for?"

The guard pointed to a screen. "There. Don't worry. You can see everything's fine."

Kane was just turning to leave his office when his private line rang, and he answered it. "MacGregor."

"Where the hell's your cell phone?" Bishop demanded in lieu of a more polite greeting.

Surprised by the ferocity, Kane said, "In my pocket, but the battery's probably dead. It's been a long day. What's up?"

"Where's Faith?"

"With me. Noah, what is it?"

"Richardson said you were planning to stop by the office, so I took a chance. Those prints he sent up here?"

"Yeah?"

"Belonged to one Jedidiah Sanderson."

"Then Faith was right. It wasn't Jed Norris."

"Let's say rather that Jed Norris wasn't who he appeared to be. Sanderson's prints are on file because he had a record. A few arrests, mostly strong-arm stuff, and going back years. But not in Atlanta."

Kane drew a breath. "Seattle."

"Seattle."

"Then he's the connection we've been looking for?"

"Sanderson was Faith's boss, Kane. He ran that construction company she worked at, took over when the younger brother who started it was suppos-

dly killed in a fire. Didn't do too well with it. He
declared bankruptcy not long after Faith's family was
killed, and blew town before anybody could stop
him."

"And came to Atlanta. Okay, but I still don't
see—"

"When I dug into the fire that killed his younger
brother, I found an arson investigator who was certain but couldn't prove the fire had been started deliberately. The insurance money was paid, and it was a
lot. But Sanderson never seemed to have any money
afterward, just a company he couldn't keep in the
black. I started wondering where the money went. I
found a photograph of the younger brother and sent
it to Richardson. He recognized it right away. Kane—
it's Max Sanders."

"Max." Kane felt curiously suspended, caught
between a moment of realization and one of dawning
fear.

"Yeah. I have a hunch the younger brother was
the corpse Dinah was about to start looking for. She
was probably looking at the Seattle end a lot more
closely than we've been, and she was suspicious of
that fire and the insurance money. I don't know
how close she was to the answers, whether she suspected Sanders or was just looking for a connection
to Seattle and somehow alerted him. We may never
know."

"Christ."

"And correct me if I'm wrong, but doesn't Max
Sanders have a key to the gate at the job site? And
official clearance to get into your office building so he
can roam wherever he damn well wants?"

Kane swung around to stare at the open door of his office. The fear was clawing at him now. "Jesus."

"Kane—"

But Kane dropped the phone, the rolled blueprints, and bolted for the door. He reached the hall just as Sam charged past with a worried look on his face. As Kane joined him, he barely took in the bodyguard's hurried explanation that Faith "should have been visible on the hallway monitor by now."

They turned the corner together, seeing a long corridor stretching before them. And Faith's shoulder bag lying on the floor beside the emergency exit that led to the stairwell.

"A mirror," Sam was saying bitterly, staring up at one of the video cameras. "He used a fucking mirror!"

Kane bent to pick up Faith's bag, feeling as though something was dragging at him, slowing him down when he needed to be moving fast, so fast, because they had her and the thought of what they'd do to her ripped at his sanity.

"No," he said clearly. "Not again."

SIXTEEN

Whatever he'd used to knock her out—chloroform, she supposed—Faith hoped it hadn't kept her unconscious for long. She couldn't be certain since there was no clock in the room where she awoke.

It was a powder room. Pedestal sink, toilet, not much else.

Head pounding and nausea churning, Faith got her hands underneath her to push herself up off the cold tile floor, and only then realized she was handcuffed. She managed to sit up, but it was a long while before the dizziness passed enough for her to struggle to her feet.

She tried the door, which was locked, then decided to splash cold water on her face to wash the cobwebs from her mind.

Afterward, she almost wished she hadn't, because with clarity of mind came terror.

She hadn't seen who had grabbed her; it had all

happened too fast. But she had no doubt she was in deadly danger. The fact that he had knocked her out rather than killed her told her he wanted something from her. He wanted whatever it was she had taken from him, the elusive thing still lost somewhere in the darkness of her mind.

She would be tortured. Like Dinah.

Faith wanted to pound on the door, to scream and scream, and it took all her strength to keep herself from doing just that.

Don't be an idiot. And don't expect the cavalry to come riding to the rescue, either. That only happens in the movies. If you want to live through this, you'll have to help yourself.

Faith pressed her ear to the door but heard nothing.

Move, just move. Look for something that might help you get free, get out of here.

There was no medicine cabinet or linen closet, and not even a picture on the walls to offer her a bit of useful wire.

Remembering suddenly, she worked her cuffed hands around until she was able to dig into the right pocket of her jacket. It was there, a thin, flexible piece of metal.

A lock pick.

It felt familiar in her grasp, and her fingers moved with swift, sure skill that required no thought. Within seconds she was free.

For a fleeting moment, Faith wondered where on earth she had learned such a thing, and why, but there would be time enough later to ponder that.

She hoped.

The locked door was more stubborn than the handcuffs, but she kept working at it.

If this damned thing would stop slipping, I could—There!

She returned the lock pick to her pocket and carefully eased open the door.

She was facing a fairly long hallway that was a solid wall on the other side and on her side boasted only one other room, its open door spilling light. At the end, she thought she could make out stairs leading upward.

She was in a basement.

She heard the voices. There were two of them, angry male voices that were a bit muffled. They came from the other room.

Her first impulse was to run as fast as she could, her instincts urging her to race from danger, to flee while she had the chance. But intellect prevailed. She stood a better chance of escaping if she moved cautiously and silently to slip past that open door unnoticed by the men inside.

Hardly breathing, keeping close to the wall and moving with utmost care, Faith eased down the hall toward the lighted doorway. As she neared it, the voices became distinct.

". . . You must have been out of your mind to hang around MacGregor and Payne all day!"

There was something familiar about that voice, but before she could probe her memory to identify it, the second man spoke.

"At least I was doing something useful! I wasn't hiding in my nice little lake house praying no one would find me!"

A coldness deeper than anything Faith had ever felt

before washed over her, and the dizziness returned far worse than before, forcing her to lean against the wall and close her eyes, to swallow the sick terror welling up from a dark nightmare place inside her.

She remembered the voice from her painfully violent vision: *Careful! She can't tell me what I want to know if she's dead.*

Faith heard her breath catch, and the tiny sound was just enough to free her from the paralysis of sheer terror. It was him. The man who had lurked in the darkness as Dinah was being tortured, who had ordered the one hurting her to break her fingers or something else, anything else, whatever he had to do to make her talk . . .

And she had sat in Kane's office with him without recognizing his voice, without realizing that Dinah's tormentor was talking briskly to Kane about structure and construction materials. Max Sanders.

The need to run was overwhelming, but Faith forced herself to move slowly, one step at a time, down the hall. As she crept nearer, the voices grew louder, more distinct.

"I've told you—you're moving too fast, allowing Kane and the police to panic you. If you'd just been willing to sit tight, to keep your mouth shut—"

"I'm not the one who killed Jed, goddammit! What was that if it wasn't panic?"

"It was our only option! It has to look like *he* was the one blackmailing Cochrane, and that Cochrane found out and killed him. That's the only way we'll distract the police *and* Kane. Once I finish planting evidence for the police to find, it'll be crystal clear that Jed was the blackmailer. Dinah found out somehow, and he kidnapped and killed her—in one of Cochrane's warehouses—intending to pin the blame on Cochrane."

"He was my brother!"

"He was a fuck-up and we both know it!"

Brother? Jed and Max were brothers?

There was a moment of tense silence inside the room, and Faith edged closer. Were they facing away from the door? Could she slip past without being seen?

"I had to take the heat off us, Max. You'd done a damned fine job of stirring everybody up until we could hardly breathe, until it was only a matter of time before Kane or one of his bloodhounds figured it all out."

"So I took a chance with the pipe bomb, so what? What was I supposed to do after she hooked up with Kane—ignore it? Sit around like you wanted to, Connie, and wait to see if she got her memory back and spilled everything to Kane?"

Connie. Oh, God . . . it is *Conrad.* That realization stabbed through Faith; she knew how this would hurt Kane.

"You could have waited! For Christ's sake, Max, even an idiot could have realized that every time you went after her and failed, you gave them more reason to look for answers—and more time."

"Look—"

"No, *you* look. I had to scramble to find evidence to make the story hang together and point away from us. Jed had to be sacrificed. It would have worked, Max. But then you had to blunder in once again, grab the girl from under Kane's nose. And if you don't think he's turning Atlanta upside down right this minute looking for her—"

"So what? He didn't find Dinah, did he?"

"You're a fool," Conrad said.

Faith risked a quick glance into the room and felt her heart sink. They were facing each other no more than a few feet inside the door, and chances were very good that both men would see her if she darted past.

"I just want the box back, Connie, that's all."

"If she remembered where she'd put it or knew where Dinah put it after that accident, don't you think it would be in the hands of the police by now?"

"She'll remember quick enough once I get my hands on her. She'll talk then."

"Oh? The way Dinah talked?"

"Surely you don't think this one will be that tough? She's no bigger than a minute, and it's easy to see she'd jump out of her skin if anybody yelled boo."

"She survived that car accident, didn't she? She came out of a coma when she should have ended up a vegetable. I wouldn't underestimate her if I were you."

"She'll talk," Max repeated stubbornly. "We'll get the box, and then we'll be safe. If you think it's necessary, we can plant the box so it looks like Jed had it— all that clear evidence of blackmail. He gets the blame for that, Cochrane gets the blame for killing him, and we lay low for a few months."

"And what about Faith Parker? They'll know *exactly* when she disappeared, Max, and you told me yourself Cochrane's still at the police station being questioned. He has an alibi for the time she vanished."

"You can fix it so it looks like he hired somebody," Max said, impatient. "You've always been able to fix things, Connie, ever since we were kids back in Seattle. Should be easy enough."

Conrad swore viciously. "Easy? Do you realize how many rabbits I've already pulled out of my hat for you? Christ, if you'd just killed her in Seattle or, better yet, hadn't been careless enough to leave that envelope in the office where she was bound to see it—"

"How was I to know Jed had hired a secretary with too much curiosity for her own good? Once she saw the note from me to him it was only a matter of time before she figured out the insurance scam. I had to get rid of her."

"But you didn't get rid of her, did you? You didn't even make sure what she looked like, killed the sister instead and the mother with her."

"Look, never mind all that, it's water under the bridge. I've got her now, and I don't intend to stop until she's told me where that goddamned box is."

You hid it in the only place you felt really safe. That's why I couldn't tell him. He wouldn't have been able to get into Haven House, and so he would have burned it down to destroy the evidence. They would have been killed, all of them. Karen and Eve, Andrea and little Katie. I couldn't let that happen. . . .

Faith closed her eyes briefly, then opened them and tried to figure out her options. She had to get past the open door and the men inside the room . . . and she had to get out of this house. Unaware of where the windows and doors were, she was bound to make mistakes, especially if she was running.

But what choice did she have? She risked another

look into the room. Conrad had turned toward a desk against the far wall, and Faith could have laughed aloud when Max turned in the same direction. Both their backs were now to the door.

Now or never.

Holding her breath, Faith slipped quickly and silently past the doorway.

"If you're determined to be stupid, at least don't be insane," Conrad was saying angrily. "To bring her here! There's no way I'll allow you—"

"I didn't know if you wanted another body pinned on Cochrane, so . . ."

Faith reached the foot of the stairs and went up them swiftly. From what had been said in that room, she gathered she was at Conrad's lakeside vacation home somewhere outside the city. Which meant she had no idea where she was.

Away. Just get away. Worry about where you are later.

At the top of the stairs she found herself in a small hallway, which led to a dining room and a kitchen, where there appeared to be an exterior door. At the end of the hall was a living room, with another staircase going up.

Don't go up. The nitwits in the movies always climb the stairs, and how they expect to get off the roof when someone's chasing them—

"I know," Faith whispered. She continued to move carefully, desperate to make certain no squeaking floorboard betrayed her to the men below. The front door, she thought, was probably near the living room, but this door out of the kitchen was closer.

As soon as she opened it, Faith detected the unmistakable odors of a garage. A closed garage. And garage doors were very noisy when they opened.

She swore inwardly and drew back into the kitchen, just as she heard heavy, quick footsteps on the basement stairs and Max swearing grimly.

With no time to do anything else, Faith slipped through the door into the garage, closing it silently behind her.

He's very good at playing cat and mouse. Don't hide. Get away.

The garage was dark; Faith had to feel her way. Moving as fast as she dared, she nearly fell over the hood of a sports car. Were the keys in it? She tried the doors but they were locked.

Growing accustomed to the darkness now, she made out the garage door, which was closed, and two windows, which were high up and also closed. Nothing to stand on.

Was there an automatic door opener? She peered up at the tracks above the car and made out the box. So there would be a remote in the car, most likely, and one by the door to the kitchen.

She felt her way back to the door, fear growing, horribly aware of the minutes ticking away. She heard the voices inside rise in a violent argument, heard them get louder as Max and Conrad came in her direction, and then a deafening gunshot.

Terrified, Faith punched the panel of the garage-door opener. Instantly, the garage was filled with bright light, and the big door began to move up laboriously and loudly.

Nearly blinded, Faith lunged for the garage door and ducked under it just as the kitchen door opened and she heard a curse behind her.

She ran.

It was dark and cold and wet; the rain must have stopped only recently, because water dripped everywhere. The drive was narrow, hardly more than two rutted tracks, and treacherous because of the mud. The woods pressed in toward her on both sides; she had no idea in which direction the lake lay.

She ran.

All she could hear was her heart thundering, her breath rasping in her throat, but Faith was certain he was behind her, gaining on her. Maybe he'd be in the car, maybe he was on foot, but he was behind her, she knew that. More than once she slipped, but miraculously kept her footing well enough to continue moving forward, away from the house.

Something loomed up out of the darkness ahead of her, reaching for her, and for an instant of sheer terror Faith thought one of them had circled around and gotten ahead of her.

"Faith. Jesus, Faith—"

She found herself caught tightly in Kane's arms, so tightly she wasn't sure if it was her heart or his pounding so wildly, and gasped, "Behind me. He's behind me—"

And then everything happened very, very fast. Kane swung her around so that his large body shielded hers. She heard an engine roar, and bright lights stabbed suddenly through the darkness, pinning her and Kane in the stark glare. She heard the sounds of tires spinning wildly on slippery ground, saw headlights coming drunkenly at them, and then the engine screaming louder, and she saw Kane's arm stretch out, saw something gleaming in his hand.

His first shot made glass shatter, and then there were other guns, other shots, and he was moving, carrying her away from danger as the car careened off the drive and plowed into the trees with a sickening crunch of metal.

The engine screamed again, then gurgled and died.

"It has to be later than midnight," Faith said. "It just has to be. This has been the longest day of my life."

"I wish you'd let me call a doctor," Kane said.

"You heard the EMS medic. I'm fine. No injuries, no shock, not even aftereffects of the chloroform." Faith curled up in the big chair before the fire Kane had lit while she'd been in the shower, and watched him as he stood gazing at the flames.

"Still," he said. "Like you said, it's been a very long day."

"And I should be exhausted. But I'm not." She paused, aware of his silence and the tension between them. "Did you say Bishop was flying down in the morning?"

"Yeah. He would have come tonight, but we were able to find you fairly quickly. Guy already had the information on Conrad's lake house, and I couldn't think of any other place he'd go, so . . ."

"The cops were shooting too, Kane. It might not have been your bullet that killed Max Sanders."

He turned his head and looked at her. "I hope it was mine."

"Revenge?"

"Justice. Now he'll be rotting in the ground."

She drew a breath. "What about Conrad? They say he might pull through."

"I hope he does," Kane said calmly. "I want him in prison. I want him to spend the rest of his life in a small, bare cell."

"He probably will. Once Richardson sorts through their blackmail box, he's bound to find Conrad's prints on the photographs and papers. He and Max wouldn't have been so desperate to get the box back if they hadn't been positive what was in it could convict them."

Kane shook his head. "All this time, the box was hidden in Haven House."

"The only place I felt really safe," Faith murmured. "I'm sorry, Kane. Sorry I dragged Dinah into this, sorry I didn't tell her that I'd found the box snooping in Conrad's office because I'd seen Max go in there. I'm sorry it's taken me so long to remember."

"Do you remember everything now?"

It was her turn to shake her head. "No, just bits and pieces. But it's a beginning. I guess Dr. Burnett was right—it'll all come back eventually."

Kane returned his gaze to the fire and was silent.

"Now that the story has an ending of sorts," Faith said, "I guess we won't have to worry about reporters following us around."

"It isn't over yet. I still have to arrange a memorial service."

"I . . . heard Richardson tell you they'd have the autopsy results in the morning. Then they'll release her body?"

"Yes."

Faith felt a dull ache. Well, what else had she expected? He'd said himself that no one would ever be able to take Dinah's place. And now that it was over, now that he had his puzzle virtually put together and she had the satisfaction of knowing the murderer of her mother and sister was dead, they would go on with their lives.

Their separate lives.

Faith looked down at the floor. Why had she even gotten dressed after her shower and come in here? Why hadn't she just gone to bed and left him alone? He obviously wanted to be alone. "I guess . . . now that the danger is past, I can go . . . home. Back to my apartment."

"I don't want you to go," he said.

She felt her heart skip a beat, but kept her gaze determinedly down. "I know I just moved into your life for a week, and I want you to know I'm grateful. I would have been so frightened on my own, and probably dead by now—"

"I don't want you to go," he repeated slowly.

She had to look up then, and met his gaze with a sensation of being stripped naked of more than her clothing.

Even more slowly, in a tone of realization and reluctance and acceptance, he said, "I . . . don't . . . want you to go."

Don't question. Not yet. Not now.

Faith was on her feet before she realized she was going to move, and he was turning toward her, putting his hands on her shoulders.

"I didn't plan this," she said.

"I know. Neither did I."

"I . . . I'm not . . . I couldn't stay if it was only because—"

"It isn't."

Faith pulled breath into lungs starving for air. "Are you sure? It's only her red polish, her earrings, but I'm not—"

Kane lowered his head and covered her mouth with his.

She heard a broken sound, and realized it came from her, from deep inside where something had let go. She felt the hardness of his body against hers, felt her fingers slide into his hair and her mouth come alive beneath his, and there was something so familiar and intimate and wildly arousing in his touch, his kiss, the strength of his arms around her, that she wanted to cling to him with all her might, all her will.

"You'll stay," he muttered against her lips.

"Yes."

He raised his head and stared down at her, gray eyes molten. He framed her face with his hands, and she could feel them shaking.

Fierce, he said, "I won't be so careful this time, do you understand? I won't bite back what I want to say because I'm afraid it isn't what you want to hear. I won't stop myself from touching you because I'm not sure you want to be touched. And most of all, I won't let you shut me out of the parts of your life that *matter* to you."

Faith reached up to touch his face. "I love you."

He caught his breath, then kissed her again, his mouth hard now, insistent. He lifted her, carried her from the living room to the bedroom.

She was hardly aware of being set on her feet beside the bed, of helping him pull off her sweater and slide the pants down her legs. She was unbuttoning his shirt, tugging it from his pants, and gasped when his hands pushed aside her bra and held her breasts.

Her hands fumbled, but she managed to push his shirt off his shoulders, unfasten his pants. She touched him and heard his indrawn breath, felt the wildly spiraling tension inside both of them wind even tighter. Touching him was necessary; it fed the starving need inside her.

"Ah, God," he muttered, hoarse and desperate.

They were on the bed somehow, the covers thrown away, pillows scattered. The lamplight let them see, but their hands saw more, moving everywhere, shaping and fondling and caressing. Lips never more than a whisper apart. Bodies straining to be closer, to merge, to meld.

He felt so right to Faith. So right touching her. So right inside her, filling an emptiness she hadn't known was there, claiming that part of her for himself.

"I love you," she whispered, and knew she always had.

SEVENTEEN

"So I guess it's all over now," Dinah said.

"I guess so."

"Puzzle completed, treasure found. Bad guys vanquished."

"You might have been more help," Faith accused.

Dinah smiled. "It had to happen the way it happened. Things do, you know. So don't feel bad."

"About Kane?"

"You love him. I wanted to, but . . . I couldn't, not the way he deserved."

Faith was surprised. "Why not?"

"Because I knew what was going to happen to me. I'd known for a long time."

"Couldn't you change it?"

"No. Like I said. Things have to happen the way they happen. And there was you. I knew as soon as we met that you'd play a part in all of it. I just didn't know how."

"It's my fault, what happened. I'm sorry."

"I'm not."

Faith was surprised. "No? But—"

"When you come to the end, you understand what's really important." Dinah looked at her intently. "You understand."

"But all the pain. The fear. I'm sorry you had to go through that."

"As I said, things have to happen the way they do."

"But I'm sorry you died."

Dinah seemed to hesitate, then said, "Something always has to die so that something else can live. You do understand that, don't you?"

Faith began to feel uneasy. "Yes, but . . . I remember now, you said once you found the MacGuffin, you wouldn't be dead anymore."

"Yes, that's what I said."

"But—"

"I'm not dead, Faith. I never have been, not really. You're the one who's dead."

Faith stared at her, at the odd little smile, the compassionate blue eyes. She reached out instinctively, and froze when Dinah reached out as well. After a moment, Faith forced herself to go on, to stretch her hand slowly toward Dinah's.

When their fingers touched, she felt the cool, smooth surface of a mirror.

Faith opened her eyes and stared at the ceiling. She was wide awake, so wide awake that she felt as if she'd never sleep again. Slowly, she turned her head on the pillow and looked at Kane. He slept with the absolute stillness of utter exhaustion, muscles totally relaxed. It was no wonder. This was probably the first decent night's sleep he'd been granted in weeks.

And, of course, they had made love until nearly dawn, again and again, unable to get enough of each other. She thought he had memorized the texture of her skin, and she was certain she would always know him, forever, even in total darkness.

Carefully, she eased out from under his arm and sat up on the side of the bed. The clock on the night-stand said it was just after eight-thirty.

She made sure he was covered and still sleeping deeply, then gathered her things and slipped from the bedroom. She took a shower, allowing the hot water to ease the ache of muscles unaccustomed to love-making, to all the unusual exertions of the day before, then dressed and went to the kitchen.

His special blend of coffee. She stared at the bag for a moment, then dumped an approximate amount into the filter, poured water into the top chamber, and waited for it to drip through to the pot below.

When it was ready, she fixed a cup with her cus-tomary load of cream and sugar, then carried it into the living room. She looked at her bare wrist, then grimaced slightly. No watch, ever, because they never wanted to keep running for her. Somebody had told her once that it was the magnetic or electrical field of her body. Faith's body.

The clock on the VCR said quarter after nine. She picked up the phone and called the hospital, asking them to page Dr. Burnett for her. He was there, of course. Even early on Saturday, he was there.

"Faith, is anything wrong?" His voice held a bit of an edge and it took her a moment to remember their last meeting.

"There's something I need to ask you," she replied, sweeping his anger aside.

"What is it?"

"Before I came out of the coma, did you believe I would?"

"Faith, I told you how unusual—"

"You know what I'm asking you."

He was silent for several moments, but her patient waiting seemed to drive him to answer finally. "There are certain criteria we use to determine patient viability. Certain minimum levels of brain activity, for instance—"

"Was I below those minimum levels?"

"Faith, there's no absolute in medicine."

"Was I below the minimum levels?" she repeated steadily. "Was I considered a viable patient with a future?"

"No," he said, then hurried on. "But there was a flicker of brain activity, and I'd told Miss Leighton on her last visit that there was always a chance. I'd seen some remarkable things . . . and you were breathing on your own, so of course there was no question of—of—"

"Nobody was going to unplug anything?" Faith finished, her voice shaky now.

"No, of course not. And Miss Leighton refused to give up hope. She was very upset when she left that last day, but still determined. I've never seen anyone so determined to save another person. If strength of will could have done it, you would have awakened that day. As it was, only a couple of weeks passed before you did." He paused. "It's a shame she never knew she was right."

"Yes. A shame. Thank you, Dr. Burnett."

"Faith . . . about what happened the other day—"

"Don't worry about it," she said. "We were all a little touchy that day." She cradled the receiver gently.

After a moment, she got up and carried her coffee to the piano. She sat on the bench and flexed her fingers, looking at them with a little frown. Then she touched the keys tentatively, one here, one there, not a recognizable tune.

The buzzer sent her quickly to answer the intercom so that the sound wouldn't disturb Kane, and a few minutes later she opened the door to admit Bishop.

"I didn't think you'd be so early," she said. "Kane's still asleep, and I'd rather not wake him."

Bishop eyed her thoughtfully and smiled. "I see."

Faith uttered a soft laugh. "This time, I doubt it. But never mind. There's coffee—mine, I'm afraid, but help yourself or make a fresh pot, whatever suits you."

Bishop watched her retreat to the piano, his smile fading and brows drawing together. "I stopped by the station on my way here," he said, coming farther into the room. "Richardson filled me in. He also . . . showed me the results of Dinah's autopsy. Nothing really unexpected. Except—"

"Except time of death," Faith said, pressing a key gently with one finger.

Bishop came to the piano and stared down at her. "Yes."

"She hadn't been dead a few days. She'd been dead a few weeks. About . . . four weeks."

Slowly, Bishop said, "The coldness of that bomb shelter, the lack of air and humidity—all slowed the rate of decomposition, made it appear she'd died recently. But the autopsy proved otherwise. The M.E. wasn't willing to estimate closer than three to six weeks."

"Four," she said softly. "Just about four."

"Faith—"

"You know, it's the strangest thing." She placed all ten fingers on the ivory keys, then looked up at him. "Just a few days ago, I could do it, but now . . . I've forgotten how to play the piano."

Bishop gazed at her silently.

"Isn't that strange? And isn't it strange how I was able to pick those locks last night, when a few days ago I didn't even know that was a lock pick in the pocket of the jacket? Isn't it strange that I keep looking at my wrist as if I should be wearing a watch, when I know I've never been able to? Why I keep using my right hand instead of my left?"

She took her fingers off the keys and held one hand out to him. "How's your bullshit detector?"

Bishop hesitated for only an instant before taking her hand. They stared at each other, her green eyes calm and his silvery ones penetrating, searching.

He sucked in a breath suddenly, and his face whitened. "My God."

Faith drew her hand gently from his. "Isn't it strange," she whispered.

Bishop seemed not to know what to say at first, but finally asked, "Does Kane know?"

"I think . . . he wonders. I think he's sensed something. But who could *know* such a thing? Who could
even imagine it to be possible?"

"It's a second chance," Bishop said. "How many
of us are granted that?"

She shook her head. "It isn't that simple and you
know it."

"It should be that simple."

"Really? And how would you feel? Put yourself in
his place. He's getting ready to bury her, Bishop. He's
spent weeks grieving, letting go of her because he
thought he had to. What am I supposed to say to him
now? Never mind?"

Bishop looked at her curiously. "Her?"

Faith's smile twisted. "Put yourself in my place. Do
you really think anything—anybody—could ever be
the same again? Could ever be what they were
before?"

"No, I suppose not."

In the silence of the apartment, they both
heard the distant sound of the shower starting, and
Bishop said, "I think it would be best if I made
myself scarce for a while. I'll go back down to the
station, see if there's anything I can do to help
Richardson."

"Coward," Faith said with a stab at humor.

Bishop smiled, but his eyes were grave. "It might
be . . . best . . . to wait awhile, you know. Give it
some time, allow both of you to adjust."

"No," Faith said. "Not after last night. This time,
we have to be honest with each other."

Bishop didn't ask any more questions. He reached
over to touch her hand, then said, "I'll be around."

"I know. Thanks."

He got as far as the door before she said his name quietly, and he paused to look back at her.

Faith touched an ivory key softly, but she was looking at him. "You'll be going back to Tennessee."

"Will I?"

"Yes. Pretty soon, I think. After the first of the year."

"What will I find there?" he asked slowly.

"Evil. And something else, something you've been searching for for a long time."

Bishop took a quick step toward her, then pulled himself up short. In a very controlled voice, he said, "I don't suppose you can tell me how it all turns out?"

"No," she said, lying. "Just—be careful, Bishop."

He was motionless for a moment, then nodded abruptly and left without another word.

Faith stared at the door a long time after he'd gone, then got up to freshen her coffee. What was the use of knowing what was going to happen before it did? Fate seemed to have a stranglehold on events; no matter what she'd done in the past to try to avert tragedy or even disappointment, it always seemed to happen just the way she'd seen it.

"Be very careful, Bishop," she whispered.

When Kane came into the living room a few minutes later, she was sitting on the couch watching a news program on television detailing the exciting events of the previous night.

"I made some lousy coffee," she said, offering him a faint smile.

He leaned over the back of the couch, sliding his fingers into her hair and drawing her to him for a kiss. The kiss held hunger, and something else, and when she could, despite what she'd told Bishop, Faith involuntarily said, "Tomorrow is soon enough, isn't it?"

Kane stroked her cheek, then came around the couch to sit in the chair across from her. "Soon enough for what?"

"To say whatever it is you feel you have to say."

He shook his head, his eyes never leaving hers. "It's between us, Faith. I don't want anything between us."

She braced herself. "What's between us?"

"This guilt."

Faith knew, but asked anyway. "Guilt?"

"Guilt. Because Dinah's been gone not even two months. And I'm in love with you."

Now that the moment had come, she wondered how on earth she could tell him. How she could convince him when even a part of her still didn't believe it. But she had to try.

It sounded so simple in her mind, so incredible when she said the words aloud. "Dinah isn't gone. She's here. She's me."

Kane didn't move, didn't seem surprised. But he said, "How is that possible?"

She drew a deep breath and let it out slowly. "The human will is . . . a remarkable thing. Dinah wanted to survive, wanted it very badly. But her body was . . . It wouldn't survive. She knew that. She had known for a long time it was going to happen. And she knew something else, something Dr. Burnett told her just hours before they grabbed her. That . . . Faith . . . hadn't really survived that crash. That only the barest flicker of brain activity could be recorded, just enough to keep the body breathing, the heart beating. A living shell without a mind or a soul."

Kane said unevenly, "But two separate women . . . You can't expect me to believe—"

"You already believe. You *feel* it's true even if everything you've been taught about life and death and the soul insists it can't be possible."

"How? How is it possible?"

She shook her head. "I don't know how. I know there was a . . . connection between Dinah and Faith before the crash, a closeness that was immediate and powerful. I know that each of them was psychic to a degree and in different ways." She shook her head again. "Maybe that had something to do with it. I don't know how. I only know that it happened."

"You speak of Dinah and Faith as if . . . as if you're neither of them."

She thought of her words to Bishop, and conjured a smile. "In a way, I'm . . . the third point of the triangle, created when the other two touched. I woke up without a memory, and for a while I was caught between the two people I had been, neither one nor the other but with shadowy recollections and half-conscious mannerisms and muscle memories. I could even play the piano. For a while."

Kane glanced at the piano and remembered her sitting on the bench looking lost and bewildered. Still, he said, "This is so . . . unbelievable. How do you know it isn't what you believed all along, a psychic connection? That it isn't as simple as you remembering things Dinah said to you while you were in the coma?"

Softly, she said, "Dinah sat by the bed and talked

to an empty shell, Kane. There was nobody there to hear, nobody to remember what she said."

Unable to be still a moment longer, Kane rose and began moving around the room. He knew she watched him with grave green eyes.

How could she claim—How could she *believe*—

"Faith—" He stopped, looked at her.

Understanding, she said, "I've gotten used to the name. We've all gotten used to the name."

In a raw voice, he said, "I saw her *body*. I see it torn and mangled every time I close my eyes. I have to plan a memorial service so everybody who knew her can say goodbye."

"I know. I'm sorry."

Kane walked to the window and stood staring out. "I told you I'd say what I had to, even if it wasn't what you wanted to hear."

She closed her eyes. "Yes."

"I can't—I don't know how to accept this, Faith. I don't know if I can."

She wanted to tell him it was all right, that she would wait until he came to terms with it all. Wanted to tell him again that she loved him, had always loved him. But she hurt too much and her throat was too tight to allow her to say anything at all.

Her purse was on a chair near the door. It was all she needed, really; most of the clothing she had here didn't fit—one way or another. And she was starting over anyway.

She picked up her purse, and she walked out.

Kane heard the door close quietly. Without turning, he said to the empty apartment, "But I don't want you to go."

.   .   .

It just didn't seem like Christmas with a temperature of nearly seventy and brilliant sunshine, but the insistent carols on the radio warbled again and again that it was beginning to look that way and Santa Claus was coming and bells were jingling. . . .

Faith turned off the radio and thought how perfectly understandable it was that the suicide rate went up around the holidays.

Alone, she wouldn't have been able to bear it. Thank God for Haven House, where she had spent hours helping decorate and bake and wrap presents for the kids. Thank God for Katie, who had been puzzled by Faith's sudden inability to play the piano, but forgiving.

There weren't many blanks left now. There was even, finally, acceptance. And gratitude.

Faith went back to trying to concentrate on the college-course catalog, silently debating whether to put her writing skills to good use in a communications field other than journalism. Or maybe advertising. Even if she had to take just general-interest courses until she made up her mind, she fully intended to sign up for the next semester. She needed to get on with her life.

She had ordered a pizza to be delivered, so when the doorbell rang she went to answer it with a twenty in her hand.

"I never take money from redheads," Kane said.

"I was . . . expecting a pizza." Faith hoped she wasn't staring at him as hungrily as she thought she was. Then again, maybe he'd think she was longing for pepperoni and cheese.

"May I come in?"

"Oh—of course."

"Very nice," he said, looking around at the comfortable overstuffed furniture and elegant but casual decorations. "This looks more like you."

Faith was afraid to probe that remark. "I needed to . . . start over here. A clean slate."

He looked at her for an unreadable moment, then said abruptly, "I saw you at the memorial service."

"Yes. It was lovely." She had seen him, too, but had kept to the fringes of the crowd. She had spoken to Bishop briefly; she had forced herself not to ask him anything about Kane, and he had volunteered nothing.

"It was . . . closure," Kane said.

"Was it?"

He took a step toward her. "I told you I'd say what I had to this time."

Faith swallowed hard. "Yes."

He reached out to her, his hand sliding under her hair to lie warmly alongside her neck. "And that I won't stop myself from touching you this time because I'm not sure you want to be touched."

She closed her eyes and pressed herself harder against his hand in mute pleasure.

"And that I won't let you shut me out of the parts of your life that matter," Kane finished unsteadily, and kissed her. "Not again. Never again."

When she could, Faith said, "I'll never try to shut you out of any part of my life, I promise."

He kissed her again, his hunger intense, unhidden,

his arms drawing her close, holding her as if he meant
never to let her go. "What I have to say is that I love
you, Faith. Whoever you were, whoever you are or will
ever be—I love you. And that's all that matters."

Faith looked into his eyes, deep enough to see the
love and the beginnings of belief, of acceptance. She
reached up and touched his face, the backs of her fingers stroking gently.

"That's all that matters. I love you, Kane."

The pizza delivery boy thought he must have been
given the wrong address, because even though he
rang and rang, nobody ever came.

If you loved

HIDING IN THE SHADOWS

you won't want to miss a taste of her next heartstopping thriller,

SENSE OF EVIL

coming from

BANTAM BOOKS

in hardcover in August 2003!

PROLOGUE

The voices wouldn't leave him alone.

Neither would the nightmares.

He threw back the covers and stumbled from t[ ]
bed. A full moon beamed enough light into the hou[ ]
for him to find his way to the sink in the bathroom.

He carefully avoided looking into the mirror, but w[ ]
highly conscious of his shadowy reflection as he fur[ ]
bled for a drinking cup and turned on the tap. He dra[ ]
three cups of water, vaguely surprised that he was [ ]
thirsty and yet . . . not.

He was usually thirsty these days.

It was part of the change.

He splashed his face with the cold water again ar[ ]
again, not caring about the mess he was making. [ ]
the third splash, he realized he was crying.

Wimp. Spineless coward.

"I'm not," he muttered, sending the next handful [ ]
water to wet his aching head.

You're afraid. Pissing-in-your-pants afraid.

Half-consciously, he pressed his thighs together. "I'm not. I can do it. I told you I could do it."

Then do it now.

He froze, bent over the sink, water dribbling from his cupped hands. "Now?"

Now.

"But . . . it's not ready yet. If I do it now—"

Coward. I should have known you couldn't go through with it. I should have known you'd fail me.

He straightened slowly, this time looking deliberately into the dim mirror. Even with the moonlight, all he could make out was the shadowy shape of his head, dark blurs of features, faint gleam of eyes. The murky outline of a stranger.

What choice did he have?

Just look at yourself. Wimp. Spineless coward. You'll never be a real man, will you?

He could feel water dripping off his chin. Or maybe it was the last of the tears. He sucked in air, so deep his chest hurt, then let it out slowly.

Maybe you can buy a backbone—

"I'm ready," he said. "I'm ready to do it."

I don't believe you.

He turned off the taps and walked out of the bathroom. Went back to his bedroom, where the moonlight spilled through the big window to spotlight the old steamer trunk set against the wall beneath it. He knelt down and carefully opened it.

The raised lid blocked off some of the moonlight, but he didn't need light for this. He reached inside, let his fingers search gingerly until they felt the cold steel. He lifted the knife and held it in the light, turning it this way and that, fascinated by the gleam of the razor-sharp serrated edge.

"I'm ready," he murmured. "I'm ready to kill her."

The voices wouldn't leave her alone.

Neither would the nightmares.

She had drawn the drapes before going to bed in an effort to close out the moonlight, but even though the room was dark, she was very conscious of that huge moon painting everything on the other side of her window with the stark, eerie light that made her feel so uneasy.

She hated full moons.

The clock on her nightstand told her it was nearly three in the morning. The hot, sandpapery feel of her eyelids told her she really needed to try to go back to sleep. But the whisper of the voices in her head told her that even trying would be useless, at least for a while.

She pushed back the covers and slid from her bed. She didn't need light to show her the way to the kitchen, but once there turned on the light over the stove so she wouldn't burn herself. Hot chocolate, that was the ticket.

And if that didn't work, there was an emergency bottle of whiskey in the back of the pantry for just such a night as this. It was probably two-thirds empty by now.

There had been a few nights like this, especially in the last year or so.

She got what she needed and heated the pan of milk slowly, stirring the liquid so it wouldn't stick. Adding in chocolate syrup while the milk heated, because that was the way she liked to make her hot chocolate. In the silence of the house, with no other sounds to distract her, it was difficult to keep her own mind quiet. She didn't want to listen to the whispering there, but it was like catching a word or two of an overheard conversation and *knowing* you needed to listen more closely because they were talking about you.

But she was tired. It got harder and harder, as time went on, to bounce back. Harder for her body to recover. Harder for her mind to heal.

Given her druthers, she would put off tuning in to the voices until tomorrow. Or the next day, maybe.

The hot chocolate was ready. She turned off the burner and poured the steaming milk into a mug. She put the pan in the sink, then picked up her mug and carried it toward the little round table in the breakfast nook.

Almost there, she was stopped in her tracks by a wave of red-hot pain that washed over her body with the suddenness of a blow. Her mug crashed to the floor, landing unbroken but spattering her bare legs with hot chocolate.

She barely felt that pain.

Eyes closed, sucked into the red and screaming maelstrom of someone else's agony, she tried to keep breathing despite the repeated blows that splintered bones and shredded lungs. She could taste blood, feel it bubbling up in her mouth. She could feel the wet heat of it soaking her blouse and running down her arms as she lifted her hands in a pitiful attempt to ward off the attack.

I know what you did. I know. I know. You bitch, I know what you did—

She jerked and cried out as a more powerful thrust than all the rest drove the serrated knife into her chest, penetrating her heart with such force, she knew the only thing that stopped it going deeper still was the hilt. Her hands fumbled, touching what felt like blood-wet gloved hands, large and strong, that retreated immediately to leave her weakly holding the handle of the knife impaling her heart. She felt a single agonized throb of her heart that forced more blood to bubble, hot and thick, into her mouth, and then it was over.

Almost over.

She opened her eyes and found herself bending over the table, her hands flat on the pale, polished surface. Both hands were covered with blood, and between them, scrawled in her own handwriting across the table, was a single bloody word.

HASTINGS

She straightened slowly, her entire body aching, and held her hands out in front of her, watching as the blood slowly faded, until it was gone. Her hands were clean and unmarked. When she looked at the table again, there was no sign of a word written there in blood.

"Hastings," she murmured. "Well, shit."

Read on for a peek at

ONCE A THIEF

*Kay Hooper's newest page-turner featuring
a dangerously charismatic master jewel thief,
available from*

BANTAM BOOKS

Museum exhibit director Morgan West is days
away from unveiling the much-anticipated Mysteries Past show—a priceless jewel collection on
loan from millionaire Max Bannister. But when
Morgan discovers that a criminal mastermind is
waiting and watching for just the right time to
strike, the stage is set for a complex game of cat-
and-mouse . . .

Barely feeling the cold, hard marble beneath her feet, Morgan darted through one of the two big archways without immediately knowing why she'd made the choice. Then she realized. There had to be more than one of them and they'd be after the most portable valuables, wouldn't they? Jewelry, then—and a large display of precious gems lay in the direction she hadn't chosen.

Along her route were several larger and less valuable—to the thieves—displays of statuary, weapons, and assorted artifacts, many large enough to offer a hiding place.

She made another desperate turn through an archway that appeared to house a room dimmer than some of the others, and found herself neatly caught. A long arm that seemed made of iron rather than flesh lifted her literally off her feet, clamped her arms to her sides, and hauled her back against a body that had all the softness of granite, and a big, dark hand covered her mouth before she could do more than gasp.

For one terrified instant, Morgan had the eerie

hought that one of the darkly looming statues of
ierce warriors from the past had reached out and
rabbed her. Then a low voice hissed in her ear, and
he impression of supernatural doings faded.

"Shhhh!"

He wasn't a security guard. The hand over her
nouth was encased in a thin, supple black glove, and
s much of his arm as she could see was also wearing
·lack. Several hard objects in the vicinity of his waist
.ug into her back painfully. Then he pulled her impos-
ibly closer as running footsteps approached, and she
istinctly felt the roughness of wool—a ski mask?—as
.is hard jaw brushed against her temple.

Better the devil you know than the one you don't . . .
·he thought ran through her mind, but for some reason
he didn't struggle in the man's powerful embrace—
·robably because she didn't know the devil out in the
.allway any better than she knew this one. Instead, she
oncentrated on controlling her ragged breathing so
hat it wouldn't be audible, her eyes fixed on the arch-
vay of the room. She realized only then that she'd
·olted into a room with only one door. Her captor had
.terally carried her back into a corner and in the shad-
·ws behind one of the fierce warrior statues, and she
·oubted they were visible from the doorway.

The footsteps in the hall slowed abruptly, and she
·aught a glimpse of a rather menacing face further dis-
·orted by an angry scowl as her pursuer looked into the
·oom. She stiffened, but he went on without pausing
·nore than briefly. As the footsteps faded, she began to
·truggle; the steely arm around her tightened with an
·dditional strength that nearly cracked her ribs.

Three breathless seconds later, she realized why.

"Ed." The voice, low and harsh, was no more than a
·ew feet down the hallway.

Morgan went very still.

There was an indistinguishable murmur of at lea:
two voices out there, and then the first voice becam
audible—and quite definitely angry.

"I thought she came this way. Dammit, she could b
anywhere in this mausoleum—the place is huge!"

"Did she get a look at you?" Ed's voice was calmer.

"No, the hall was too dark. When I tapped he
boyfriend to sleep, she ran like a rabbit. Why th
hell did he have to pick tonight to come here?
he wanted romance, he should have taken her to h
place. Judging by what I saw of her, she'd have ker
him busy between the sheets for a week."

Feeling herself stiffen again, this time indignantl
Morgan was conscious of an absurd embarrassmer
that the man holding her so tightly against him ha
heard that lewd comment.

"Never mind," Ed said impatiently. "We're coverin
all the doors, so she can't get out, and the phone line
have been cut. Go back to your post and wait. We'll b
finished in another half hour, and out of here. She'll b
locked in until morning, so she can't do us any harm."

"I don't like it, Ed."

"You don't have to like it. And stop using my nam∢
you fool. Get back to your post."

There was a moment of taut silence, and then Ed
unhappy minion passed the archway on his route bac
to his post, an even more distorted scowl darkenin
his face.

Morgan heard his footsteps fade into silence; strai
as she would, she couldn't hear anything from Ed. A
least five minutes must have passed, with agonizin
slowness, before her captor finally relaxed slightly an
eased her down so that her feet touched the cold floo

His voice sounded again, soft and no more than a sibilant whisper, next to her ear.

"I'm not going to hurt you. Understand? But you have to be still and quiet, or you'll bring them down on us."

Morgan nodded her understanding. As soon as he released her, she took half a step away and turned to confront him. "If you aren't with them, what are you—" she began in a whisper, then broke off as the question was answered.

He was a tall man, an inch or two over six feet, with wide shoulders and a wiry slenderness about the rest of him that spoke of honed strength rather than muscled bulk. She'd felt that strength. Enveloped in black from head to foot, he had a compact and very efficient-looking tool belt strapped to his lean waist. And from the black ski mask gleamed the greenest pair of eyes she'd ever seen.

"Oh." She knew then what he was doing here. "Oh, Christ."

"Not nearly," he murmured.

Morgan felt a burst of pure irritation at his ill-timed humor but somehow managed to keep her voice low. "You're just another thief."

"Please." He sounded injured. "Such a commonplace word. An ugly word, even. I prefer to call myself privateer."

"Wrong," she snapped, still in a low voice that would have been inaudible a couple of feet away. "This isn't a ship on the high sea, and we aren't at war. You're a common, ordinary, run-of-the-mill *criminal*." She could have sworn those vivid green eyes gleamed with sheer amusement.

"My dear young woman," he said, that same emotion threaded through his soft, unaccented voice, "I a neither common nor ordinary. In fact, I'm one of th last of a vanishing breed in these uncomfortably o ganized high-tech days. If you must attach a noun t me, make it 'cat burglar.' However, I'd much rath you simply called me Quinn."

Morgan stared at him. Quinn? Quinn. She knew him. Of *course* she knew him! For nearly ten year the name of Quinn—along with assorted aliases an journalistic nicknames in various languages—had bee synonymous with daring, nerveless theft at its mo dramatic. If the newspapers were to be believed, h had smoothly robbed the best families of Europe, r lieving them of fine baubles and artworks with a del cate precision and finicky taste that made the "cat" i his preferred noun an apt choice. And in so doing h had bypassed some of the most expensive and con plicated security systems ever designed with almo laughable ease. Also according to the newspapers, h never used weapons, had never injured anyone, an had never come close to being caught—all of whic made him something of a folk hero.

"Hell," Morgan said.

"Not yet." He seemed even more amused. "I se that my reputation precedes me. How gratifying. It nice to know that one's work is appreciated."

She ignored the levity. "I thought you were a Eurc pean thief exclusively."

"Ah—but America is the land of opportunity," h intoned in a reverent voice.

She didn't know whether to laugh or swear agair It disturbed her to realize that she—be it ever s reluctantly—found him amusing. With her own lov of ancient artifacts and priceless artworks, she ha never felt the slightest urge to romanticize the theft c hem. And no matter how rapturous certain journalists seem to be in describing the daring exploits of thieves with taste and without any leaning toward violence, she saw nothing of a Robin Hood–type myth clinging to this one: No one had ever implied that Quinn shared his spoils with the poor.

"What are you doing here?" she demanded.

"I rather thought that was obvious."

Morgan drew a deep breath. "Dammit, I meant— Stop staring at my chest!"

Quinn cleared his throat with an odd little sound, and in a suspiciously pensive and humble tone said, "I have held in my hands some of the finest artworks the world has ever known. Had I but realized a few moments ago that so exquisite a work of nature herself was so near . . . May I say—"

"No, you may not," she said from between gritted teeth, fighting a mad urge to giggle. It cost her something to stop him, because the words were certainly lovely enough if one cared for that sort of base flattery—not sure that she was impressed by them, of course.

"No, naturally not," he murmured, then added sadly, "there are certain drawbacks to being a gentleman burglar."

"Oh, now you claim to be a gentleman?"

"What's your name?" he asked curiously, ignoring her question.

"Morgan West." Oddly enough, she didn't think about withholding the information.

"Morgan. An unusual name. Derived from Morgana, I believe, Old Welsh—" This time he stopped himself, adding after a thoughtful moment, "And familiar. Ah, now I remember. You're the director of the forthcoming Mysteries Past exhibit."

She raised a hand and shook a finger under his nose "If you *dare* to rob my exhibit," she said fiercely, "I wil hunt you to the ends of the earth and roast your gen tleman's carcass over perdition's flame!"

"I believe you would," he said mildly. "Interpol itsel never threatened me with more resolution."

"Never doubt it." She let her hand fall, then said in an irritable tone, "And you distracted me."

Still mild, Quinn said, "Not nearly as much as you distracted me, Morgana."

"It's Morgan. Just Morgan."

"I prefer Morgana."

"It isn't your name—" She got hold of herself. Ab surd. Of all the ridiculous . . . Here she was in a dark museum that was being systematically looted by ar organized group of thieves. Her dinner date had been at the very least, knocked unconscious; she'd been chased through marble halls by a man who probably wouldn't have been nice if he'd caught her; and now she was defending her name preference to an interna tionally famous cat burglar who had too much charm for his own good.

And hers.

Doggedly, she tried again. "Never mind my name. If you aren't with those jokers out there, then why are you here?"

"The situation does have its farcical points," he said amiably. "I'm afraid I dropped in on them. Literally. We seem to have had the same agenda in mind for tonight. Though my plans were, of course, on a lesser scale. Since they outnumber me ten to one, and since they are definitely armed, I chose not to—shall we say—force the issue. It breaks my heart, mind you, be cause I'm almost certain that what I came here for is now neatly tucked away in one of their boring little leather satchels. But . . . *c'est la vie.*"

Morgan stared at him. "What did you come for?"

Quite gently, he said, "None of your business, Morgana."

After a moment, she said speculatively, "I don't suppose you'd let me see your face?"

"That wouldn't be my first choice, no. Quinn is a name and a shadow, nothing more. I have a strong feeling that your descriptive powers are better than average, and I don't care to see a reasonable facsimile of my face plastered across the newspapers. Being a cat burglar is the very devil once the police know what you look like."

And watch for the sequel to

ONCE A THIEF

The thievery continues in June 2003 with

ALWAYS A THIEF

ABOUT THE AUTHOR

KAY HOOPER, who has more than four million copies of her books in print world wide, has won numerous awards and high praise for her novels. Kay lives in North Carolina, where she is currently working on her next novel.